Blinding Trust

(A Mitchell Family Series Book 7)

Written By: Jennifer Foor

Copyright © 2013 Jennifer Foor

All Rights Reserved

Cover Art By : Wicked Cool Designs – Robin Harper

Check out the other books by Jennifer Foor

(Contemporary Romance)

Letting Go - A Mitchell Family Series Book One

Folding Hearts – A Mitchell Family Series Book Two

Raging Love – A Mitchell Family Series Book Three

Risking Fate – A Mitchell Family Series Book Four

Wrapping Up – A Mitchell Family Series Novella 4.5

Wanting More – A Mitchell Series Book Five

Saving Us – A Mitchell Family Series Book Six

Hope's Chance (Contemporary Romance)

The Somnian Series (YA Paranormal)

Books 1-5

Hustle Me (A Bank Shot Romance)

Hustle Him (A Bank Shot Romance)

Diary of a Male Maid

This book is dedicated to anyone who has ever known someone with, loved someone with or lost someone to breast cancer. One in every 8 women will be diagnosed in their lifetime. Early detection is the key.

I'd like to take this time to acknowledge and appreciate some of our friends and loved ones that have battled Breast Cancer.
Thank you to everyone who participated in the organization of this list.

Each of the follow names below were provided through my author and personal pages. They are in no certain order, but are all equally honored.
God Bless all of the family's that have suffered pain and loss from this terrible illness.

Penny Gillespie * Jaye Sheldon * Beverly Sims * Shirley Bohannon * Bonnie McBride * Linda S * Teresa Kelley * Helen Harden * Alice Duddy * Freida Baynard * Louise Jensen * Leslie Crawford * Lorena Van Auken. * Lesa Ann * Patricia Balmer * Ann Borunda * Jenea Clark * Wanda Lee Bullock * Heather B.* Tina D.* Brooke K.* Theresa M.* Karen * Janell C.* Deborah M. * Ezell Nobles Smith * Karen Jean Meyers * Vivian Brown * Sandra Kelly * Lana Turner * Sandy Bean ***Mary Geraldine DacocoWoodruff** * Gretchen DeWalt * Mary Ann Briguglio * Joan Callender * Judy Campbell * Beatrice Verone *Barbara Hayes * Nancy Cummings * Wini McBroom * Maureen Sandifer * Joy Zaben * Mary Becchelli * Lucy Lucidi * RuthAnn Rushworth * Luella Menard * Robbie Phipps * Ruth Gillespie * Jean Wilson * Vickie Swankie * Party Redmond * Tracy Kirby * Dixie C. * Linda Lysk * Dorothy Oihus * Becky Vasquez * Sandra Davila * Shirley Carlson * Brenda Crane * Cedar Bluff * Helen Pierce * Teresa John * Nancy Inmon * Julie Savage * Natalie Wehrs * Joan Setser * Judy Compton * Jennifer Walden * Marianne Anderson * Patsy Zenker * Susan Jones * Ellen & Lale * Dina Maio * Andrea Ramirez * Patricia Elliott * Tara Bencomo * Joy Padilla * Chris Lively * Melinda Rees * Kimberly Muresan * Della & Patty * Susan Lonon * Jessica Holmes * Janelle Larkin * Kristi Murphy * Amy Schneider * Grace Frome * Katie Boyles Martin * Alice Chernetzki * Faye Campbell * Fern Sprouse * Alice Zittle * Alice (Pam Duddy's Mom) * Liz Dewalt Piper's Mom * JoAnn Coleman * Lessie Adams * Teena Slingluff * Susie Simms * Leigh Anne Miller * Ida Buchanan * Jackie Pierce * Elizabeth Fields * Julie Tuttle Donovan's mother-in-law * Margie Crosby * Betty Kieran * Joan McClure * Ann Berg * Linda Bradford * Michelle Dunlap * Barbara Bradford Himelright's friend Joan, her Aunt Ruth and cousin Heather * Julia Bowden * Carlene Grant * Barbara Disharoon * Dianne Cheverie * Barbara Jones * Linda Adams * Betty Ann Crabtree * Jeanette * Courtney * Delores * Patricia * Tina Brown Shawler * Susan * Sherrell Kennedy * Jennifer Johnson Polo * Elaine Parker * Marilyn Berard * Deb Gallogly * Tamara Yarbrough * Elizabeth Stien * Pamela Anderson * Brunilda Colón Frewerd * Annette Perez * Diane Tu * Doris Arwilda Massey * Mary Reddick * Connie Proudfoot * Debbie Newman * Marcella Moore * Johanna Schryer * Maryann Liberatore * Wendy Lou Fox * Mary King * Olga Towers * Jamie V * Mary Allen and her family * Narelle Schulz * Dorothy Massey *Bonnie * John * Roy * Darline * Alberta * Joyce Maxwell * Dana Loebel * MaryEllen Martin *

Sue Morgan * Louise Wood * Deborah Castaneda * Leroy West * Concepcion G * Jenny * Patty * Laura Garrison * Patsy Rider Lane * Iris Rogers * Mary Mcbride * Jennifer Coleman * Jodi Chevarella * Gillian Washington * Donna * Marilyn Kurman Rosen and her family * Nancy Cordes * Karen Falls Hill * Rhonda Ainsworth * Gloria Dufour * Linda Smith * Monica Flick * Marie Walter * Pam Calhoun

Beta Readers

Margo Lomeli, Amy Haigler, Karrie Stewart, Jennifer Harried, Erica Willis, Sarah Thompson, Mechelle Lovell Jackson, Kim Eckley, Kim Person, Milasy Mugnolo and Stephanie Horning

Web Design and Marketing by: Amy Haigler

Thanks to all of my new friends on my FB, Twitter and Goodreads.

Author: Amanda Bennett, Author: Elizabeth Buchanan

Author: Emily Snow Author: Michelle Valentine Author: Michelle Leighton

Author: Heather Gunter

Thank you for spreading the word and all of the support you give.

Thanks to all of my other Independent Author Friends. (you know who you are)

Thank you to all the book bloggers out there spreading the word for me and others who write.

Maryse Book Blog, Into the night Reviews, Book Bitches, Word, Rockstars of Romance, Kindlehooked, Shh Mom's reading, Totally Booked, Word, Reading is my time out, Stick Girl Book Reviews, Wolfels World of Books, Dirty Books and Dirty Boys

Book Broads, Book Studs, Books Books Books, Reality Bites Books, Naughty Mafia Vegas, Smutty Book Whores,

What to read after fifty shades

Special Thanks to:

Everyone who has made this series the success that it is. I am forever grateful. Thanks to my family and my faith. With them, all things are possible

Chapter 1

Savanna

I couldn't believe that it had been five years. None of us expected Conner and Amy to end up with a house full of kids, probably because we remember how he was before Amy came into the picture. When that happened, everything changed.

They'd gone through a lot to be together. Between her still being married and the fact that they hid their relationship, it wasn't exactly easy for them.

I think once Amy got pregnant with their first child, Cammie, was when they knew that they were going to have to start making decisions.

Our family had been through so much, so the drama with Amy was nothing new to us. It was unfortunate what they all had to go through, but they persevered and came out stronger than ever before.

I was especially sad when they made the choice to move back to North Carolina. I understood that Conner wanted to be near his sister, so that they could raise the kids together, but I had become so close with Amy that I knew I would miss her terribly.

Lucy and my mother-in-law kept me busy, when I wasn't running after the kids.

Noah was very athletic. I found myself taking him all around the state of Kentucky. Colt was great about making his games. He even coached him during football season.

The girls usually tagged along. They played so good together and Noah was always a big help.

Due to one of his games, we were late getting to Cammie's birthday party. By the time we got there, the whole family was there, already celebrating. It was great to see everyone together. Actually, it was great to be out of the darn car. You know it's a long drive when you have three kids that have to pee more than physically possible.

Ty was the first one to greet me, like always. He grabbed me and pulled me into a spinning hug. "There's my sexy cousin." He kissed me on my cheek.

Bella was still wearing her uniform from a game she must have had earlier in the day. She saw Noah and the two of them wandered off together. It was amazing how close they still were. It was also hard to believe that Noah was almost eleven and Bella was ten. Since coming into our life, Noah had been such a blessing. He taught me how to be a mother and, since his mother had died when he was three, I was the only one he had.

Colt loved all of our children, but I think he shared a special bond with Noah. Maybe it was because they were the men of the house. It could have been that Colt still felt guilty for not being there the first three years of his life. It wasn't his fault. We didn't even know he had a child.

Through the years it was almost like I forgot that I hadn't birthed him myself. I love him just as much as my own girls. Our family just wouldn't have been the same without him in it.

Ty smacked me on the butt and grabbed Christian. "There's one of my pretty nieces. Uncle Ty missed you!" He kissed her on the cheek, too.

Miranda came out of the house and walked up to me, while Ty met Colt on the other side of the truck, to wait for him to get out Addy, who was almost four and still had to be secured in a booster seat.

"Hey, cuz." Miranda always smelled of the best shampoo. Since her and Amy's salon was here at the house, they never really had to leave the kids. Ty's mother had her own daycare center between Ty's kids and Conner's. She seemed to be in heaven when she was with them.

After our hug, I pulled away to look at how beautiful she was. "What is your secret? You look ravishing. Your hair is so shiny."

She played with her hair. "If I told you, you may throw up."

"Seriously? It can't be that bad."

Ty walked past quickly, spatting out one word. "Cum!"

I almost threw up in my mouth. Miranda started to laugh as she followed her husband. "Told ya. It's full of proteins. You should try it."

Still trying to not throw up, I shook my head. "No thanks!"

Colt cocked his eyebrow, while carrying Addy. "Sick! That's what they are."

"Yeah, but there are family and we have to love them, right?"

"Sometimes, darlin', that's debatable."

I loved my mature husband. Ty and Conner still acted like teenagers. Miranda and Amy seemed to like it. After a while, it got on my nerves. Colt and I were settled and content. We didn't need to act like them to be happy.

Our family was huge. Growing up, mine was so small. Even when I married Colt, his family wasn't that large. It was now. All of our children had made it triple in size.

I heard screaming and went running toward the sound. A mother knows her own child's screams. Colt and Miranda had just got into the house, which was full of people being loud. I knew he couldn't hear what I was hearing.

Jake had Christian by the ponytail and was swinging her around. He saw me and dropped the bunch of hair. "Hi, Aunt Van." Just like his father, when he did something wrong, he'd look so innocent.

"Jake, why were you pulling your cousin's hair. You know that's not nice!"

"She said that my breath smells like skunk."

I wanted to giggle. Christian had been on this kick where she told everyone how she felt. Sometimes her truthful confessions were downright offensive. "Well, that doesn't mean you should pull her hair. How about telling an adult next time."

He shrugged and went to pull away, but his father grabbed the collar of his shirt and pulled him back. "Not so fast! Did you brush your teeth, like I told you to?"

"Yeah!"

Ty looked at me and then bent down. "Let me smell your breath."

The things we do for our children. I watched Ty make a face like he was going to throw up.

"Your breath smells like the dog took a crap in it. Boy, how many times did I tell you to brush your teeth?"

He shrugged again and wouldn't look up into his father's eyes.

Ty looked over at me. I had nothing to say, since he was already embarrassing Jake. "Go tell your mother what you *didn't* do. I'm sure she will have a good idea what to do with you."

I laughed with Ty as we watched one of his sons pout his way into the house. "That poor kid. You probably didn't brush your teeth when you were his age either."

He put his arm around me as we walked into the house. "Even as kids you have to admit that my breath was always fresh enough for you to want to kiss me, Van."

I rolled my eyes and turned my attention to the house full of family. Miranda was walking around the living room, talking to her mother, with her hand in Addy's. We talked or text messaged just about every day and she was just crazy about my girls. I missed seeing all of them, but we all had lives. We still got together often; it was just never often enough.

Cammie was wearing an outfit that was both cute and an eyesore. I was positive that she must have picked it out herself. Josh was playing on the floor with his cousin Jax. They had a Lego tower over two feet high. I followed the southern accents to the kitchen, where Colt and Conner were already talking about work.

Colt smiled when he saw me walk into the room. We didn't get a lot of alone time with the kids always running around. Usually, the girls would end up in bed with us. There had even been several times where we ended up having our alone time in one of their twin beds. For my tall husband, it wasn't the most comfortable of situations.

One thing I never had to worry about was my husband straying. Since he worked at our family's ranch, he never even went anywhere except on our property. When we went into town, we were always together, with our children in tow.

Even through the years, Colt was still as handsome as ever. Some of his whiskers had a couple grays, but I kept quiet about it. Ty already gave him enough grief about being over thirty, even though we were all hitting that pivotal mark.

It didn't matter to me if Colt's whole head turned gray. He would always be the hottest man that I would ever know. He knew it too. When we were alone and I gave him that look, like nobody else in the world existed, he knew what it meant. I was still madly in love with my husband. He was an excellent father and a great partner.

Through the years, Colt had built a beautiful life for us. Our house was perfectly designed for a family, even though we hadn't even come into Colt's life yet when he built it. Even through out minor struggles, our love always saw us through. The longer we were married, the more I believed that we could get through anything.

With his arms wrapped around me from behind, he kissed the side of my cheek. "What was wrong with Christian? That was her screaming, right?"

I turned to look at him. "You didn't run when you heard it?"

"I did, but I saw that you and Ty had it under control. Once I knew who the culprit was, I went back inside. You know how Ty's sons are."

"Actually, it was Christian who started it. She told him he had terrible breath."

Colt made a face, like he wasn't surprised. "That kid is goin' to get herself into trouble, if she keeps this up."

"I told her!" We'd both told her. She just had to tell people the truth, all of the time.

"Maybe you should just teach her to lie," Conner teased.

I reached over and pushed him. "Don't even joke about that!"

"You guys joking about shit without me in here?" Ty walked into the kitchen, followed by Amy. Her belly was so cute. I caught Conner giving her a look, like they were the only ones in the room.

I poked him in the arm. "I saw that! Now I know why she's always pregnant."

The room filled with laughter.

"She's just jealous cause she never gets any." Ty made Conner and Amy laugh, but I could tell the look on Colt's face without even looking at him. He didn't like the fact that I talked about our sex life to Miranda and Ty when he was listening in on our conversations. It wasn't like I directly called him to complain.

"Shut up! Colt and I are perfectly happy." I was afraid to look at my husband, so I backed my body up into his. Thankfully, I felt his large hands reaching around my waist again.

"I happen to like waking up to a bed full of family." I think Colt realized how that came out the second he'd said it. But, it was already too late.

Ty was on him like a fly on shit. "Dude, that's just wrong! I'm out of here!"

Conner covered his face and laughed, while Colt got mad and walked into the living room.

Amy was putting candles in her daughter's princess cake. She was shaking her head and laughing as well. "He does it to himself, you know. Ty and Conner just wait for him to say the wrong thing and they pounce every time."

"I know. You'd think after all these years, he'd learn." I grabbed the matches and started lighting the candles. "Sorry we were late getting here."

"It's no biggie. You're here now and that's all that matters."

I followed behind Amy, who was carrying the cake, while attempting to sing 'Happy Birthday', so that everyone else would join in. Finally, the chaos that filled the house, turned to give their full attention to the birthday girl. Her face lit up when she saw her cake. She ran over toward the dining room table and sat down in front of the lit up masterpiece.

All of the kids filled in the chairs around the table and got excited that they would all soon be eating cake and ice cream. Our family loved sweets. Jake and Jax had the cavities to prove it.

Noah and Bella came walking inside together, halfway through the song. They were too caught up in each other to care what was going on with their younger cousins. I didn't mind, since they didn't see each other very much. Well, not counting talking on their matching iPads, that my mother-in-law had to buy them for Christmas.

The kids were spoiled, all of them. Colt's mother had nothing else to do with her time. Aside from taking trips with my parents and her own sister, she spent her free time taking the kids different places. She even treated the whole family to two trips to Disney. It was what she lived for, so we didn't get on her about it.

Even with being spoiled, mine and Colt's children knew their place when it came to being home. They knew they couldn't get away with things like at Grandma's house.

We stood around, getting each child situated with plates of pure sugar. I think only the females realized what was going to happen in thirty minutes. The boys were going to be bouncing off the walls.

When I was growing up, one Ty was hyper enough. Now there were two of them running around. One drop of sugar and they could bring down a house. God, they were so ornery.

Once the kids had finished eating, I helped Amy and Miranda clean up the mess. Ty's mom took Addy and put her down for a nap, which was nice of her. Through the years we'd built a new kind of relationship. I'd learned to love her and appreciate what she'd always done to protect her child. There wasn't anything that I wouldn't do for mine. It sort of puts things into perspective when you have one of your own.

Speaking of parents, mine moved to Kentucky last year after my father retired. I thought they would be more sad about leaving their life here in North Carolina. Instead, they were thrilled to move close to us. When I say moved, I mean they moved onto the ranch.

Colt's mother offered for them to move into her huge house, but they insisted on not being a burden. They paid for a nice modular to be built near Karen's old house. Karen had also offered her house, but my parents wanted Miranda and Conner to always have a place to come with all of their kids.

It worked out great. My mother still worked everyday. She got a job working at one of our produce stands. Actually, she sort of fell into managing it. She loved the job and it gave her the opportunity to meet people from town. They also started attending our church, which gave them even more new friends. I swear they socialized more nowadays then ever before.

Since we were staying at Ty and Miranda's, we got the kids gathered up and headed over. It was just across the Mitchell property, but far enough where you had to drive.

Ty came over to the vehicle and helped Colt carry our bags. He smacked me on the butt when he walked past me.

"Is it necessary to touch my wife every time you're near her?" Colt seemed offended, which was weird to me. He'd hadn't been like that in years.

"Dude, it ain't like that. I'm just messing around. She likes it."

I walked in the house and left the two of them to their conversation. They were too old to start rolling around in the dirt, like they used to. Besides, they had no reason to fight. We were all completely happy.

So I thought.

For the rest of our visit, Colt seemed on edge. I had no idea why and I didn't want to stir the pot by asking. I figured that when we got home, we could discuss it in private. Except when we got home, all Hell broke loose.

Chapter 2

Colt

I didn't tell her because I didn't want her to worry when it could have just been nothing. Savanna considered Noah hers. It wasn't a secret to anyone that Krista was his birth mother. We just didn't talk about it anymore.

It wasn't until I got the phone call, a week before we went to North Carolina, that things started to worry me.

When Krista and me were a couple, her little brother came to live with us. Their dad was too drunk to even care. He wasn't a bad kid. In fact, as soon as he got the chance, he got out of Kentucky to pursue his dream of being a rockstar.

Apparently, big things had happened for him and suddenly his band, which I didn't know he was a member of, had made it big. Since I didn't follow that kind of music, I had no idea who his band was. I certainly didn't recognize his name when he left the message with Savanna. All she could tell me was that someone name Zeke Marlo had called and said it was urgent.

Even after I dialed the out of area number, I still didn't recognize the voice of the person that picked up. He had to actually explain who he was. We talked for a while, catching up and talking about how he'd been for the past ten years. The topic of his sister dying was short. I could tell it was a sore subject.

Zeke, which is what he legally changed his name to, told me that they were coming to Kentucky for a big charity concert. He asked if I would come out and visit with him while he was there. I didn't see any harm in it, until he asked if I could bring Noah.

Now, for some reason, that bothered me.

Noah had never met Zeke. I didn't even own a picture of him except from when he was a kid. So, I did what every curious parent would do. I went on the internet and checked him out.

He hadn't been lying. Zeke was a big star. His band, Dodging Bullets, had even had a platinum song called "Gutter Love". I was proud of him for his accomplishments. He'd come from nothing and made a life for himself.

Here was the problem.

After reading about his success, I discovered that his road to fame hadn't been as harmonic. He got into drugs so bad that he was hospitalized and been to rehab three times in the past five years. His first wife left him and the second one was also an ex-addict.

I wasn't a fool. Living in that kind of life had to be hard. I just didn't think I was ready to school my son about it. I also didn't want him idolizing his uncle. I wanted more for my son and he already had a vivid imagination. Thinking that he could be a rockstar too, would have been right up his alley.

I think Savanna sensed right away that I was keeping something from her. I became on edge and it showed even more when I got around my cousin Ty. His constant flirting with my wife had always just been in fun. He loved to tease her. I shouldn't have gotten offended about it. Except I did.

I felt like jacking his ass up in front of the whole family.

I pretty much avoided him the whole time we were visiting and by the time we left, Savanna was even giving me the cold shoulder. I knew once we got home, she was going to give me hell.

I wish that was all that happened.

I could handle my wife and I knew just how to make things better. She was the love of my life and without her I was nothing. We never fought about things and we also made it a point to not keep things from one another.

I know that's why she was more than pissed when we got home and had an unexpected visitor, waiting at our door.

I wouldn't have even recognized him, had it not been for my internet snooping. Zeke had dyed his blonde hair black. He was covered in tattoos, even on his fingers. Some kind of ring was through the center cartilage in his nose and both of his ears were pierced. His leather pants and shirt that looked like it was made from flecks of metal, were also a dead giveaway that he wasn't just a neighbor, looking for help.

Savanna climbed out of the vehicle, but didn't get the kids out. She looked up at our porch and then over to me.

I scratched my head to think of what I could say to her, but nothing came. I should have told her.

Zeke walked down a couple steps as I approached him. I heard Savanna telling Noah and Christian that they had to stay in the car. I reached out my hand and reluctantly shook his. "Good to see you."

"You too, Colt. It's been too long, man." I would have been okay if I never saw him again. It wasn't because I was being an asshole. I was trying to be a good father. I wanted to protect my son. Uncle or not, this guy was trouble. I just knew it.

"We're just gettin' back from North Carolina. If I would have known you were comin', I would have been able to tell you that."

He shrugged, while still smiling. "No biggie, man. I just wanted to stop by. My wife wanted to see where I'd spent some of the good parts of my childhood, that's all. I knew you might not be home. Honestly, I didn't want to bother you."

That would have been terrible if he'd showed up when Savanna was home alone. She would have freaked out. I looked around the yard and didn't see a car. "Where'd you park?"

He pointed toward the back of the house. "I had my driver pull out back. It's easier for him to turn the limo around back there."

Limo? Now I knew I had to explain to my family who this guy was.

I looked over at Savanna and took a deep breath, knowing she was going to be so pissed off at me. "Darlin', come here. There's someone that I'd like you to meet."

She smiled one of her unsure smiles and came walking toward me. Honestly, I think he scared her. She put her hand into mine, before I could introduce them. "This is Zeke. He's Krista's brother."

I watched the color leave my wife's face. She tried to swallow the lump in her throat, but as words never came, I knew she couldn't. I squeezed her hand, still waiting for her to say something.

Zeke reached out his hand for her. It took her a second to finally reach out and shake it. "So, is your name Darlin, or should I call you something else?"

We both smiled at his way of breaking the ice. I didn't know if he sensed her animosity, and I didn't care, as long as she didn't pass out or start ripping his eyes out of his head. I'd imagine though, that his eyes were worth a pretty penny to some crazed fans. My wife wasn't one of those people.

"Nice to meet you. I had no idea that you were in town."
She turned to give me that look where I better not have known
or she was going to go off on me later.

I could hear the kids starting to whine.

"If you'll excuse me, I better get them out." I watched
Savanna go over and start to unbuckle Addy. In a matter of
seconds, I saw Christian running from the other side of the
vehicle, followed by her brother. A terrible feeling shot directly
through my stomach when I realized that I'd have to tell him
who this guy was. There was no way out of it.

He ran past us, taking two steps at once. When he got to
the door, he tried to pull it open. "Dad, can you unlock it? I have
to pee."

Zeke just stared at my boy. Now, I know when he was a
baby it was probably difficult to tell, but Noah looked identical
to me.

I walked up to unlock the door and hesitantly turned
around. "Did you want to come in?"

Zeke looked around at the girls and then back to me. "I'll
come back before I leave town. You guys are just getting back
and I don't want to just barge in."

I shook his hand. "Next time, just call first."

I watched him walk toward the back of the house and
before the girls were on the porch, a large black limo drove
down the dirt lane.

Savanna looked right at me as she walked up the porch steps. "If you knew about this, so help me God, Colt."

"Darlin', I can explain."

She carried Addy over to the couch and turned on Disney for her and Christian, before walking into the kitchen, folding her arms, and waiting for my explanation.

Noah came running in the room. "Dad, who was that guy? Did you see his car? He must be rich!"

Noah didn't understand enough about money to realize that our family had it, as well. I knew what he meant. He meant that the man was famous rich. "Yeah, he must be, buddy. Can you go into the livin' room and keep an eye on your sister's for a second?"

He rolled his eyes and stomped into the living room. "Why do I always have to watch them?"

"Boy, don't you get smart."

After I knew he wasn't around, I turned my attention to my angry wife. "Colt, tell me you didn't know he was coming."

"I didn't. I mean, I knew he was in town, but we never talked about him stopping by."

Her eyes got big and if she could have, she would have been breathing fire. "What do you mean, you knew? How long have you known? Is he the person who called you? How could you not tell me something like that?"

I grabbed both of her arms and pulled her close to me. "I didn't say anything because I thought he would leave town and forget all about seeing Noah."

She pushed me away. "WHAT? Did you tell him he could?"

I held my arms up, trying to get her to calm down. "I didn't exactly tell him yes. You're makin' it sound way worse than it is, darlin'."

She turned around and started loading the dishwasher. "Don't you even call me darlin right now!" I could hear it in her voice that she was crying.

"Savanna, Noah knows that you're his mother. We haven't kept Krista a secret though. I don't see how this could change anything. Just calm down and be rational. Noah's home is here. He's happy. Just because his rockstar uncle wants to meet him, doesn't mean anything is goin' to change." I wrapped my arms around her waist and kissed the inside of her neck. "I'd never let anything happen to our family."

She finally turned around and let me hug her the right way. "I know. I just don't want to lose him, Colt. I love him so much."

"You're never goin' to lose him. Never!"

My wife had finally calmed down, but that was just the beginning of what was to come. Zeke was going to keep trying to see Noah and I knew that the actual visit was going to kill Savanna.

I got it. I understood that she didn't want her little boy tainted. We'd always let Noah know that his mother loved him. Having an uncle that was still living, and a rockstar, well that was going to excite him. The tractors that he collected could soon be stashed away in a closet and replaced with band posters and guitars. It was something that even I wasn't prepared to handle.

That night, before the girls woke and ended up sleeping between us, I cuddled up next to my wife. She was playing some game on her kindle that she played every night before bed. "The kids are all asleep in their rooms, for a change."

"I know. I helped put them there." She giggled.

"Are you goin' to put down that game and give me some lovin', or do I have to take what I want while you're still playin'?"

She cocked her eyebrow. "The second choice sounds kind of hot."

I grabbed the waist to her pajama pants and yanked them down past her hips. She lifted up her ass to help get them down easier. I pushed up her little top to reveal her belly button and placed tender kisses all around it. She bit down on her lip like she always did. Her panties came down next, well, after I licked them until they were wet on the outside. With each stroke of my tongue, I felt her body pushing into me. I wasn't the only person who was horny in our bed. That made it even hotter.

Once she wasn't wearing any bottoms, I took it upon myself to slowly take her top and push it over her breasts. I need to see them; to feel them with the palms of my hands. I knew when I'd gotten to her nipples, because they hardened with my first touch. I heard her little reading device hit the floor and knew I had her complete attention.

Savanna ran her hands through my hair, gripping it as I pinched both of her nipples and kissed the inside of her left leg. She lifted it, allowing me to kiss even further inside. Her body reacted to my touch the same way it always had. I could still tickle her with my kisses and drive her crazy with my touch.

It was more than just being with Savanna, nowadays. Since the kids were always around, we had to be more spontaneous.

Before getting myself too invested, I climbed off the bed and headed over to lock the door. We didn't want any little visitors catching us naked together.

Savanna, who was now totally naked, was sprawled out on our bed waiting for me to return. I licked my lips, just knowing how much pent up desire I had for her. I hated that we never had alone time and I know it drove her crazy as well.

Once I climbed back on the bed on top of her, she grabbed me by my arms and pulled me into her, so that our kisses started immediately.

Her skin smelled of a fresh shower and her hair was still wet at the ends. I grabbed a handful and pulled back enough to have a full view of her neck. It didn't take me long to lick and kiss it from the base up. She moaned with my every touch, making my erection hard as a rock. I pressed it against her, letting her know that we didn't need foreplay; not that we ever did. All she ever had to do was bend over, and if it had been a long time, sometimes just smiling at me did it.

Savanna reached down, taking my shaft into her warm hands. She stroked it as our tongues mingled together. Her breathing became heavy and when I reached down between her legs again, all I could feel was how ready she was for me. Wasting no time at all, I drove myself inside of her, making sure to kiss her during my first thrust. She squealed, taking my whole size, like she'd practiced for all these years.

I licked one of her nipples, getting more aroused by the way it felt sliding against my tongue. I could tell she liked it. She licked her own lips and watched me, while my rock hard cock found it's pace.

The slower I moved, the faster my release came. We never had time to waste and it was a good thing I was so close, because little knocks started coming from our door. "Mommy! Daddy! I can't get in," Christian cried.

I knew at any moment Savanna was going to lose her concentration, so I did what every good husband would do. I took two fingers and started rubbing at her little clit until I sent her bucking into me. With my other hand over her mouth, to prevent her screams of passion to be heard by our daughter, I let go and filled my wife with a weeks worth of sexual tension.

I wished that we'd had time to lay there and catch our breath, but since one child was knocking and yelling, another started screaming from her room. Savanna sighed as she jumped up and started getting dressed. I felt my pajama pants hitting me in the head as she made her way to the door and waited for me to slip them on. This was what our sex life had come to.

Chapter 3

Savanna

I was still upset with Colt, but sex wasn't just about pleasing him. I had needs too. The whole Zeke thing was overwhelming me so much that I was unable to sleep. I tossed and turned, aside from having four little feet kicking me all through the night. Finally, at around four in the morning, I went into Christian's room and went back to bed in peace. Exhaustion had set in and I was happy to be able to close my eyes and finally drift off.

When I woke up nothing had changed. Zeke was in town and Noah was going to have to meet him for who he was. I'd be a bad mother if I tried to prevent it. We would have to sit down and tell Noah all about his uncle and go from there.

He was a smart boy and I hoped that it wouldn't cause problems within our family.

Since no one was awake yet, I tried to fall back asleep, until I felt someone little touching my face. I opened my eyes to see Christian standing over her bed looking at me. "Hi, Mommy."

I reached out and grabbed her little hand. "Hi, baby. Is Daddy awake?"

"Yes. He took Addy downstairs. She said she wanted food."

I sat up and pushed the hair out of her face. "I love you."

She giggled and started swaying her body. "I know." Her little green eyes sparkled just like her fathers did.

I followed her down the stairs and found Colt and Addy in the kitchen. He had her in a chair and was feeding her bananas cut up and scrambled eggs. Her hair was a rat's nest and even after she saw me, she continued to stuff her face. That girl could eat.

She smiled, allowing some of the mashed up bananas to escape out of the sides of her open mouth. "Hi, sunshine. Are you eating naners?"

She smiled and shoved another handful into her mouth. "Yes!"

Colt put his arms around me and turned my body around to face him. He hadn't shaved yet, probably because Addy woke him up. "Good mornin', darlin'."

His lips pressed into mine and I instinctively closed my eyes. His lips were always so soft when we kissed. As I pulled away, I opened my eyes to see him staring at me. "Good morning to you. Thanks for letting me sleep."

He laughed and turned around to flip a couple strips of bacon. "It's seven, Savanna. It ain't like I let you sleep all day. I knew Christian was goin' to find you and get you downstairs. You know how she is."

"Yeah, I do. So, after breakfast, I think we need to sit down with Noah and have a talk. The longer we wait, the harder it will be for me. I say we just tell him about his uncle, let them visit, and forget about yesterday. I don't want to fight with you over something that we need to deal with."

He turned around to look at me again, after making sure his bacon wasn't going to be too crispy. "I know you don't like this. I just want you to know that I'm worried too. I don't want our son to be corrupted by his crazy lifestyle. You know that he's goin' to think that kind of life is interestin'."

"I think you're jumping the gun. Noah loves his life. It ain't like we're goin' to lose him." I hear the fear in Colt's voice as he tried to calm me. It wasn't reassuring when he was worried about the same thing.

We spent the rest of the morning dealing with our normal routines. It wasn't enough to keep my mind off of things, but a mother's job is never done. Colt made plans to invite Zeke and his wife over for dinner. It was disturbing enough that they were coming, but to top that, Colt handed me a list of everything they didn't eat. I'd have to make a special trip into town just to be able to feed the people that I didn't want in my house.

Colt headed out about nine in the morning to do his daily checks on everything. I knew he'd be back by lunchtime, since we usually spent the afternoons in the office doing paperwork. When I needed someone to vent to, I called the salon, where Miranda and Amy would both be.

Scissor Sounds. Are you callin' for a cut or color? Miranda had the cutest southern voice. I almost wanted to play like I was an old lady and set up a fake appointment.

It's just me. How busy are you?

I just walked in. Amy is doin' a foil treatment. What's up?

You are never going to believe what happened. I still can't believe it.

Are you goin' to tell me or do I just have to hear you upset about it?

Sorry! Krista's brother is back in town.

Krista? Like Noah's Krista? I forgot all about that kid.

Yeah, and that's not even the worst part.

Does he want to see Noah? Oh my God I know you are freakin' out.

I'm not freaking out about that as much as the fact that Krista's brother changed his name. He goes by Zeke Marlo now.

Why does that name sound familiar?

Because he is the lead singer and guitarist for that rock band that Conner is so crazy about.

Shut up! Are you for real?

Can you not be so excited about it? I called you for moral support.

Sorry. It's just...well he's famous. It's kind of cool.

Not when he and his wife are recovering addicts.

Noah doesn't have to know that. He'll just be excited about meetin' his famous uncle. Wait! Am I supposed to be against it all together?

YES!

So an autograph is out of the question?

Amy is so much better at being on my side! You suck!

Sorry. Can you at least tell me why we are against it?

Just because! I mean, what if he wants to go stay with him? What if they have booze and pills all over the place? What if he wants to be a rocker or dye his hair black and pierce his face up? My God, Colt will have a heart attack and die.

I think you are reading too much into this. Maybe he just wants to meet Noah because he is the only family he has left. Just because he looks different than us, doesn't mean he is a terrible guy. He was always a nice kid. I'm not sayin' that he hasn't changed, but at least let them meet. You never know. Noah might get freaked out and not want to see him again.

I'm a horrible mother.

No! You're a great mother who is worried about her son going in the wrong direction. It's good that you care. Listen Van, Noah is a smart kid. He knows you and Colt love him to death. Just take some deep breaths and be positive about the visit. The more negative you are, the more he will want to do it. I know it's hard, but you have to try.

It makes me feel like I am losing him. I respect Krista for having him and being his mother, but she's gone and I have been that boy's mother since he came to live with us. I love him like he is my own flesh and blood. He helped me get through one of the hardest points in my life. I can't imagine not having him.

He isn't going anywhere. He loves you. You know that.

I better go, Addy will be up from her nap soon.

Okay. I love you. Deep breaths and call me if you need me.

Love you, too!

I felt a little better after we hung up, but I was still worried.

Once Addy woke up from her nap, we headed out to the grocery store. It took me forever to get everything on the list for dinner, since I had no idea how to even pronounce some of the foods.

While standing in line at the checkout, I noticed Zeke was on the cover of two tabloid magazines. I threw both of them on the counter and paid for them with my groceries. If this man was going to be around my kids, I wanted to know everything about him.

When I had all of the groceries loaded into the SUV, and my daughter in her booster seat with a cookie, I opened up the first magazine and started reading. Addy started to whine, so I turned on a video of a dancing purple dinosaur and she calmed down. As much as I hated hearing those songs over and over, they sure did calm my child down. She missed it when her sister went to kindergarten. She only had preschool three days a week.

The first tabloid paper was a picture of Zeke, surrounded by two half dressed bimbos. He had a cigarette hanging out of his mouth and a bottle of booze was in his hand that was hanging over the shoulder of one of the girls. It made me cringe to think about my almost eleven year old idolizing this guy. He wasn't supposed to fall in love with bands and music until he was at least in middle school.

After reading the whole three page article, I learned that Zeke owned a couple of houses. This particular picture that I was looking at had been taken at his L.A. property. Apparently, while his wife went on some tour with other recovering addicts to talk to teens in different cities, he was busy living it up without her.

One of the women were claiming that he fathered her unborn child.

I felt nauseous that someone his age could still be so irresponsible. He made Ty look like a saint, that's for sure.

I put that magazine down and grabbed the next one. This particular magazine was well known and all about musicians. Zeke and his band were on the cover, wearing only pants. They were all covered in tattoos, and not the pretty kind, like Colt had. Two of the members had one side of their heads shaved. They had their tongues out and were holding up live rats like they were going to eat them whole. Zeke had his arms crossed and was looking over with a sly grin on his face. He rubbed me the wrong way and it wasn't just because I was being a selfish mother.

I opened the article and read about all the members and what they had come from. Zeke met the twins while doing a show in New Orleans. Once the three of them got together, they were signed and added the last two members. The story went on to talk about how fame had caused the band to have troubles. All of the after parties, the drugs, the booze and the women, had created a group of men that barely had working livers.

It went into each member in detail, finally ending with Zeke being the last. I read all about his alcoholic father and what he went through as a kid, relying on just his sister to be fed each day. They talked about his first wife and how she couldn't handle the lifestyle any longer. He'd met his second wife at one of his rehab trips and they'd had a very public affair, not caring who knew or how many people they hurt.

It went on to say how he and his wife had reconciled and they were seen at a fertility clinic. The article was claiming that a child would calm down the troubled star. I thought the article was crap. You can't bring a baby into that kind of environment to act as some sort of last result therapy. It appalled me.

When my phone started ringing, I realized that I had completely lost track of time. I was certain that my frozen items had melted all over the back storage compartment.

Hello?

Hey, darlin', it's me. I'm just checkin' on you.

I looked at the clock and saw that it was eleven thirty. *I am leaving the store now. Do you want me to pick up lunch?*

I can make us something and have it ready when you get here.

Okay, we'll see you in about twenty minutes.

Alright, darlin'. See you then.

Addy was in the back watching the dinosaur show, not paying any attention to me in the front seat. I started on our way back to the ranch, feeling worse than I had before I read the articles. I was scared to even show Colt. I knew he was worried too.

Once we pulled up at the house, Colt came out to help with the bags. Sure enough, ice cream was dripping out of one of them. He held up the bag in the driveway.

I gave him a guilty look and handed him the articles. "I sat in the parking lot reading all about our visitor."

He cocked his eyebrow and grabbed some more bags. "I don't want to know, do I?"

I grabbed Addy out of her seat. She'd fallen asleep and I was trying not to wake her. "Not really," I whispered.

As soon as I had laid our daughter down for her nap, I headed into the kitchen to find Colt examining the things that I had purchased. He was reading one of the labels when he noticed me standing there. "This stuff sounds disgusting. Meat has to be better for you than what's in this stuff. There ain't no way in Hell that I would eat liquid beans instead of beef."

I laughed, thinking about Colt being a vegetarian. "Darn. I was thinking about changing our diets."

"To hell with that. I'd rather starve. My kids are eatin' good food, not this imitation shit."

I helped put the non-perishables away and sat down at the table. Colt put a plate with a tuna sandwich down in front of me. Then he sat down across from me with his plate and a bag of chips. "I talked to Miranda today about what was going on."

"What did she say?" He popped a chip in his mouth.

I took a bite and waited until I swallowed to answer. "She thought it was cool, at first."

"It ain't cool. I just want this visit to be done and over with. When Zeke leaves, we need to sit Noah down and let him know that we are not okay with him growin' up and wantin' that kind of lifestyle."

Colt took a huge bite of his sandwich and just stared at me. What he was doing was thinking about something. I'd seen him do it a million times. "I love you."

"Your lunch is that good, huh?"

We both laughed. "The house is really quiet." It usually was when the two oldest were at school. It wasn't until they all got home that it got chaotic. "We could go upstairs."

He dropped his sandwich down on his plate and brushed off his hands. "We could?"

I bit down on my lip and gave him that look. "Uh huh."

He stood up and reached over the table to grab my hand. I sat my sandwich down and let him lead me up the stairs to our room.

This was exactly the distraction that we both needed in order to go through with our day. I wanted my son to know his family. I just didn't want him being corrupted by him.

It was going to be a long night.

Chapter 4

Colt

My wife didn't have much faith in people. I couldn't blame her. She'd been through a lot, and even though she was fully recovered, that kind of traumatic event changes a person. She had lost her ability to see the positive in things, which left her dwelling on all of the negatives.

I felt that it was important for me to keep her as distracted as physically possible, so when she offered a quickie, I was all over it.

Savanna didn't waste any time once we got up to our bedroom. With no little one's being able to walk in, we left the door open and went right for our bed. While standing on either side facing one another, we proceeded to undress. I couldn't take my eyes off of Savanna eagerly taking off her clothes.

She wanted this distraction so badly.

Once I'd kicked off my boots and got down to my boxers, she was already crawling up on top of the bed in nothing at all. "Do you know how crazy you make me, woman?"

She reached over and grabbed my hands, so she could pull me onto the mattress with her. Once our faces were almost touching, she took her lips and lightly brushed hers against mine. "I have a pretty good idea."

I avoided touching her and let her take the lead. We were kneeling on the bed, until she guided my body down to lay on my back. In one swift move, she was straddling my hard cock. She let her body rock over the stiff erection. I ran my fingers up around her waist, letting them glide up to her smooth breasts. She reached over and jutted her tongue in my ear. I needed to kiss her and she knew it was what I wanted, because she pulled away, teasing me and not letting me have it.

I reached my hands around, grabbed her plump ass and squeezed it. She grinded herself into me again, leaning back so that her tits were right in my face. I flicked her nipple with my tongue, then bit it with my front teeth. She ran her hands through her hair and moved her body so that her other nipple could get the same attention. I watched her as I sucked it in between my teeth.

My pulse was racing as I drug my wet lips over her hardened nipple. She moaned and ran her hand into my hair. Finally she let me kiss her. Her lips were full of passion as she opened them, letting our tongues finally touch. The first sensation of our passionate embrace was always the same. Even as a grown man, who had been with this woman for so many years, she still got me on a level that I couldn't even explain.

I reached my hand down and inserted one finger between her folds. Her body reacted to my touch. While still inside of her, I used my thumb and started rubbing on her little clit.

My erection needed attention and my wife knew just what to do. She leaned down and pressed her lips into mine again, before sliding down, forcing my fingers away from her wet pussy. When she was down facing my hard cock, I watched her taking it into her hand. She stroked it a few times, before putting her lips around my shaft and letting her saliva lubricate my whole length.

I watched her tongue, running up and down the vein located in the back of my shaft. I grabbed the top of her head and held it as I felt her moving up and down my hardness.

I had to take advantage of what Savanna was doing. She rarely had the time to do anything like this and I could tell that her drive to please me was coming from the stress of what she was feeling. At any rate, I was a man. I wanted her in any way I could get. Forgetting that I had my hand on her head, and was pushing it down, I heard her starting to gag. She pulled her head up and started to laugh at herself.

That gag reflex always caused her problems.

She licked her lips and attempted to put it back in her mouth, like she was starving for it. I grabbed her hair and kept her within inches of my erection. She stuck out her tongue, trying her hardest to make contact with my skin. "You want it?"

She looked right at me and moaned. "Yes."

"Oh yeah, I know you do, darlin'."

When I let go of my hold on her, she took me back into her mouth and began stroking me hard and roughly, while using her mouth as a tool to get me off.

Try as I might, I couldn't hold in the pounding explosion that was about to happen. Thankfully, she pulled away for a second and I saw my window to change things around. I grabbed her by the underneath of her arms and lifted her up to be straddling me. She wasted no time positioning her pussy against my cock, enabling it to slide right in.

I heard her gasp, right before I felt her body rocking back and forth. She started using her folded legs to bounce up and down. She still didn't know how beautiful she was to me. While my wife took control of our afternoon delight, I ran my hands all over her sexy physique. Her soft breasts continued moving all around as the motion of her body sped up.

Savanna closed her eyes and ran her hands from her abdomen up to her breasts. I watched her biting down on her lip as she concentrated on the way my being inside of her was making her feel. I reached my arms around and pulled her close to me again, so that I could feel her lips against mine. I grabbed onto her ass again and grinded her body roughly into mine. Our skin was rubbing in all the right places, causing a friction that sent me over the edge. I held her body firm while my release burst inside of her tight walls.

It was hard to breathe, and even harder when she leaned down and continued kissing me.

Since we still didn't hear a little one crying for us, we lay there together in each other's arms. Sure, we had a bunch to do before our unwanted guests arrived, but we just needed time to ourselves.

A few hours later, Savanna had gotten herself involved in cooking with ingredients that we had no idea what was in them. She was determined to make things perfect, even when I knew she hated the idea of having Zeke and his wife over for dinner.

While she had involved herself in such a big task, I took Addy on the golf cart to get the kids from the bus stop. She loved going places with me and I enjoyed spending time with my youngest child. She was my little ray of sunshine. She liked to sit on my lap and steer, so I got her situated and let her take the wheel.

We still hadn't told Noah all about his uncle, so he had no idea that we were expecting him to show up shortly. Since my mother had heard of our news, she insisted on taking the girls for the night, giving us time to deal with whatever may happen.

Savanna took a break and gathered everything for me to take over to my mother's house. Of course, Noah started asking questions right away as to why he couldn't stay with her.

I think Savanna would have liked to have time to think about what she wanted to say to Noah. Unfortunately, he was too nosey to wait and be calm about it. We sat him down in the kitchen across from both of us. I held my hand on Savanna's knee knowing how worried she was about it. "Dad says that you have to talk to me. I knew my teacher was goin' to call. I didn't do anything. It was Billy."

I looked at my wife and lifted my eyebrows. "Boy, what are you talkin' about?"

"I didn't put the gum in Lisa's hair. Billy did it and told the teacher that it was me."

I put my hands over my face and took a few deep breaths. "That's not what we need to talk to you about, Noah. Me and your mom have somethin' that we need to tell you and it's important that you listen."

Noah folded his hands and looked right at me. "So, I'm not in trouble?"

Savanna held out her hands and reached for his. He gave them to her and also turned to give her all of his attention. "Sweetie, do you remember talking about your birth mother?"

"Yeah. Her picture is in my room."

"Did you know that you had an uncle?" Savanna looked over at me, like she wanted to know she was going about this the right way. I winked at her, but felt just as uncomfortable as she did. Noah was mine and after not knowing that I had a son for his first three years of life, I wasn't sure I wanted to share him. I realized how selfish I was being, but it was the truth.

"I have lots of uncles," Noah replied.

"No, not them. Your birth mother had a brother. He lives really far away and we haven't heard from him since before you were born." Savanna was doing a good job.

"Why not? Didn't he know I was alive?"

"Yes, buddy. He knew your mother gave birth to you. He was just trying to make a life for himself and couldn't get back to get to know you. When your mother passed away, you were brought to us. I never heard one word from your uncle until last week." Noah needed to know the whole truth, except it was hard to explain to a kid his age that someone isn't a good role model, especially when they were famous.

"Why did he call you? How come he didn't just call me?"

"Because I am your father and he knew he'd have to get in touch with me to set up a time to come and visit."

"He's that guy from the other day, right?" Noah played with his fingers while we talked. I knew he was curious and I couldn't blame him. Family was always the most important thing to me, so naturally he would think that this was a good thing.

"Yeah. He's that guy."

"He looks weird." He'd only seen him clothed. After looking at Savanna's magazines, I was even afraid of what he may have under cover.

"He lives a different kind of lifestyle than we do. Your uncle is into music. He's in a band." Right away I saw Noah's eye light up. This news excited him and I could feel the pull of losing him starting to take place.

"Is he on the radio? Is he famous?" My son was now leaning into the table, hanging on my every word.

"Yes."

He ran over and grabbed his IPod. "What does he sing? I need to download the songs to my playlist.

Savanna and I looked at each other and I could tell she was starting to freak out. "Your uncle is in a grown up band. They are uncensored and it isn't appropriate for someone your age." She explained it exactly how she should have.

Noah got an agitated look on his face. He tossed his IPod on the table. "Forget it then!"

"Don't treat your belongings like that, Noah. We will not buy you a new one if you break it!" I wasn't taking his attitude because he couldn't do something that he wanted.

"It's not fair!"

"How about you meet your uncle tonight and spend some time with him? I'm sure he will be willing to sign things, so that you can share them with your friends." It was all I could think to offer him. Dealing with someone his age wasn't exactly easy. They wanted to act like they were grown up, but had no idea how to do it properly.

"Does he live in a mansion? I bet he has a tennis court. Will his band be here for dinner too?"

"Go get your chores done and you can ask him all about it when he gets here." Savanna had finally had enough of Noah's excitement. I was clenching my jaw the whole time myself, so I couldn't imagine how frustrated she was.

We watched Noah run out of the kitchen before we said anything to each other. I reached my arm around my wife and kissed her cheek. "It's goin' to be fine, darlin'."

She started to cry. "You don't know that, Colt. Our son is going to be so caught up in this guy. You know how he gets."

I wiped the tear making its way down her cheek. "It's for one night. Then he will be out of our lives and probably never call again."

She nodded and leaned her head on my shoulder. "I hope you're right."

"It's just a visit. How much harm can he do in one night?"

She turned around and looked right at me. "I'm scared. Noah is such an influential soul. I don't want him tainted by this guy. I know it's wrong to judge people, but this guy is just horrible. He lives his life different than we do. I just can't fathom our son wanting to grow up and be like that. I know you think it's going to be okay. I'm just worried about him."

I stood up and started massaging her shoulders. I got that it was different for her. She always kept Noah close because he wasn't her blood. I don't get why she always feared losing him when the kid loved her so much. "Stop overreacting, Savanna. Everything will be fine. Let's just appease this guy and let him see Noah. No harm done."

She stood up and hugged me. "I hope you're right."

I rubbed the small of her back. "We've dealt with much worse, darlin'."

I left Savanna in the kitchen and headed out to find Noah. He was feeding the horses when I found him in the barn. "Hey, Dad."

"Hey, Buddy. You need any help?"

He put the bucket that he was holding down and wiped off his hands. "Nope. Sam's helping me just fine."

I laughed when I looked down at my old dog. She was turning twelve and for a lab that was old. Most days she laid around on her bed until the kids got home. She'd run after them for a few hours and then sleep for the rest of the night. The only help she was offering Noah was companionship. He did love that dog though.

"Do you think my new uncle rides horses? Does he have kids?"

"Noah, to be honest with you, I don't know much about your uncle. I haven't seen him since he was your age. When he comes over tonight, it will be like I'm just meetin' him too. How about we wait and ask him all of those questions?"

I put my arm around my son and we walked back to the house. I could only hope that no matter how exciting Zeke seemed, Noah would see him for what he really was.

Chapter 5

Savanna

I had to take a Xanax thirty minutes before Zeke and his wife showed up. Noah kept asking when they were arriving about every five minutes, making me on edge. At one point he came in the kitchen and whispered to me if he could download just one of the guys songs. I was reluctant to tell him no, but only because I didn't want there to be any animosity between him and I before his uncle showed up.

When I heard the car pulling up out front, I had already opened a bottle of wine and filled a glass for myself.

The more I continued to try to be positive, the more I feared the worst possible outcome.

Voices filled the living room and I knew they had arrived. I washed my hands and took a deep breath before heading out to greet them. Unlike his normal self, Noah was hiding behind his father as the couple entered. The dog was going crazy, so Noah took her by the collar and locked her in the office. It was weird, because Sam loved people. However, she did not like them.

I smiled when I caught eyes with his wife. Unlike her husband, she was able to make herself look more presentable without seeming emo. Her blonde hair had streaks of black through it, but it wasn't anything that Miranda hadn't done to her own hair. She had her nose pierced and a tattoo on her wrist, but wearing long sleeves had hidden all of the rest of her skin. I reached my hand out to her. "I'm Savanna."

"Hi, I'm Piper. Thanks for having us over. Zeke has been talking about this for a while now."

I put on a fake smile, trying to ignore the lump in my throat. "Noah is very excited,"

He had come back into the room as I said it. I put my hands on his shoulders and waited for Zeke to talk.

He reached his hand out for Noah. "What's up, little man?"

"You're my uncle?"

Zeke laughed. "Yeah, I am. Your mother was my sister."

It was another punch in the face for me. I know it was selfish. I had no right to claim him as my own, but I did it anyway.

"I don't remember her." He didn't seem sad; just making the statement out loud.

Zeke looked at me and then back to Noah. I guess he was trying to be respectful and I did appreciate it. "I can tell you stories about your mother, if you'd like. She was real special to me."

Piper seemed like she felt out of place. She kept looking around at the walls and pictures in the house. I walked over to where she stood. "So, I'm trying to get this recipe right with all these organic foods. Do you think maybe you could help me in the kitchen for a minute? I will just die if it tastes like dirt."

She smiled and followed me into the kitchen. "I like your house. It's so cozy. None of our houses look anything like this."

I wasn't sure how to take that. Was she saying that our house was crap, or was she missing living a normal life. "So, what do they look like?"

Her eyes got real big. "Don't you watch Cribs on MTV?"

"No. I haven't watched that channel since I was in college. Once I met Colt, I just lost interest. It's not exactly the kind of thing to watch with little kids around."

I handed her a spoon and let her taste one of the items I had made. She blew on it before putting it near her lips. "Wow. You did great. Zeke will love this."

"That is a relief. Do you like it?"

She looked toward the doorway and then back to me. "What you made tastes good. Zeke is all about eating this way. If it were up to me, I'd have a hamburger and fries."

We both laughed together.

"It must be crazy being married to someone famous. Do you mind me asking how you met?"

She shook her head. "You know, I really thought you'd have checked us out online or something. Don't you read magazines?"

I felt embarrassed for buying those tabloids, so I didn't bother sharing the things that I had learned about them. "I read Better Homes and Gardens."

"It's probably a good thing. Some of those papers just like to cause drama. Half of the things you read in those articles aren't true. In fact, I'm pretty sure that they cause most of Hollywood's divorces."

I started thinking outside of the box, realizing how hard it must be. "So where are you originally from?"

We sat down at the kitchen table. It was better than me having to go back into the other room with the guys.

"I was born in Berlin and then my parents moved to America when I was two. My father started a small bakery and he and my mom still run it together in Richmond, Virginia."

"Have you been back to Berlin?"

She tapped her fingers on the table. "Not until I married Zeke. We were the last of my family to come to the states, so we never had a reason to go back. My parents moved here for a better life."

"How did they feel when you married a rockstar?" I just had to know how her parents felt about her marrying someone so rough looking.

She shrugged. "They stopped talking to me. Picture the most old fashioned parents in the world and multiply that times ten. Then you will have my parents. It wasn't just the tattoos, or the piercings. I think they could have lived with that. It was the fact that he was married when I met him. My mother is very serious about her beliefs and extramarital affairs aren't acceptable. I kept it a secret from them until I landed on the cover of one of those supermarket tabloids. My parents only spoke to me one time since they saw that picture and it was to tell me that I was no longer a part of their family."

I felt so sad for her. I could see the pain in her eyes. "That's horrible. I'd do anything for my kids, no matter what."

"It's fine. I'm used to it. Besides, I was the one who decided to live this life. The night I met Zeke, I wasn't even supposed to be where I was. I lied to my parents so that I could sneak out to a concert with my girlfriends. I had no idea I was going to meet him."

I remembered reading about her meeting him in rehab. It was hard to wonder if she was telling the truth, or the tabloid. I held up my hands. "I'm not judging you, but were you like a groupie?"

She laughed. "No way! Groupies are little sluts who just want to sleep with the band. I wasn't promiscuous at all. In fact, I wasn't very experienced. When I met Zeke, I was standing in the corner of the room, avoiding the drinking and drugs that were all around me. He took me up to the roof and we spent the rest of the night just talking."

"So, you got together then?"

She smiled and shook her head. "No. I didn't see Zeke again until a year later. I didn't exactly hang around with the good crowd, so it was no surprise that one of my friends had to go into rehab after drunk driving and killing someone. Part of their sentence was to spend eight weeks in rehab. On one of the visitation days, I saw Zeke sitting outside smoking. Of course, I didn't think he would recognize me. He'd been drinking the night we met and he was around so many women that I never thought I'd made an impression. My hair was a different color and I even dressed differently." She laughed out loud. "He called me by name when he saw me. I was floored. That's actually the day that our picture was taken and my parents disowned me."

"Without a place to go, Zeke moved me into one of his houses. The paparazzi went wild, taking photos whenever we were together. I knew he wasn't a saint. He'd cheated on his wife a million times, but I didn't sleep with him until he had filed for a separation. You probably think I'm terrible."

The thing was, I actually didn't. For some reason, I really liked her. Of course, I wouldn't have chosen her life, but she seemed like a nice girl. You can't help who you fall in love with, or when it happens. "Don't feel bad. When Colt and I got together, I had kind of promised myself to his cousin. We'd known each other for years, but something happened between us and we just couldn't stop it. I've been with him ever since."

"He's very handsome. I can see how he'd be hard to resist." She looked like she was embarrassed for saying it.

"He was. My ex was also very good looking and he was in a coma. Now you probably think I am the horrible one."

She put her hand over her mouth, like she was in shock.

After a few seconds, she finally dropped her hand back down on the table. "Did it cause problems in the family?"

"Only for a little while. We're all best friends now. He's very happy with his own family." I wasn't even going to explain that Ty had married Colt's cousin Miranda. That was just too hard for people to interpret.

We talked for a little longer about our parents and then she helped me set the dining room table. The guys were still in the living room and I was completely fine keeping Piper occupied. Besides, it gave me a chance to get to know her more. I had to admit, she was sweet and seemed to be more normal than I ever could have expected.

When it was finally time to eat, I heated up Noah some chicken tenders, so that he wouldn't have to eat the concoction that we all had to. I saw his lip curl when he saw me open up the pot. It didn't smell bad, but I was sure it didn't taste good.

Watching my husband trying to swallow the mystery food was so hard to do without laughing. He tried his best to keep an even face, but as each spoonful hit his mouth, I could tell he wanted to spit it out. The texture and taste were nothing like we'd even eaten before.

"This tastes great, Savanna. Thanks for going to the trouble. Next time I can have my chef make it for us, so that you don't have to spend the whole day in the kitchen. I know it's time consuming, but it's so good for the body."

He didn't look anything like a guy that took care of his body. "It was no trouble. I'm glad you like it."

"You have a chef at your house?" Noah seemed amazed.

"I do. He goes where we go," Zeke explained.

"Wow! How much money do you have?"

"NOAH!" We both yelled at the same time.

Zeke put his fork down. "It's okay. He's just curious." He gave all of his attention to Noah. "Every time the radio plays one of my songs, I make money. When I perform in concerts, I make money."

"You make money when you sleep?"

Zeke laughed. "Yeah, I do. It's pretty rad huh?"

"You're like, the richest man in the world."

We all laughed at that one.

"No, I'm not. I've worked hard to make it where I am, though. It's not as easy as you think; just ask my wife." Zeke nudged Piper.

"Whatever. You get to buy whatever you want. You have a limousine. All we have is tractors and trucks. You're so cool!"

I think Colt felt like he got kicked between the legs. He cleared his throat and excused himself from the dinner table, using the excuse that he had to use the men's room. I knew that if I went after him, it would only cause them to be alarmed, so I chose to ignore my husband, when I knew he needed me. I felt horrible about it, too.

Noah continued to ask Zeke a million questions. Most of the things he asked were just absurd, but the guy kept answering him. When they finally settled back into the living room, and started talking about Krista, Colt took me out on the porch swing.

He put his arm around me as we rocked back and forth. "You alright, darlin'?"

I shrugged. "I'm hanging in there. How are you?"

"I'm tryin' to be fair. They're family and it's important that they know about each other. Zeke seems alright. He ain't all strung out like I thought he would be. He seems to have his problem under control. What about his wife? Does she seem alright?"

I leaned my head against my strong husband's shoulder. "She's nice, actually. I don't know how the two of them fell in love, but she seems like she has her head on straight. She told me a whole different story than I read in that tabloid."

He started laughing at me. "I think maybe we both overreacted about all of this, Savanna. Aside from his weird ass food that he eats, the guy seems fine. Maybe we shouldn't even be worried about him being in Noah's life. It ain't like he's got him listening to devil worshippin' music and wanting to tattoo his body."

I pushed him. "My God! I hope not. He's just a kid."

He grabbed my hand and kissed it. "I'm just playin' with you. It's all goin' to be just fine. Once they leave town, everything will go back to the way it was. You're always goin' to be that boy's mom."

After all of the worrying, I was feeling like it was possible. I leaned my lips up to Colt's and kissed him before standing up and heading for the front door.

Noah met us at the door. He grabbed my hand and started pulling me. "Mom, come on. You have to help me pack."

I looked back at Colt, feeling confused. "Pack for what?"

"Uncle Zeke said I could go stay at his house. Can you believe it? I'm goin' to see a real rock stars house."

Everything wasn't going to be okay. In fact, it was far from being okay.

Chapter 6

Colt

It took Savanna a while to get Noah settled down enough to go up and get a shower. The last thing he wanted to do was say goodbye to his new, famous uncle. When we knew he was upstairs, I led Zeke and Piper into the kitchen to talk.

Savanna wasn't doing well. She always lost it when it came to our kids. She sat there just staring off until I started speaking. "I think we need to talk about some things, Zeke. I think we might not be on the same page here."

"Sure, man. What's up?"

I opened up my hands that were sitting on the table. "Look, don't take this the wrong way, but I don't think it's a good idea for my son to go stay with you."

He crossed his arms. "Why is that? You've known me for years. I didn't tell him he could come with me tonight, but I think I deserve to have a relationship with my nephew."

"I knew you when you were a child. Times have changed. Savanna and me are goin' to have to talk about this first. Noah ain't never been somewhere far away from us. He just met you and it's obvious that you live a different kind of lifestyle."

He got up from the table and started pacing around my kitchen. "I get it. You think I am going to corrupt your kid. You know, Colt, I may look different than you, but I'm still that same guy you knew before."

Savanna couldn't take it anymore. "As much as I want to believe that you both are good people, I have to keep my guard up when it comes to my child. I think before Noah can go to stay with you, he should get to know you here, where we know he is safe."

"Safe? Lady, I don't know what magazine or news channel you get your information from, but I'm not some child molester or serial killer. I'm his blood. It's way more than you share with him."

I banged my fist on the table. "Enough! This shit is not happenin'. You will not come into my house and degrade my wife in front of me. That woman has been the only mother that kid has had since he was dropped off at our doorstep. She loves him as much as if she had him herself. You need to leave, before I remind you how we handle things around these parts and I can promise you that you're not goin' to like it."

"Colt, don't threaten me for stating the facts man. I have every right to know that kid."

"Where have you been for the past ten and a half years of his life? I know I haven't seen you for almost seven. You knew where we lived. You could have sent cards. Hell, my number is still the same. You never gave a shit about him." I wasn't going to tolerate him any longer. This guy had come into my house and been disrespectful. He needed to get the hell off of my property.

"Things have been tough for me. I had a lot of problems and I didn't want to taint our relationship with them."

Who did he think he was? "We never had a relationship, Zeke. You were a child when you lived here. I helped your sister take care of you, for a short time. I owed you nothing and my opinion doesn't even matter. This is about my son. Your sister didn't even bother to tell me about him. Do you have any idea what that was like for me, for my wife? No, you don't! You couldn't, because you were out getting drugged up. I reckon that's how you had to deal with her loss, but that ain't how I do things. She should have told me about him. I would have taken care of them."

Savanna walked out of the room and sat on the couch. I didn't mean it like I wanted to be with Krista. I think she'd just had enough for the night. "Look, I think it's best that we just sever ties. Noah has met you. If you want to see him, it's going to be here. I don't want my son knowin' your lifestyle. It's not the place for a kid."

"So he can't come and stay with us?"

"No!"

Zeke grabbed his wife by the arm and almost pulled her out of the kitchen. "If you're going to refuse me to see my own nephew, I'm going to have to contact my lawyer. Do you really want to go about it that way, Colt?"

"You do what you gotta do! No judge in his right mind is goin' to think that Noah bein' around all that partyin' is a good idea."

Zeke shook his head again. "I hoped this would go better, I really did."

Once we watched them pull away, I hugged my wife. "It's goin' to be fine, Savanna. He's just mad that we wouldn't let him take Noah. He'll calm down and it will be fine."

"I hope so," She cried with her face tucked into my chest.

Our kids had never been threatened like this. I didn't know what to think. On one hand, I was hoping that it was just some phase that the guy was going through. Maybe after he left and calmed down, it would just all blow over and he would decide it wasn't worth his time or his money. It wasn't like I forbid him to see my son. I just said it had to be on my terms. I'm his father. He had to know that I would throw that card out there. Any good father would have done the same.

It also wasn't because Zeke's appearance. I knew there was a good guy somewhere in that tough armor he wore. The problem with Zeke was the package that came with him. He may not have been using and he could have been married to a princess for all I cared. It was the crowd of people that surrounded him wherever he went. It was the type of things that his songs implied.

He couldn't get away from the life he'd made for himself.

I got that he broke down after losing Krista. It made sense. The kid came from nothing and she was his only lifeline. Before they stayed with me, it was Krista who fed him and made sure he went to school. Their dad wasn't much of a father at all. They had no supervision.

"The bottom line is that Noah is our son. We decide what happens."

Savanna turned and looked at me. She was so serious and I knew what she was going to ask. "Colt, I am going to ask you something and I need you to tell me the truth, no matter how much it would hurt me."

"Don't do this Savanna. I know where you're goin' with this."

She put her hand over my lips and was already starting to tear up. "When I was going to marry Ty and your father had his fall, what would you have done if Krista was on your doorstep, pregnant with your child?"

"I would have done the right thing." She was starting to get up. I pulled her back down beside me. "You wanted the truth and you of all people know what kind of man I am. As much as I was in love with you, I'd have to take care of them. I would have felt obligated."

She covered her face and I could hear sniffling. "I get it. You're a good man, Colt. I just can't imagine coming here and the pregnant woman at your door not being your cousin. I can't imagine a life without you in it."

"You don't ever have to, because you're right where you belong, darlin'. I didn't say I would ever love Krista. She came from nothin' and if I wanted my child to be taken good care of, it would have been under my roof."

She still wouldn't turn to look at me. "It doesn't bother you that things could have turned out so differently?"

"If your askin' if I would have showed up for your and Ty's wedding, I'm not goin' to answer that." I wasn't that guy that runs in and breaks it up, even if it was what I wanted to do. "I'd never get over you, Savanna. Losin' you would kill me."

She finally turned to face me with a face full of tears. I brushed them away as she spoke. "You're saying that after being with me for over ten years. You don't know what it would have been like back then. Having a baby with someone changes people."

"I know what I know. You were always the one. Thinking about you bein' with Ty still makes my blood boil."

"Well, I feel like I've been kicked in the stomach when I hear you say that you would have just been with Krista."

Why did she even ask if she knew what path I would have chosen. Women were so difficult. "Oh, so it was alright for me to go to sleep in that carriage house while you were showering with my cousin?" It was a low blow and I knew that my frustration had caused our disagreement to escalate. She stood up and started walking away from me. I tried to grab her arm. "Wait!"

Savanna turned and pointed at my face. "How dare you! You knew how hard it was for me. I wasn't showering with Ty. He came into the bathroom. Why are we even rehashing this, Colt. It was years ago!"

"You started this!"

"Screw you!" She threw her little temper tantrum while walking away.

I followed her and grabbed her from behind. "We shouldn't be fightin'. Everything turned out the way it should have."

Just as Savanna finally started to relax her shoulders, we both caught a glimpse of Noah standing on the stairs. His eyes were wide open and he had tears in them. "You wished my mother dead!" He ran up the stairs and we heard his door slam shut.

Savanna followed me up the stairs to Noah's bedroom. He'd locked the door, so I knocked to get him to open it. "Open the door, son. We need to talk about this."

Silence.

"Noah, I'm not kiddin'. If I have to break down this door, you're goin' to be sorry."

I heard footsteps and then the door knob jiggling. He didn't open it. When I pushed the door ajar, I saw him jumping back on his bed, face first. "Are you goin' to talk to us?"

"I heard you, Dad. I heard you say it turned out right. You wished her dead! You wished my mom dead so you could be with her!" He pointed at Savanna and then threw himself back down on the bed.

The damage was done. Savanna walked out of the room and I was so mad at Noah that I couldn't think about running to her. "You watch your mouth, boy! Savanna is your mother and you don't..."

"SHE'S NOT MY MOTHER!"

His words hurt me and I knew she heard them too. I grabbed him by the shirt and lifted him off the bed to a sitting position. "Don't you ever say that!"

"I hate her! She took my mother's place. I wish she never even lived!"

My bare hand made contact with Noah's mouth faster than I could realize what was happening. I'd never been so upset with him before. He covered his mouth and started crying.

When I stood up and got to his door, I turned back around and looked at my son, laying on his bed, bawling his eyes out. "You will stay in this room until you can apologize to your mother. Savanna may not have had you, but she is your mother in every way possible. What you just said to her, you can never take back. You remember that, Noah." I started to walk down the hallway. "And you can forget about seein' your uncle again. This is not happenin' anymore!"

Savanna was in the bathroom, in a ball, in the corner. Her head was in between her knees and she was hysterical. I couldn't imagine the pain of Noah's words and how they had affected her. She didn't deserve that; not after everything she'd done for that kid. In one sentence, he had ripped her whole world apart. Nothing was more important to my wife than being a mother. I knelt down beside her. "Darlin', he didn't mean what he said."

She pulled her knees away. "Yes he did."

"Oh hell, Savanna. He couldn't live without you. None of us could. He's just mad and he's a kid, so taking it out on us is all he knows to do."

"Please just leave me alone," she cried.

"No!" I picked her up and carried her to our bed. Once I had her on it, she turned and put her face in the covers so I couldn't see her. "He will apologize and everything is goin' to be alright. I promise!"

She looked up at me, with makeup running down her face. "Did you see his face, Colt? I know Noah and I know when he's serious. He meant what he said. He meant every word of it." She cried harder. I watched her face scrunch up as the tears poured out.

What was I supposed to say to her? Noah was probably still crying because I'd hit him. Naturally, I just wanted to walk away and come back when it was all settled. Unfortunately, I was right in the middle of it all.

I left Savanna and Noah crying and headed to my mother's to get the girls. At least if Savanna had them to keep her busy, she wouldn't have time to be so emotional.

My mother had this intuition about her. She knew when something was wrong. I'd no sooner walked in the door when she started asking me questions. "What's wrong? It didn't go well?"

"Mom, nothin' about it was well. Zeke wants to take Noah home with him. Noah told his mother that she wasn't his mother. He said he hated her." I shook my head in disappointment. "I slapped him."

She walked over and hugged me. Right away my daughter reached out for me to pick her up. She was getting entirely too big to be carried around. I looked down at the couch and saw that Christian was asleep and laying on Lucy's leg. Christian didn't get naps like her sister, so she was always the first to conk out. Lucy smiled but stayed quiet so she didn't wake her. "Son, this is what being a parent is all about. There is good and there is bad. I hate to tell you this, but the rebelling doesn't go away over night. I'm afraid this is probably just the beginning."

"Savanna is never goin' to forget this. I'm afraid this can't be undone."

"Time heals all wounds. You and I both know how much that kid loves her. He reminds me of someone I know." She patted me on the back.

"What did you do when I got mouthy?"

"I hit you with a wooden spoon!"

I suddenly remember running from the wooden spoon. "You never caught me."

"No, but your father's belt did the trick, didn't it?"

That was something that I could never forget. He used to snap it to scare me. I learned to mind what I said, in fear of getting that leather smacked across my bare ass. "Yeah." I finally smiled.

"Get the girls home and just be there for your wife. Everything will work itself out. You have to have faith, Colton."

I kissed my mother and Lucy goodbye before getting the girls back to the house. Savanna and Noah were both in their bedrooms. It was difficult to carry both of them, but I was used to the task. Once I got Christian in her room, I carried Addy straight to her mother. When I laid her down beside her, she started to stir and it got Savanna's attention. She wrapped her arms around our daughter and kissed her little head. She was still sobbing, but I knew that this was the best thing for her. She needed to feel that motherly connection, even if it was with another one of our children. "Why you cryin', Momma?"

"I was just sad."

"It's okay, Momma."

We didn't know why she'd started calling Savanna that, but my wife loved it.

I wrapped my arms around Savanna and Addy, but said nothing to her. I just wanted her to know that I was there for her.

As far as Noah went, well, I left that kid in his room without checking on him. He needed to feel left out, because he'd hurt her so badly. This was going to leave scars and I wasn't okay with that.

Chapter 7

Savanna

I wanted to wake up and it all have been a nightmare. Noah's words repeated over and over again. It was breaking my heart each time. Then there was the fight with Colt. I knew we'd both been too frustrated to have that sort of conversation, but I forced it anyway.

Now he was mad, at not only Noah, but me as well.

It felt good to have his arms around me, and even better to have Addy in bed with us. It also reminded me of the child in the other room, who had broken my heart. I never thought I would hear him say such awful things to me. Hearing that he hated me was just indescribable.

When morning came, I was afraid to get out of bed. I didn't know what to say to Noah. I just loved him so much and if he didn't love me, I didn't know how I could handle that.

Colt took Addy downstairs early. I could hear him talking to Christian when I started walking down the stairs. Since she had no idea what happened the night before, I put on a happy face. "Good morning, pretty girl."

"Hi, Mommy. Grandma and Aunt Lucy let me stay up and watch the show with the duck mans in it."

"The duck men, you mean?"

"Yeah, that's what I said."

She loved watching the men with the long beards goofing around. Colt never missed an episode and now he had the whole family watching it. Of course, Ty and Conner took their love for the show to a whole different level. On several occasions they had a whole conversation with each other by only using lines from the show.

At first it was funny but, after a while, it became so annoying.

"Did you have fun with Grandma and Aunt Lucy?"

She nodded and started playing with her doll. Addy had a handful of banana and was shoving it into her mouth. Her eyes lit up when she saw me smiling. It melted my broken heart a little.

Colt smiled as I poured myself a cup of coffee. "Mornin', darlin'."

I smiled back at him.

"So, I talked to Noah this mornin' and told him that he wasn't comin' out of that bedroom until he thought long and hard about what he said to you. Until he apologizes, he is not to step foot outside that room unless he has to piss."

"Piss! Mommy, is piss a bad word?" Christian asked calmly.

Colt shook his head, smiling, as I gave him one of my looks, like he should have known better. Addy put her little hand over her mouth and started laughing. I feared that soon they would both be saying it in unison.

"Yes, honey. It's a bad word. Let's try not to say it again."

"When I'm a big girl, can I say piss?"

"Christian, your mother said not to say it. Daddy is sorry for slipping. I will put a dollar in your piggy bank." Colt was trying not to curse in front of the kids at all. To help with that process, he would give each child a dollar if he cursed in front of them.

Soon they would need new piggy banks.

"How was Noah when you checked on him?" As hurt as I was, he was still my son and it mad me sad that he was stuck in his room, even if it was because of something that he deserved to be punished for.

"I woke him up to talk to him. He didn't say much."

I handed him a rag to wipe off Addy's face. Our little piglet always got more on her face than in her mouth. She was getting too big to eat like that. She moved her head to the side. "No! Stop it, Daddy." It was cute how she talked.

"Your face is dirty. Maybe if you'd eat slower you wouldn't wear it," Colt teased.

She jumped down from her seat and went running after her sister. It was great that they were finally old enough to play together. They still fought and got jealous of each other, but other times they were the best of friends.

Colt had to make his run around the farm, like he did every day. He kissed me goodbye and said bye to the kids, before leaving. I took a deep breath and walked up the stairs to Noah's room.

He was putting on his shoes when I entered. "Your dad made breakfast. You need to hurry and eat so we don't miss the bus."

He stood up and walked by me, like I didn't exist. "Noah, I know what your father said to you."

He grabbed his book bag by the front door and stormed out. I put on a pair of flip-flops and ran out on the porch after him. That kid was already on his electric scooter and halfway down the dirt road. The girls were at the door, making sure I wasn't leaving them there.

Knowing that I still had to get both of them ready for school and pre-k, I couldn't take the time to chase after my son.

The girls were good for me and we climbed on the golf cart to head to the bus stop.

"Mommy, look it's Noah." Addy pointed toward her brother. He was leaning against the ranch sign with earphones on his head.

"He's grumpy, so I want you both to leave him alone today."

"Why is he grumpy?" Christian asked.

"He just is. Boys can get grumpy sometimes." Thankfully, the bus pulled up.

Noah held his hand out and walked Addy onto the bus, like he did everyday. At least he wasn't mad at his sisters, like he was at me. Addy sat down in one of the first seats, like the preschoolers had to. Christian sat in the seat behind her and Noah went to the back of the bus. When it started to pull away, I saw him looking directly at me. His eyes were filled with hate.

I was so upset over it, that I took the golf cart straight to my parent's house. They were sitting out on the screen porch drinking coffee. I think they knew something was wrong. Right away, my mother made me a cup and they both gave me their attention. It took about an hour to tell them everything that had happened. They were so reassuring and tried their best to make me feel better.

After I had heard enough positives from them to aid a hurricane relief party, I headed back to the house to start on my daily routine.

Usually, by the time Colt came in, around lunch time, I'd have the house picked up and his lunch ready. I was doing good, getting all the beds made and the dirty clothes picked up from each room. It wasn't until I got to Noah's room where I got distracted.

On his pillow was a picture of Krista. I'd hung the picture for him when he came to stay with us, but after a few years, we redecorated his room and he stuck it in his closet. I didn't even know he remembered where it was.

I sat down on the bed and held the picture in my hands, just tracing the photograph. It was hard to imagine what Noah was going through. I was raised by my parents who were still living. Who knew how much of his mother Noah could remember, but it was obviously bothering him.

I hated that I was the cause. More than anything in the world, I wanted to be able to solve any problem for my children. This wasn't just about his uncle visiting. No, he'd stirred something up in Noah's mind and now the child was all broken up over it.

No matter how much I wanted to fix things for Noah, I knew that I was the last person to be able to do it. It made me feel left out, among other things. When it was all said and done, as much as I wanted to be Noah's mother, I would never be able to fill those shoes completely.

Once I was home, and had all of my morning duties completed, I filled up the large soaking tub with hot water and bubbles and sank down in it. I didn't want anyone thinking that I wanted their sympathy. One could only hope that this was just a reaction that Noah was having after overhearing his father's words. I had every inclination that it was all just going to blow over.

Colt didn't come in until after one in the afternoon, which was late for him. I could tell from the way he was slamming cabinets that his day wasn't going the way he wanted it to. I avoided approaching him as I headed in to grab an apple.

He sat down and started eating a sandwich, looking at me, but saying nothing.

I sat across from him and took a bite of my apple. We'd played this silent game before. When he was ready, he would spill and I would be there to listen.

I'd almost finished eating the piece of fruit when he sighed and took his last bite. "The damn main motor went up in the east side chicken house overnight. I had to call in the fuckin' neighbors to help clean the mess. This is the second time that the alarm didn't sound when this happened. You need to get on the phone with that damn manufacturer and raise hell. They need to come out and give me a new one. I can't have losses like this. Are they goin' to pay for me to replace the dead chickens that I'm goin' to have?"

Colt had paid an arm and a leg for the top of the line alarm system to be installed in all of the chicken houses. If there was anything that went wrong, he would get a text message or even a call. For this to have happened and him not know that it had, wasn't a good thing. The fact that I had to make the call, wasn't a good thing either.

It was just one of those days where you wake up and know it's going to be a bad day. "I'll take care of it."

He stood up and stuck his plate in the sink. "Get that frown off your face, Savanna. I can't deal with that shit right now."

I got up and walked out of the kitchen before I could say something to start a huge fight. Colt was a good man, a great father and usually a perfect husband. Unfortunately, he'd always been one to hold in his anger until he'd finally explode. The exploding almost always happened when he was around me.

I used to take it so personal, thinking it was my fault, but through the years, I'd learned to just ignore him, no matter how much it bothered me.

I went ahead and called the company, like Colt requested. Then I headed up to Noah's room again. As soon as I walked in, I could just feel the tension between us again. I started putting away his clothes, hoping to get done and get out before I started to cry again. I got that everyone thought this was just something Noah was going through, but it didn't make it any less hurtful.

When I opened his sock drawer and saw the marble notebook, I thought about leaving it be. I shouldn't have been so nosey, considering I was trying to be a great parent. It could have been filled with pictures, or school work. I wished that was all it was, as I opened it up and saw what it said. The first pages had all been ripped out, probably because it was a notebook from a previous year. In black magic marker, written in big block letters, it read: I HATE THEM! I WISH THEY WOULD JUST DIE LIKE MY REAL MOM.

I closed the book, unable to look at his handwritten words any longer. If Colt saw what he'd wrote, he would have busted his little ass, so I put the notebook back in his drawer and just stuck his clothes back on top of it.

With Colt downstairs watching television, I retreated to my room, where I started crying again. I was going to need wine to get through the evening. Hell, I was going to need wine to get through the next week.

Chapter 8

Colt

I was worried about a lot of things and problems on the ranch didn't make my day any better. I knew I'd pissed Savanna off, but I thought if I gave her a task it would take her mind off of Noah. He was just being a stubborn kid, like I was at his age. Within a couple days he would forget he even said such terrible things about her.

Aside from Savanna being all upset, I had bigger problems involving my son. It had only been one night since Zeke visited, but as soon as I left to do my daily run of the ranch, I got a call from someone claiming to be his attorney. I was so pissed that he'd gone and called the man that fast, that I told him my lawyers number and then hung up before he could get a word in edgewise.

About an hour after that my lawyer called and he didn't have good news for me.

Colt, it's Mike Trimmel. Look, I just got a call from some lawyer claiming that he tried to contact you about visitation for your son. He said you gave him my number and refused to talk to him. Tell me you know something about it.

Yeah. He called earlier.

Can you give me an idea of what's going on? He claims that you are refusing his blood uncle visitation.

That's right. Are you aware of who his uncle is?

I had to look it up, but yeah, I know who he is now.

Then you can imagine my feelin's about him takin' my son.

Colt, I realize that you are the boy's father and legal guardian, and if this was just some random citizen I would say that they wouldn't stand a chance in Hell at winning in court. The problem is, this guy has money. He has a lot of money. We both know what that means.

You can't mean what I think you do. Have you seen the type of lifestyle this guy lives? He doesn't even know my son. He hasn't been a part of his life since he was born.

Colt, I know what you're saying. I do. I'm just trying to be honest. Unless you are willing to get involved with a very costly trial, I would suggest you work something out with this uncle before he proceeds with legal papers.

So you're sayin' I should just hand over my kid whenever he wants to see him?

I'm saying that maybe you two could come up with a compromise. Perhaps it would work out if you offered to go with him when he visited.

I run a ranch. I can't just up and travel all over God's creation to hang out with someone that I don't even care for.

Take some time and think about what I said, Colt. I would hate for you to be involved in something that could become a media spectacle. We can't always agree with our family, but at the end of the day, that's exactly what they are. I know what you went through when Noah came into your life. Try to put yourself in his shoes. He has an uncle that he didn't know about. Maybe letting them get to know each other won't be such a bad thing. Maybe he will figure out that his uncle isn't someone he likes to be around.

Or maybe he will want to be a rockstar too.

All children have aspirations. That doesn't mean they follow through with them.

Thanks for the advice, Mike. I get what you're sayin'. If you really think it's a good idea, I will try to contact Zeke and see if we can work something out. I don't want to do it, but I also don't want my son resenting me or his mother.

Let me know how it goes and you know I am up for it if you do need me to represent you.

After we hung up I felt angry. I thought my lawyer would tell me something completely different. Instead, he told me to allow Zeke to get to know my son. The way he explained things made it seem like I didn't have a chance in Hell at keeping Noah away from his uncle. Could money really buy verdicts like that? Were judges that careless to allow children to be around irresponsible people? It made me even more mad.

So, by the time I came in for the day, I would say that I was not a guy that Savanna wanted to be around. I knew I was being rude to her. I felt bad, but I just wanted to be alone. I had decisions to make and she wasn't going to even want to hear what I was considering.

When she finally retreated to our bedroom and had fallen asleep, I did go upstairs to check on her. She was still so beautiful and I appreciated her more than she could know. I got that I had a horrible way of showing it. Sometimes, I just needed to deal with things in my own way, even if it meant shutting her out for a short period.

I picked the kids up from the bus stop and watched my son walk right upstairs to his room, without saying a single word. I wondered how long the silent treatment was going to last.

The girls were telling me all about their day and as much as I loved hearing about it, my mind was in other places. Since their mother was still asleep, I got a movie on for them and headed up to check on her. When I knew she was still out like a light, I pulled out my phone and called Zeke.

Hello?

Zeke, it's Colt. We need to talk.

Now you want to talk?

You're damn right I do.

I assume you heard from my lawyer?

And mine.

Colt, I really don't want this to get ugly. If we could just...

We need to work somethin' out, Zeke. I realize you have a right to know your blood nephew. You need to understand the predicament it puts me in knowin' that he's never been around your kind of lifestyle. I don't approve of him being a part of it either. That is no place for a child.

I can assure you that what you think goes on, doesn't. Piper and I live a very normal life when I'm not on tour. We have a big house with a nice size pool and rarely even entertain people. Noah would be our guest at our home, not out on the road like you're thinking.

It still doesn't change the fact that he doesn't know you. I don't know you anymore, Zeke. What kind of parent would I be if I just let him hop on a plane and go see you?

I understand your concern. What do you have in mind for a compromise?

I want to come with him to visit you. I need to see where you live and how you live, before I can let my son be involved in your life. I don't mean to offend you, but I am looking out for his best interest.

I think that would be a great start. I don't have hard feelings against you Colt. You've always been a stand up guy.

We can't come until school is out. Will that be a problem?

Not at all. My tour is wrapping up and when it does, I will get in touch with you and schedule something.

So, you're callin' off the lawyers?

Of course. Look, I just wanted to get to know the kid. I didn't want to cause drama. You know how close I was to my sister, Colt. I know it's taken me a long time, but I'm trying to change my life around. Getting to know my nephew is one of those steps in making things right. I'm not trying to take him away from you. I just want the opportunity to spend time with the only family I have left.

I get it. I don't like how you went about it. Did you have to call your lawyer the second you left out of my house?

I guess I jumped the gun and for that I'm sorry. I'm used to having to cross my t's and dot my i's. It's just habit, man.

Just get in touch with me when your home. I will make sure I can take some time off.

Thanks, Colt. This means a lot. I know I'm around people everyday, but it gets so lonely. I don't have kids, or anyone that I can call family, except for Noah. I just want the chance.

I'll talk to you in a month or so, Zeke.

I didn't wait for him to reply before I hung up.

I covered my face in my hands and thought about my wife. She wasn't going to like this one bit.

Later that night, after Savanna had made dinner and we'd gotten the kids to bed, I climbed into bed next to her. She was reading, like she did every night. I kissed her on the shoulder and laid my head against her smooth skin. "I'm sorry for bein' a jerk."

She never looked away from her book. "You should be."

I smiled, knowing she was literally giving me the cold shoulder. "I need to talk to you about somethin'." I grabbed the Kindle out of her hand and finally got her attention. "It's important, darlin'."

She folded her hands and cocked her eyebrow. "Did you buy something?"

We had an agreement about buying major things without telling each other first. "No!"

"Is it good or bad, because I don't feel like having anymore bad news today, Colt. I know you think this is some phase, but it doesn't hurt me any less."

I put my hand over hers. "I need you to hear me out, Savanna."

She shook her head. "Oh God! It's bad!"

"Would you just calm down and let me talk?"

She threw her hands up. "Fine! Just tell me."

"You already know that I had a piss poor day, but you only know half of why that was." I got her attention. She turned and looked right into my eyes. "It seems that our visitors last night weren't happy with how things went. Zeke took it upon himself to contact his lawyer about having visitation rights."

Savanna jumped off the bed like it was on fire. "Are you shitting me?"

"I'm not!" I laughed at her using that word. She rarely cursed. "Keep your voice down so we don't wake up the kids."

She got back in bed and got close enough so we didn't have to talk loud. "How do you know he called his lawyer. Did he call and threaten you about it?"

"No. His lawyer called me, when I was dealing with the bullshit in the chicken houses."

Her eyes were huge and I could tell that she was scared. "What happened?"

"He was goin' on and on about Zeke bein' legally entitled to get to know Noah. I wasn't listenin' that well, on account of bein' so damn mad about it. I gave him Mike's number and hung up."

She readjusted herself. "So, that's it? Did you call Mike and ask him if he heard anything? Is Zeke going to try to take Noah away from us? Colt, I can't lose him."

I grabbed at her hands again, squeezing them inside of mine. "Mike called me." I hesitated telling her what Mike gave as advice. She wasn't going to be happy. In fact, I saw her firing my family's long term attorney over it. "Before you freak out, just listen to what I have to say."

"You're scaring me, Colt."

"We're goin' to have to let Zeke get to know Noah. There's no way around it, without things gettin' real ugly." I hated saying it out loud. Her face went from concerned to stunned in a matter of seconds.

"No judge will let that happen."

"Mike said that with Zeke's money and who he knows, there's a chance things would get ugly and we would lose. I don't want Noah dragged through magazines. I don't want him bein' some paparazzi's story."

"What are you saying?"

"I talked to Zeke tonight on the phone. He's agreed to drop everything if I allow Noah to come see him at his house, once his tour is over."

"That is not happening, Colt! Over my dead body am I going to put our son on a plane and just let him go."

I appreciated how devoted she was. "He ain't goin' alone. I'm goin' with him."

"You have to run the ranch. You can't just leave. If it has to be done, I will go."

"Savanna, I love you and you are the best mother to all three of our children, but you aren't Krista. I think it's best if I take Noah. Zeke is goin' to want to talk about her and since she and I shared a past, it's better that Noah knows that I did care about her. Right now he thinks I wished her dead. I need to fix that."

I knew it hurt Savanna. She got quiet and refused to reply. She shook her head and got up out of bed. I even tried to reach for her, but she walked out of the room with tears in her eyes.

Ever since the day that Noah came into our lives, she'd been his everything. I knew her heart was broken. How was I supposed to choose my wife's happiness over my son's safety? What kind of father would I be if I just didn't care about Noah or where he went. She had to know that I was trying to do the right thing for our family. My job was to protect them and that was all I was trying to do.

It was obvious that my wife didn't want to be near me. Maybe I should have went and looked for her. I honestly didn't know if she just wanted to be alone, or she was expecting me to run after her. Women were complicated and they played too many head games. Sometimes, I just wished she would have spelled things out for me.

I expected her to come back to bed at some point during the night, but she never did.

Chapter 9

Savanna

I was more than hurt.

I was angry.

I felt betrayed and like I was losing my hold on my own family. It felt like I was being pushed to the side, after devoting my whole life to being Noah's mother. The pain ripped through my heart, leaving me feeling so alone inside.

I sat out on the porch, in the dark, for the longest time. Colt wasn't too keen on me getting overemotional. He said that I needed to stop wearing my heart on my sleeve and grow a backbone. I couldn't help that I was a sensitive kind of person.

After all that I'd been through, I just couldn't find an easy way to change. Sure, I was better than before, but when it came to one of my children, it was a different story.

I slept on the couch, trying to avoid looking at my husband, after he'd made a major decision without including me in it. It was true, I didn't have custody or adoption papers for Noah. I should have gotten them a long time ago, but we never thought anyone would ever bother us about it. We shared the same last name and had been so open to Noah about Krista.

The next morning, I focused on getting the kids ready for school. Colt tried to be nice, but I ignored him as much as possible. I knew he was trying to do the right thing. I wasn't mad at him for his decision. I was mad because he left me out of it.

When the kids were gone and Colt had gone off to work, I did what I did every time I needed someone to talk to.

I called the salon.

Scissor Sounds this is Amy.

It's Van. I need to vent. Are you busy?

Miranda isn't coming in today. She and Ty took the kids to the zoo. I don't have a client for the next thirty minutes. What's up? You okay?

How are you even working, being so pregnant?

I'm used to it. I sit whenever I don't have a client, so it isn't so bad.

Plus, you could always walk into the house and take a nap, I guess.

That's right! So what's up?

Well, you know Zeke came over to visit with Noah, right?

Yeah, what you didn't tell me, Conner filled me in.

After it went so horribly, Zeke called his lawyer and had him threaten us with visitation rights.

What?

Yep. He knew we would be left with no other options.

You could have let it go to court and proved he wasn't fit to have visitation.

Our lawyer told Colt that he could buy the win. Do you believe that? He said it would cost us too much and we may not win. Either way Noah would have to get to know Zeke.

So, what are you going to do?

Colt is going with him when he visits.

Are you for real?

Yeah. I don't even know what to say to him right now. I feel like I have no say at all.

Van, I'm sorry you are going through this. I hate when things happen that we can't control. I'm here if you need anything.

I know. I think I just needed someone to tell me that I wasn't just being a selfish bitch.

You aren't. You have raised that child as your own. You have every right to be concerned and feel what you feel.

Thanks, Amy. I better get off of here. I have a doctor's appointment this morning.

Okay. I hope your day gets better. Love ya!

Love you, too.

It took me no time at all to get a shower and leave for my doctor's appointment. I had avoided going and rescheduled my annual pap test for two months. Just the thought of those cold metal forceps spreading me open made me cringe. I think my mind made it much worse than it actually was. At any rate, I still hated getting it done.

The waiting room was filled with pregnant women. I thought about Amy being pregnant and even considered missing that feeling. Then I remembered child birth and even what Miranda had gone through. After having the twins, Miranda had her tubes tied. It was to prevent her having to go through a dangerous pregnancy. I don't think she cared. They had three healthy children and the boys were a huge handful anyway. Ty never complained about not being able to have any more children. They were always on the same page in their marriage. Sometimes, I envied that so much, especially considering what I was going through at the moment.

When they called my name to come back, I felt that tense feeling in the pit of my stomach. The nurse showed me to my room and pointed to the sheet that I was supposed to strip down and put over my naked body. As she walked out, I turned and looked at the stirrups that my feet would soon be in.

I thought about the doctor and how many vaginas that he must look at in a single day. I didn't know what kind of person would want that job. Sure, some women were probably attractive, but most were older and had given birth. I don't know about them, but my vagina never looked how it did before I had kids. Colt never complained, but I was certain it had changed.

My doctor was in his forties. He was a nice man who always talked about family and hobbies while doing the exams.

I appreciated that he talked about his wife and kids, but at the same time, he was still looking deep into my vagina.

Maybe I had so much on my mind that focusing on one thing was the way I was trying to cope. Either way, when he stepped into the room and stuck his cold hands under the sheet to feel my breasts, I immediately felt uncomfortable.

It didn't help that I'd just read this erotic thriller about a doctor that seduced his patients. My mind was making me think crazy things and all I wanted to do was get dressed and get out of there.

At first, I thought it was my imagination that he was spending way too much time massaging my left breast. His eyes were focused on the wall and it didn't seem to be turning him on at all. "Savanna, I'm going to send you to the diagnostic center to get a mammogram. I'm feeling something out of the ordinary and I just want to check it to be on the safe side."

"I'm not even old enough. Is it really necessary?"

"I don't think it's anything you have to worry about, but let's get a better look at it."

"Should I be worried?" I didn't want anything to be wrong.

"No. I don't think it's anything. I just want to be sure."

After documenting his findings in his computer, he shut the laptop. "The front desk will give you the paperwork to have the test done. If you can, try and schedule it when you leave today. It usually takes a couple of weeks to get an appointment."

I was so shaken up that I almost forgot to pick up the paperwork at the front desk. I knew my doctor said not to worry, but it was hard not to. I sat in the SUV and felt around for the whatever it was he felt. When I couldn't feel anything out of the ordinary, it made me feel a little better. I was sure it was going to turn out to be nothing. My family had no history of breast lumps or cancer.

I decided not to tell Colt or my mother about the mammogram. They were both so worried about the Noah situation that I didn't want to concern them. Colt wouldn't notice that it was on my mind, since we were already dealing with other problems. Plus, I didn't want to worry the family if it wasn't necessary. They would all band together and make the situation ten times worse than it was. Ty and Conner may even ask to do their own examination, which in turn would cause Colt to have a heart attack. Joke or no joke, he hated their crude sense of humor.

I got home a little after one, since I had to go to the grocery store. Since I'd left Colt a note telling him where I was going to be, I didn't seem surprised when he hadn't called to check on me.

As I started carrying the heavy bags in the front door, I saw him sleeping on the couch, with ESPN blaring. The slam of the metal door caused him to sit up straight. He jumped up and grabbed the bags out of my hands. "Is there any more?"

"Yeah, it's in the back."

We walked into the kitchen, where Colt left me to go get the rest of the groceries. While starting to put them away, I looked down at our large kitchen table and thought about our beautiful family. As much as I didn't want to, I started to cry. I felt like out of nowhere everything was crumbling around me. We'd been such a perfect family, never taking one another for granted. Noah had never given me lip or a hard time. My girls were the cutest little things. I suddenly became overwhelmed thinking about us being broken.

Colt's strong arms wrapped around my waist as I turned to face him. He held me close, not saying anything at first. After he let me get it out, he kissed the top of my head. "You know I hate when you hurt, Savanna. I wish I could make things easier for you."

"I know. I shouldn't be so upset about it. I just feel like I'm losing him and I hate it. He just doesn't understand how much he means to me. The thought of losing him is just killing me inside." It wasn't just Noah. It was everything.

Colt kept holding me and kissing me on the top of my head. I knew he was thinking of what to say, but the words just wouldn't come to him. He couldn't understand what I was going through, even the parts that he knew about. Noah was always going to be his flesh and blood. "I hate to say this, darlin', but maybe you need to talk to Ty. If anyone knows what you're feelin' it's him."

I was utterly shocked that he would suggest that. Colt and Ty were close, but when it came to me, Colt always kept his guard up. He wasn't jealous of our friendship, it was more like he just was aware of our history. "He will just say I'm being a baby and to get over it. You know how he is."

"Actually, when it comes to you, I'd think he'd be pretty nice about it. He cares about you and you obviously need someone you can talk to, especially if I have to leave town. It would put my mind at ease if I knew that you had someone that understood your side of it all."

"I appreciate that, Colt. I know you don't like admitting that."

"It's water under the bridge, Savanna. You're my wife and he is our cousin. If you can't turn to your family then something is wrong." Colt grabbed the rest of the groceries and started loading them up in the pantry. For just a second, I forgot about everything I was feeling and thought about being caught with him that Thanksgiving a while back. It was those moments in my life that I cherished. I could have done without the getting caught part, but the moment was unforgettable.

"You do know that after all these years, you have nothing to worry about. My whole world revolves around you and our children. I'd never stray from that."

He cocked an eyebrow and brushed the hair out of my face as he got close. "I never said you would."

He leaned in and kissed me, almost making me weak in the knees. His lips were powerful persuasion for me to forget what was going on. Whenever my last breath on earth was going to be, I wanted it be in this man's arms.

I pulled away slowly. "The kids are going to be home shortly."

He leaned in and kissed me again. "Noah will hold their hands and start walkin'. I want you, Savanna."

He lifted me up on the countertop and immediately started lifting my shirt over my head. Colt tugged on the cups of my bra, freeing my breasts for his lips to explore. I held my head back and let him work his magic. With each little kiss, my body went into little frenzies. I needed what was happening. My hands had reached down to unhook his belt buckle, even before my mind had told them to do it. Our lips met again, this time allowing our tongues to meet and mingle.

The room became hot as I tugged at the waist of his jeans, to loosen them enough to get his big boy out. It was already standing at attention, just ready for me to spread my legs. Colt pulled down my cotton yoga pants and underwear with one swift movement. He pulled my ass just far enough off of the counter and moved his hard erection right between my legs to my sweet spot. The more it pressed against my eager sex, the more I burned with desire for it to be inside of me.

By making a few thrusts myself, I was able to get him positioned perfectly without even touching it.

It wasn't like I didn't want to touch it. I wanted to guide it in and feel it as it went in and out of me. I was dripping with anticipation of what was about to happen. When he entered me, I gasped, feeling his length overwhelming me.

His kisses became manic and I matched his movements, as even our teeth began brushing together. His hands gripped my ass cheeks and he kept them there to help better guide himself. His thrust were vigorous and his breath was weakened when his movements increased even more.

I grabbed his hair and ran my tongue along his Adams apple. I could taste the sweat on his skin and the salty taste made me want to lick him again. My legs wrapped around his ass as I leaned back and grabbed one of my breasts, sliding my fingertips across my nipples. At first they were still soft, but by the time I squeezed them they were rock hard and in need of his attention. He licked his own lips before letting them coat the tip of my nipple with his saliva.

My head fell back, even as I tried to concentrate and enjoy his simple touch. He had me so turned on that I couldn't hold back the urge to let the tension of everything go. I could feel the warmth growing between my legs. The tickles became more apparent and my legs began to lock up.

Colt steadied his pace, making sure to hold out until my body stopped jerking.

I could feel him losing control. Little sounds were escaping his mouth. Finally he collapsed his head into my chest.

We both just stayed locked together trying to catch our breath. Our moment may have been over and some stress had been relieved. As much as I would have liked for it to solve all of my problems, it only reminded me of how good things could be between me and Colt if I'd only let them.

Things were going to be okay. I couldn't stand to live without this man or any of our children. It just wasn't an option.

Chapter 10

Colt

Things between Noah and Savanna didn't get much better as the week progressed. Even though they spoke to each other, anyone could sense the distance between them. I hated to admit that it hurt me to see them acting that way toward each other.

By the time the weekend came, I think Savanna just needed a break. Since her parents lived here on the ranch, even visiting them wasn't good enough. Since Noah and Christian both had things to do, Savanna took Addy and headed to North Carolina for a couple of days.

While she was gone, I was determined to smooth things out between her and Noah, even if I had to beat some sense into him. Regardless of their blood, the two of them were family and nothing was going to change that.

Christian had a birthday to attend on Saturday, while Noah had a lacrosse game. Once I had my daughter dropped off, we headed to the ball field. Noah was quiet at first, but he piped up when I started talking about his uncle. "I spoke to your uncle this week and he asked if you could come stay with him once his tour was over."

"Really?"

"Yeah, really. This is how I see it though. Since you've been treatin' your mom so terrible, I think it's best that we wait a few more months. I don't think it's a good idea for you to be rewarded for the way you've been actin'."

Right away, I could tell that I'd hit a nerve. "But, Dad! I really want to go."

"Well, your mother really wanted her son to respect her. Do you think it's right for me to reward you right now, Noah? Do you have any idea how much you've hurt her?"

He shrugged. "Not really."

"Boy, I don't know what's gotten into you, but you best get back to the right way of actin' before I take away more than a damn trip. Savanna is your mother and you know that. She's loved you since the first moment you came into her life. Do you know how lucky you were to have her just accept you the way she did?"

"She wanted kids anyway. She told me that."

"Son, she had just lost a baby. Did you know that? Before you came into our lives, we had just dealt with a serious situation. Your mother was kidnapped and held against her will by some very bad people. She tried to escape and ended up getting hurt. When she was found, she'd already lost the baby." He hung on to my every word and I could already see the concern in his eyes as I told him about her horrific past.

"Was she sad?"

It made me sad to even talk about it. I pulled into the parking lot at the field and turned off the truck, but we just sat there. "We were both real sad. We'd been trying to have a baby for a while and nothin' happened. Then when she finally got pregnant, tragedy hit. It ripped her heart apart. She couldn't deal with it."

"So how did she get better?"

"One day these people came to our door with a little boy. That little boy asked her if she was going to be his mother and from that moment she got better."

"I don't remember, but I know you're talkin' about me, dad." He seemed sad.

I reached over and patted his shoulder. "Noah, you healed her. You healed her heart even when I couldn't do it. She loves you unconditionally and she doesn't deserve what you're puttin' her through right now. You need to figure out how to make things better." This was his mess and if he thought he was old enough to say those kind of things, then he needed to step up and figure out how to eradicate his wrong doings.

"What do I do? Does she want me to apologize?"

"It would be a good start. She thinks you don't love her anymore." I knew he still did. The kid would be devastated if anything happened to her.

"It's not that! I was just mad. I didn't know I had an uncle and he seemed so cool. He's all famous and stuff and mom kept saying how she didn't like me around him. Then I heard you both sayin' stuff about Krista and it made me mad."

We could see his team already warming up. "Look, Noah, it's important to make things right with your mother. I could never regret Krista havin' you, but you need to know that we were never goin' to stay together. We were too different. Savanna never took Krista's place. I never even knew I had a son because she kept it from me. I get that this is hard for you and I know we need to go through this, but shutting out Savanna, who has been your only mother for the past ten plus years, just isn't a way to solve things. She's all you got kid."

I heard him start to sniffle and looked over to see him crying. It took me back to a time when I said that I hated my father. I couldn't remember why I'd said it, but I remember my mother telling me that I would never get another one.

"I'm sorry, Dad."

"Tell it to your mother when you see her. Go on and get out there before you have to do extra laps." I watched him hop out of the car and grab his gear, but I didn't follow him. Savanna was out of town and all I could hope was that when she returned things were going to be resolved between her and Noah.

After the practice and the birthday party, we grabbed a pizza and went home. When Addy wasn't around, Christian liked to act like she was one of us guys. The last time Savanna had left her with us, she'd tried to pee standing up and made a mess all over the bathroom. To make matters worse, I learned that Bella had done the same thing.

To imagine two little girls in our family wanting to be boys was just wrong in so many ways.

Even over the phone I could tell my wife thought it was funny. It was so good to hear her laugh. She was going through Hell and needed time to heal. Some people could let things go and move on. For Savanna, it took a while longer.

Since we had the whole day Sunday, I decided to put the kids to work. We started cleaning the house and ended up in the garage. I'd straightened it up before, but after years, I'd collected too much junk. Shelves full of old memories covered a whole wall. My goal was to get half of the stuff thrown away. I was tired of storing all of our Christmas decorations in the attic and shed because they wouldn't fit in the garage. Savanna gave me a fit about it.

I started on the top shelf and handed each kid a box and then grabbed one for myself. We each sat down on the concrete floor and started looking through it. Noah had a box full of my trophies. He pulled each one out and read what sport it was for.

Christian had gotten a box that had some old toys from my mother. Honestly, I'd known that's what it had in it. I just wanted her to feel like she was helping. In no time at all, she started playing with some old GI Joe figures.

My box was from my college years. It was full of pictures of me and my ex that we never mention. She'd cheated on me with my best friend and had a kid by him. She was my first love and my first heart break. It was devastating to me and for the longest time, I truly believed that I never wanted to feel that way again.

Krista had just become someone to fill the void of being lonely. I knew I didn't love her and I think she knew it too. Still, we stayed together for a while anyway. Her and her brother needed someone to look after them, and at the time, it gave me something to do.

Krista only stuck around until she couldn't deal with me anymore. I wasn't forthcoming and I had no intentions of ever being serious with her. It's a shame that I didn't know she was pregnant. Even though I knew we weren't going to work out, I would have taken care of her and little Noah.

She didn't have a right to keep that from me. I don't care what her reasons were.

I sat there looking through some old pictures, but my mind was on the day I arrived in North Carolina and got my first glimpse at a very grown up Savanna. I wanted to resent her, but from that very first day, I think I knew she was special.

"Daddy, do you have clothes for this doll?" Christian held up a naked GI Joe. Thank God Mattel or whoever made the damn things put plastic underwear on them.

"Sweetie, boys don't change clothes on their dolls. Joe was a soldier. He protected us."

"Why? What if he gets dirty?" She looked so confused.

Since he was the same size as her Barbie's, I just decided to appease her. "I bet he can fit into Ken's clothes. Why don't you go in the playroom and see?"

She jumped up and ran toward the kitchen door. "Okay!"

Noah laughed and shook his head once she was gone. "Don't laugh at your sister, or I will tell her how you used to love playing Barbie's with Bella."

"Did not!"

"Did too! Now, let's put the box of trophies in the throw away pile."

He picked up the box, but sat it back down again. "Can I have them?"

There was at least twenty trophies in total and probably another box somewhere else. "It's too many, Noah. Your mother wants me to clean out the garage, not put everything somewhere else in the house."

"Can I have a few to keep? How about just your favorite ones?"

I had to laugh at him for wanting my old junk. I got that he wanted to be like me, but it was just surreal to be someone's idol. Still, in that very moment, I felt blessed to have him look up to me and not his rockstar uncle. It could all change after our visit, but for now, he was my little protégé.

I scooted over next to Noah and grabbed a couple trophies out of the plastic box. The first few were from college, but as I dug down, I got to the ones from when I played little league. My first championship trophy came when I was in first grade. I located the trophy with the big baseball at the top. "This was my first little league championship win. I pitched the last three innings, and it was a big deal back then because it was our first year out of coach pitch. I struck out six players that game. I remember my dad making it to the game. He was so darn proud of me that he took the whole team out for ice cream afterwards."

Noah had a smile on his face that changed as quick as it came. "Do you miss your dad?"

"I miss him every day. I know he's up in heaven lookin' down at us. Sometimes, I think he keeps us safe."

"Do you think Krista, my mom, is watchin' over me?"

I rubbed his head. "Buddy, I know she is."

"Do you think she's mad at me, too?" He looked bent out of shape over it.

"I think that she wants you to be happy and loved, which you are." Every once in a while Noah would have these type of conversations with me. The older he got, the less they happened, but I never turned away from his questions. I knew it was important for him to always be 'in the know' about his mother.

"Yeah. I wish I could remember her. I only know she was pretty because I have pictures."

"Your mother was a looker. When guys walked by her their heads would turn. She had big dimples on both of her cheeks and even when she wasn't smilin' you could tell they were there. Her eyes were light and beautiful and her hair had never been colored. It was naturally blonde."

"Was she prettier than Mom?"

It was a weird question and I felt uncomfortable answering for the first time. "They are very different, but both very beautiful."

"What if you had to choose?"

"Noah, you know that this question has no right answer. If I say Savanna then you get your feelin's hurt. If I say your mother, all Hell would break loose if she found out. Your mother and I were more friends than lovers. We lived together and got along just fine. I wasn't her forever and she wasn't mine. I know you don't remember this, but your mother was getting married. Her new husband was trying to adopt you."

"So I wouldn't have been a Mitchell?"

"Well, he found out he couldn't do it without my permission and that meant your mom had to tell me about you. I learned that she was planning on introducing us right before her accident." I hoped he was old enough to understand the things I was telling him. If Savanna came home and things were worse with Noah, I wasn't sure what could happen.

"Would you have said yes? Would you have let him adopt me?"

"Are you kiddin' me? You're my only son. I loved you from the moment I first laid eyes on you. I'd never let anyone else be your father. I know you would have had a step-dad, but I wanted to be your father. I should have been there when you were born."

He leaned over and hugged me. "I'm glad you're my dad."

It was a touching moment until Christian came walking out into the garage with GI Joe in a dress and my cell phone in her hand. "Okay, Mommy. Here's Daddy." She handed me the phone. "Mommy wants to talk to you."

I covered the phone with my hand. "What happened to Joe?"

"He told me that he wanted to be a princess." She was brushing the little hair he still had.

I shook my head, thinking about my daughter turning my beloved GI Joe gay. Poor Joe!

Hello.

Hey, babe. I just wanted you to know that I won't be home until late. Ty's making a big dinner for the family and they also wanted me stay.

How about you just stay another night and drive home in the mornin' I don't want you out on the roads so late.

Are you sure? I miss you and the kids.

Give Addy a kiss for me and I'll see you tomorrow. I love you, darlin'.

I love you too. Tell the kids I love them. See you in the morning sometime.

She sounded relaxed and I didn't even care if I had to get the kids ready for school the next morning. Maybe her time away had helped.

Noah was looking at me when I hung up the phone. "Mom says she loves you and she'll see us all tomorrow."

Noah smiled and I saw love in his eyes again.

Chapter 11

Savanna

I was reluctant, at first, about going to visit everyone in North Carolina. With all of the drama happening with Noah, I hated leaving. Still, I needed a break from it all. Colt, being Colt, offered to take Christian to her friend's birthday party and Noah to his game. Addy was so excited about seeing her cousins that she totally forgot about her sister not being with us.

I think once I hit the North Carolina state line, I felt like I could breathe. When I pulled into the farm, I actually felt excited.

After sending a text to Colt, letting him know we had arrived safe, I could hardly keep Addy from busting out of her booster seat. "I want to see Cammie and Callie, Mommy. Hurry!"

"Just a second, honey. We aren't at their house yet."

She looked around and pointed. "There they are!"

Sure enough, the girls came running out of the barn toward my vehicle.

With Addy being drawn away from me, I headed toward the house to see my family. Loud music was coming from inside as I entered, I found out why.

Ty and Conner where standing in the living room. They had spiked their hair and put on black makeup all around their eyes. They both wore black ripped up outfits and in their hands were cardboard guitars. The music was something that I'd never heard, but I noticed the CD sitting on the table and saw that it was Zeke's band. As the two of them continued to jam out and play the air guitar, I walked over and turned off the stereo.

Laughing filled the room. "Pretty rad, huh?" Ty stood there like he was famous.

Conner just kept smiling. I knew which one of them thought this little bit would be funny.

Ty came up and tried to hug me, but I pushed him away. "You are an ass!"

"Miranda gave me permission to sign your tit." He pulled out a black sharpie from the front of his pants. I cringed as I watched him open the cap with his teeth. "Left or right?"

I backed away from him more. "Get your nasty ass pen away from me!"

"You really are against famous people. Some people would kill to have me sign their tits."

"Where are the girls?" I rolled my eyes and tried to ignore him.

Ty lifted up his shirt to display his abdomen. "You want me, don't you?"

"Stop it!"

He cornered me in the room. "Conner is into pregnant chicks, but I have room for a groupie like you."

I took my knee and brought it up between his legs. He did this thing where he laughed and moaned at the same time, as he hunched over and tried to catch his breath. "You can't take a joke, Van! You suck!" Ty grabbed himself between the legs and held his hand there as he walked toward the kitchen.

The house filled with female voices as Miranda and Amy came walking in. Amy looked like she was about to burst at the seams. They each walked up and hugged me at the same time. "It's good to see you."

Miranda turned around and took a look at Ty and Conner. "I told you both not to do that!"

"We couldn't help it, sis. It was a kickass idea!"

"You both are asshats!" Amy pointed at them and shook her head.

Miranda's scorning did nothing to make Ty wash off the makeup and change his clothes. In fact, he and Conner walked around for the rest of the day like that.

I spent the night in the guest room at Ty and Miranda's, while Addy chose to stay with her cousins. Even though the mattress wasn't as soft as mine, it was a great night's sleep.

I woke up to the smell of cooking bacon and a conversation between Miranda and Ty having to deal with nipple sizes.

"I'm telling you, baby, their like fingerprints. Each set is different," Ty said as he flipped the bacon.

Miranda sat in a chair with her knees against her chest. She had a cup of coffee in her hand and was reading something on her tablet. "That's ridiculous! How would you know anyway?"

"I am the master of tits, that's how!"

They didn't look at each other as they talked and they didn't notice me standing there, holding my hand over my mouth.

"The master of tits?"

"Shit yeah! You put a picture of your tits in a line up with a hundred other sets and I guarantee I can pick yours out!" I couldn't help but start to laugh. They both turned and looked at me.

"Van, can you please tell my husband that he's full of crap?"

"Honestly, I think you should take him up on the challenge."

"And let him look at ninety nine other sets of breasts? You've got to be jokin'. The last thing this man needs is permission to be a pervert."

Ty held up his arms like he couldn't help himself. "It was worth a try, right?"

"No!" Miranda and I said at the same time.

They retreated into the living room shortly after, while I made a cup of coffee and sat in silence. It was nice to have a little time to myself, but also made me think of the reason that I wanted to leave town in the first place.

I felt like my happy little bubble was being jeopardized and I didn't know how to make things better. With my health being in question, no matter how much I was told not to worry, I still couldn't see a way out. I think Ty being obsessed with breasts was making my morning worries heightened. As much as I tried to separate my problems from my visit, they were clearly one in the same.

In just a short time, Colt was going to take Noah for a weeks visit with Zeke. Maybe I would have felt better about it if I were included in the decision. To be honest, I felt like I didn't belong. Maybe I was being selfish. I'd known all along that I wasn't Noah's birth mother. I shouldn't have been surprised that this kind of conflict had come in to play.

Once the kids woke up, the house filled with chaos. I went outside to the barn, where I sat down on the couch and looked around, thinking of all the happy memories that we'd all shared in the place.

I don't know how long I'd been out there, but a man clearing his voice caught my attention.

Ty came and sat down next to me. He put his arm around me and I nestled my head into his chest, like I did when we were teenagers. "You going to tell me why you're here?"

I shrugged. "I just needed to clear my head."

"Van, I know you. This can't just be about Noah. You know you can talk to me. I'm not always a complete dick."

I couldn't believe that he could tell something else was wrong. "I'm fine, really. I think I am just being selfish. I mean, Noah has a right to know his uncle, doesn't he?"

Ty looked straight out at the wall, never really paying attention to me being so close to him. I appreciated that we could be like this and it didn't harbor any feelings between us. He really was a good friend to me.

He cleared his throat again. "Don't get me wrong, Van. I think it's cool and all that Noah has a famous uncle, but from what I've seen, he's not really kid friendly. What made him come around again?"

"He was in town and said that he's trying to turn his life around. I get that. I can't imagine what it's like to not have family. I just wish he didn't want to be a part of mine. I sound like a selfish bitch don't I?"

"No! You sound like you don't want to share your son with someone you don't trust. I know exactly how you're feeling."

I smiled and looked up at him. "Colt said you would."

"That's surprising, considering that when you last visited he practically ripped my head off for teasing you."

"He knew about Zeke and hadn't told me. I guess he had a lot on his mind and you were an easy target." I almost felt bad for Ty, except he was forever tormenting poor Colt.

"He's doing that shit again, where he shuts you out. You'd think he'd learn." Ty shook his head and patted me on the leg. "Maybe if you performed annilingus once in a while, he'd be more open."

"Anni what?"

"You know, where you lick each other's assholes."

I slapped him in the arm. "You are so sick!"

"Come on, Van. Don't even tell me you never did it before."

Whether I had or hadn't, it was none of his business. Besides, Ty knowing my sexual secrets was not a good way to keep Colt happy.

"No comment!"

"It's all good." He stood up and put his hands in his pockets. "I don't know if Miranda told you, but today is the church picnic. I think Amy and Conner already told Addy she could go with them. I know the pastor would love to see you."

I shrugged and stood up with him. "That sounds like fun. I mean, what else am I going to do if you're all there?"

I hadn't been back for the church picnic since before my parents had moved to Kentucky. One thing was for certain. The people would still be the same ones that attended when I was a little girl.

After calling Amy, and finding out that they were already getting ready to head there, I agreed to catch a ride with Ty and Miranda and meet them. I guess they knew all along that I would want to go, or maybe they weren't really going to give me the option to decline.

When we first got there, I was surrounded by a bunch of elderly people that remembered me, but I had no clue who they were. All of the children congregated on the big playground, while the adults mingled around evenly lined up picnic tables on the grass.

It was a perfect day for a picnic. The sun was shining and there were just enough clouds to give us random breaks from the hot rays. I got myself comfortable at a table with my family. Watching them all interact with their children was still a hoot, considering that Ty and Conner were never the type of guys that anyone could see being in devoted relationships and raising families.

I happened to look over at Ty, just as he spotted someone that he obviously didn't care too much about. "Look what the damn cat drug in. Miranda is going to flip her lid."

I followed his eyes across the lawn to a blonde looking down and talking to a boy that was about the age of Addy. It wasn't until the woman looked up that I realized who it was and why Ty had made his comment. I kept my voice as low as possible. "Oh my God, is that Heather?"

She didn't look that much different. She gained maybe ten pounds, but was still skinny and her hair was as perfect as it always had been. She was too caught up in the conversation with the child to notice Ty and me looking at her.

I turned around and looked at him instead. "I thought she moved far away?"

"As far as I know she did. Her mom still lives here. She must be visiting." Ty kept looking at Miranda, just waiting for her to notice Heather.

After the whole episode with Amy's ex, she and I had forgiven Heather for her flaws to the extent of being able to tolerate her. She had risked her life for our family, but no matter how hard she tried, Miranda would never forgive her for what she had done to her and Ty. I wasn't even sure if Miranda had seen her since that all happened.

It had been years, and with time, the wounds of her wrecking my relationship with Ty were long gone. I got that she was in love with him and sometimes people do desperate things for the people they love. I didn't agree with her actions, but we were all adults now. If the child holding her hand was her own, then she'd obviously found someone to love her.

I didn't mean to keep staring, but when she caught me, all I could do was walk up and say something.

Except...I didn't know what to say.

We were never friends.

It was always more like frienimies. We loved to hate each other.

Heather smiled, but I could see her concern as I got closer. Instead of speaking to her first, I bent down and looked at the little boy. "Well, hello there, cutie. Where'd you get those brown eyes from?"

He shrugged and buried his face into his mother's side.

"He's shy," Heather announced.

"Is he yours?"

She smiled and looked down at him. "Yep. He sure is."

"He's very handsome." I was still trying to make conversation with someone that I never should have approached.

"Thanks. He gets his looks from his daddy." I noticed that she wasn't wearing a ring and I think she saw what I was doing. "We..um...it's complicated."

I tried to play it off like I wasn't being nosey. "I just wanted to come over and say hello. I never got to thank you for what you did for Amy." I looked over at Amy. Conner was telling her something in her ear and she was smiling. "I'm sure she'd like to say hello."

"I'll wait until Ty and his wife aren't around. I didn't come here to make drama. My mom hasn't been doing well, so Jacob and I made the trip to come visit. I promised her we would stop by today, but I don't want to cause trouble for your family. We'll just visit later." She started to turn around and head back toward the parking lot.

I don't know what got in to me, but I ran after her, grabbing her by the arm. "Heather, wait!"

She turned around and looked as shocked as I did for doing it. "You don't have to be nice to me, Van. I'm not that same person anymore, but I will never forgive myself for what I did to you and your family. I ask God every day to forgive me."

I bent down again and looked at the shy little boy. "So, your name is Jacob?"

He nodded.

I held out my hand to him. "I have a little girl your age and I think she'd like to play. Do you want to meet her?"

He nodded again and then took my hand. I looked up at Heather, who seemed astonished at me for being kind.

We made it over to the swings where Addy was. She hopped off and came running toward me. "Who are you?"

At first he hid behind me.

"Does he know how to talk, Mommy?"

"I'm Jacob," he announced.

"Jacob needs someone to play with."

She started running back to the swings. "Come on then!"

My daughter was something else!

Heather waved and walked over toward her mother. As I smiled back at her, Miranda grabbed my arm and pulled me to the side. "Why is she here?"

"She's just visiting her mother."

She pointed to Jacob. "Is that her kid? Her spawn?"

"Can you be nice? We are at church, for God sakes."

"Fine! You and Amy may think she's changed, but I don't have to like her. She's still the devil in my eyes." I got how she felt and understood.

"She won't bother you, Miranda. She's here visiting just like I am. It's been years and she's obviously moved on. I'm not saying I want to be friends with her, but I've known the girl since I was a little girl. I'm just at a point in my life where I'm tired of being so angry. Without Heather in my life, I never would have been with Colt. I think in some ways I'm grateful for the life that she led me to."

Miranda looked defeated. "I get it, Van. I just can't get past it. Maybe that makes me a terrible bitch. I just can't do it."

I hugged her, not knowing what else I could do. "I love you and I know you have legitimate reasons. Let's just keep the peace today and we don't have to see her again."

Ty came over with someone I didn't recognize and pulled Miranda into a conversation. Since she was better and with her husband, I was able to run to the ladies room without having to worry about a cat fight in the church parking lot.

Heather was in the bathroom. She was on the phone and the conversation wasn't a good one.

"You said that you would come with us."

"I don't care about that, right now."

"Please don't do this to me again."

I could tell that she was arguing with someone. To not feel like I was imposing, I hurried up and tried to leave before she hung up. Unfortunately, by the time I flushed, she was leaned over the sink crying.

"Are you okay?" I asked.

She shook her head and tried to clean up the eyeliner that was running down her cheeks. "It's nothing that I haven't been dealing with for the past five years. Same shit different day. I'm fine and I know you don't really care if I had my feelings hurt. I don't expect you to ever get over what I've done to you."

I handed her a paper towel. "Do you need me to get your mother?" I didn't want to rehash something from the past. We were adults now, with children. It was time to grow up.

"No! She thinks everything is fine. I don't want her to worry about me. She found out she has cervical cancer last month. She's been going through chemo and hasn't been doing well. I can't stress her with my problems. She needs to think everything is fine."

I got quiet for a second before speaking. "I'm sorry to hear about your mom. I hope everything works out." Immediately, I started thinking about having to get a mammogram. Overwhelmed with anxiety, I started to sob. "Gosh, I'm sorry. I don't know what's come over me."

Heather just stared at me. "Van, are you alright?"

I nodded, but continued to cry. "I'm just going through something, myself. I came here to clear my mind, but my problems are still the same no matter where I go. I just feel like I can't win, you know?"

She put her hand on my shoulder and as weird as it was, I felt okay about it. "I envy your life, Van. You have beautiful children and a sexy husband to go with it. I can't imagine what's gotten you so sad. I understand if you don't want to tell me. I should just go."

We weren't friends, but I felt like I was going to explode with emotions. "I'm having trouble with my oldest son and now I have to go have a test done because my doctor thinks he felt a lump in my breast." I shook my head. "I can't believe I just told you that."

Heather used to absorb people's dirty laundry and use it against them. I regretted telling her something that my husband didn't know.

"Look, I know we aren't friends but, you need to take my advice, Van. Get the test as soon as possible. My mother waited and now she is fighting for her life. I know you have no reason to believe me, but it's good advice. Do it for your children. I'm sure you don't want them to be without you. I couldn't imagine one day without Jacob. He's my rock and he's showed me what love is all about. Now, if his father would just get on board, we would be perfect."

I smiled through the tears. My next sentence was like sticking my own foot in my mouth. "I know why you loved Ty so much and why you did the things you did to try and have him."

She was as confused as I was and I knew the topic should have been off limits. "Come again?"

"I just...I get it now. I see why you risked so much to be with him. When you love someone so much, it's so hard to accept that it isn't meant to be. People change, Heather. We grow up and we learn from our mistakes." We stood there for a while not saying anything. "I hope that man comes around. Family is what's important in life. He's a fool if he takes that for granted."

I walked out of the bathroom and got back to being with my loved ones. Spending time with Heather reminded me of my family back home. Suddenly, I couldn't wait to be back there with them.

I ended up staying until Monday, after Miranda and Amy begged me to. We stayed up late each night playing cards and listening to Ty and Conner acting like idiots together. The more I was around them, the more I believed that Ty and Conner were both hatched from an idiot egg. They never did anything without each other and the way they communicated was like they had a secret language.

Even though I enjoyed my weekend away, I think Addy and I both wanted to get home. I missed Colt and the kids and with my mind going awry I needed to be close to them.

I'd made my mind up about one thing, though. I wasn't going to worry Colt about what the doctor found in my breast. Since he said it was probably nothing, I would just wait it out. He didn't need to be anymore stressed.

I could handle it.

I had to.

Chapter 12

Colt

She was acting different and I didn't know why. I could tell she missed us, but Savanna was keeping something from me and she was doing her best to try and act normal.

I thought her weekend away was going to be enough to clear her head. Instead, she came home and seemed even more distant. At first, she seemed happy to be home and she even hugged Noah, but I could sense the animosity between them.

After hugging me, Addy ran up to play with her sister, like everything was fine.

Once Savanna had finished unpacking, she came and sat next to me on the couch. Her reading device was in her hand and she seemed more focused on it than me sitting right next to her.

I reached my arm around her and pulled her close, so that I could kiss her on the temple. "I missed you, darlin'."

She smiled but didn't look up. "I missed you, too, babe. Were the kids good for you?"

I felt annoyed that she wouldn't look at me while she talked, so I took the device and pulled it out of her hands. "What are you not tellin' me?"

She grabbed it back. "Nothing. You're being silly. I'm just relaxing. You know the ride is hard, especially with Addy."

I cocked and eyebrow and looked at her. Something was off and I was determined to find out what it was.

A little while later, I went out to the barn and called my cousin, Ty.

Sex advice hotline, how can I direct your call?

It's me. Cut that shit out. I need to talk to you about somethin'.

I thought you were Van.

Of course you did. Look, Ty, I need to know if you noticed anything off about Savanna. Did she talk to Miranda about things?

Not that I know of. I noticed she was being weird and I asked what was up. She said she was fine.

But you don't believe her?

Hell no! Look, man, I know Van and I can tell when something is on her mind. She was out of it. Maybe you should talk to her about annilingus.

What?

Jesus, you two are so naïve. Ass licking, dude.

You need mental help! Can you please be serious for a damn minute and help me out here.

Just ask her.

Yeah, well, she won't tell me what it is. I'm startin' to think that this has nothin' to do with Noah.

You're going to have to ask her. I don't know anything. I'll ask Miranda, but I think she would have told me if she knew something.

I was just checkin'. Thanks, man.

No problem. Call the sex advice hotline anytime between nine a.m. and five p.m. eastern time.

I shook my head and just hung up on him. If his life depended on being serious, he'd be dead by now.

When I went back inside, Savanna was doing the dishes, while Noah dried them. They weren't speaking to each other, but at least they were sharing a small amount of space. I leaned against the wall and watched them.

Savanna didn't understand how much I loved her for taking on the responsibility of raising Noah. She could have walked away, but instead, she threw herself into it as if her life depended on it. I appreciated her so much.

Even at his worst, Noah loved Savanna too. He was obviously going through something, but at the end of the day, I guarantee she'd be who he asked for if he needed help. We were buddies, and that was enough for me.

When they saw me standing there they both smiled. I wasn't certain, but I had this feeling that maybe they had spoke to one another. It would have been nice to get back to normal. The silent treatment wasn't feasible in our house.

The girls were being awfully quiet, so I headed upstairs to check on them. Little voices weren't coming from the playroom. They were coming from my room. I followed them into the master bathroom and found them both sitting on top of the counter. They heard the door creak and turned to look at me. Giant eyes, displaying makeup fit for two clowns just stared back at me.

"What are the two of you doin' in here?" It was difficult not to laugh. They looked hideous, and if the circus were in town, they'd fit right in.

I could hear Savanna running up the steps, so I knew that any second they were going to be in serious trouble.

They looked at each other and then back to me. "We are getting ready for a wedding, Daddy."

Savanna came in and gasped. She put her hand over her face and I wasn't sure if she was more upset at the girls for doing it, or the makeup they had ruined in the process.

I chuckled. "Who is gettin' married?"

"Barbie and GI Joe, silly. They can't live together until they get married. Are you goin' to come?"

Savanna said nothing as she walked up and grabbed a washcloth out of the closet. She ran it under the faucet and started with Addy's face. She tried to pull away. "No, Mommy!"

"I have to wash it off. You will get a rash if I don't," Savanna argued.

Addy fussed some more. Savanna looked at me and rolled her eyes, while trying not to laugh herself.

Once we had them back to normal, and cleaned up the ruined makeup mess, we all headed downstairs. Noah was in the kitchen getting a drink. He no sooner walked back out into the living room, when he tripped and went falling forward. The large glass of milk covered the hardwood floor.

He looked back and noticed that he tripped on one of his sister's shoes. "It's all your fault Addy!"

I was already picking up the broken pieces of glass from the cup, while Savanna was heading over with a towel. "Just get out of the way until we clean up the mess. Noah, it was an accident." I looked up at him and saw him pointing at Addy and mouthing 'I hate you'.

Savanna looked at me, like she'd seen it too.

"Mommy, Noah said he hates me." Addy was not one to keep things to herself. Both girls enjoyed getting Noah in trouble. I guess it was part of being a sibling. Since neither Savanna or myself had any, we didn't know what was normal.

I pointed toward the steps. "Get your ass upstairs, boy!"

Noah stood up, looking guilty. "I didn't do anything! She's a liar!"

"Noah, we saw you do it!" Maybe Savanna should have just let me handle it, but she seemed pretty annoyed.

"No you didn't. You're just takin' up for your kids!"

He didn't get another second to back talk his mother, because I was right on his ass, chasing him into his room. My belt was off before I entered through his door. He flew onto his bed and backed himself up against the wall, holding his arms over his head. "Don't dad! I'm sorry! I won't do it again!"

I took the belt and slammed it against his bed, making a sound that was loud enough to cause him to jump. He balled himself up tighter. "I am about sick of your attitude, Noah. You're being mouthy! You're lyin' all the time."

"Please don't beat me!"

I didn't want to hurt my kid. My own father used to tell me that it hurt him more than it hurt me. I understood what that meant, as I stood there with a belt in my hand. I held it up. "Look at me, boy!"

He looked up with tears in his eyes, sniffling.

"I am done with the way you've been actin'. If you don't straighten up, you're goin' to be done with lacrosse. You hear me?"

He nodded.

"You stay up here until you can apologize to your mother and sisters. If I ever hear you talk to them like they aren't your family, I will tear your ass up!"

Noah put his head down in his knees. "Yes, sir."

I left the boy in his room to sulk by himself. There was no way I was going to sit there and feel sorry for him. After all of our talks, he still wasn't acting like he'd been taught to. His disrespectful attitude was going to cause him to spend his whole summer in that damn room if he didn't shape up.

Savanna and the girls were downstairs watching an animated movie. They were cuddled up on either side of her. I stood there looking at the very clean floor, before heading over to the couch. Savanna smiled when I sat down and reached my arm around them. She and I didn't care much for animated movies, but family time was always important. Plus, we also knew that the girls would soon fall asleep and we would have some alone time.

It took longer than we both thought, but after an hour, they were fast asleep against us. I grabbed Christian while Savanna picked up Addy. They were getting heavy to carry up the stairs every night. You'd think that after three children we would have mastered the concept of bedtime. Contrary to every parenting book Savanna had read, nothing worked on our kids.

We met each other in the hallway. I reached for her hand and led her to our room. Before climbing into bed, she wrapped her arms around me and held me tightly. "I love you so much, Colt. Please don't ever doubt that."

I had no idea why she would say something like that. It was almost cryptic, like I should expect something bad to happen. "You sure you're alright, darlin'?"

I kissed her head and pushed her back far enough to be able to look into her eyes.

"I'm fine."

"You sure that their ain't somethin' you need to tell me? I feel like there is."

Savanna shook her head. "No. I'm just upset about Noah. I guess I just thought he would miss me while I was gone. I don't get how all of the sudden everything has changed."

"He's bein' a kid, darlin'. It's just a stage he's goin' through. I know the kid loves you and his sisters, too. He's bein' a little jerk and it's goin' to stop or I will have to take drastic measures to correct it myself." I hated threatening violence, but if it was what it took to knock some sense into my son, it was going to have to happen.

"I don't want you to have to go to those kind of extremes. He's just rebelling. Your mother says that you were the same way."

I was a handful. I could remember having my ass beat more than a dozen times. Once I set fire to a pile of leaves that my father forced me to rake up. I ended up burning down a tool shed and damaging a fence. Another time, I drove a four wheeler straight through a barn, with Conner on the front of it. I wasn't exactly a innocent child, but I never talked to my parents the way that Noah was talking to us. It was uncalled for and I wasn't having it in my house. My biggest problem was the way he was treating his mother. "I never disrespected my parents."

"I did a few times. I mean, I never told them off, but when they wouldn't let me do things that I wanted to do, I definitely wasn't an easy person to live with. Being an only child yourself, I suspect you did it a few times as well. Your mother wouldn't have put up with it. She probably threatened you with that wooden spoon more than you can remember."

I kissed the top of her head again. "I guess you're right. We still need to hold our ground. If Noah keeps at it, the girls are goin' to follow in his footsteps and then we're goin' to have a bigger problem to deal with." I rubbed her cheeks with my thumbs and looked deep into her eyes. "How about we take a bath before bed? I could use some quality time with my wife."

She looked up and smiled. "That sounds fantastic!"

"You take off your clothes and I will get the water started." I undressed and tossed my clothes on the floor as I walked. Since I was feeling distant from Savanna, I wasn't going to waste one second I had to be alone and naked with her.

Chapter 13

Savanna

After picking up the clothes that Colt left on the floor and making my way into the bathroom, he was already in the tub with his arms reaching out for me. I smiled as I removed the last of my clothes and climbed in to sit in front of him.

The water was so hot that it took a second to get used to, while the tub edges were cold against the underneath of my arms. Colt warmed the rest of my body as he reached his large hands around and started washing my neck, then down to my breasts. His stubbly face tickled the backs of my shoulders and I couldn't help but close my eyes while enjoying what only he could do to me.

The soap in his hands made the friction slippery, allowing him to maneuver his way up and down my arms with ease. He groaned as his fingertips massaged beneath my breasts. I felt both of his hands slide down my abdomen and continue until they reached my inner thighs. I was so eager for him to touch my pussy. I craved his attention after being away from him for days. The slightest touch to my sweet spot would send me in a frenzy. Colt must have sensed my anticipation. A small chuckled vibrated off of my shoulder as he rubbed harder on my inner thighs, never touching my pussy. I was just wanting, no needing, him to fill me with his love. The more he placed small kisses on the side of my neck, the more I could feel myself surrendering to his every touch.

Colt slowly let his fingers slip over my sex. If it weren't fully submerged in the water, I would have said that it was on fire. I was so hot for him to touch me there; to penetrate his fingers into my entrance.

He went slowly, moving his fingers up and down both sides, never allowing himself to feel what was inside waiting. I moaned each time, feeling the friction of his fingers sliding over my sensitive skin.

His strong arms surrounded my body, leaving me feeling completely safe and overwhelmed with desire for him. We were alone and all of my worries seemed to fade away with every precious touch of his lips to my skin. "I love you," he whispered into my ear.

As much as I wanted him to continue teasing me with his fingers, I wanted to kiss his perfect lips even more. Slowly, I turned to face him, never hesitating when I leaned in and pressed my mouth over his. I pulled away, opening my eyes slowly and watching him doing the same. "I missed you, Colt."

I needed this more than he could imagine. It was important for me to connect to my husband, when I felt like everything around me was falling apart. I just needed to know that no matter what happened with my health, or with our son, Colt would never stray from our beautiful marriage. I don't know why I felt insecure. For the longest time, I was certain that he would always love me. I think it was just my mind playing tricks on me, but my emotions seemed to be on overdrive. We'd come so far, after being through what no couple should ever have to endure.

I brought my fingers up to his lips and traced them before leaning in and kissing them again. He groaned and kissed me harder than before, letting his tongue finally make contact with mine. As they meshed together, so did our fingers and bodies. I wrapped my leg around my husband and straddled him, while holding both of his hands. We finally let go, but only so that we could explore each other's wet skin.

His long, stiff erection was poking me in the leg, reminding me that I wasn't the only one in the tub with needs. I reached down and grabbed his shaft, using the water as a slippery guide while stroking. Colt leaned his head back against the tub and closed his eyes.

I leaned in and kissed above one of his nipples, before running my tongue up to his neck. When I got to his stubbles, he looked down at me and grabbed either side of my face with his hands. For a few seconds, he just sat there staring into my eyes.

He leaned in and let our noses touch. I could feel his breath on my lips, but waited for him to make the first move.

Our next kisses were fueled by a mutual need. Our mouths moved in sync, matching brushes of our tongues and exploration with our hands. We were surrounded by bubbles, but I didn't need to see Colt's body to know what I was doing. I had every inch of him memorized.

Colt placed his hands under my ass and got me into the exact position for it to slide in once he sat me down. Between the hot temperature of the water and the shear size of my husband, I gasped. He cleared his throat and used his hands to guide me up and down. The water was splashing all around us as our pace became vigorous. I threw my head back and closed my eyes to concentrate on the pleasure I was feeling. Colt took one hand and ran it up to my breast. He pinched my nipple in between two fingers. I lifted my arms around his neck and teased his lips with my tongue. They tasted of sweat from the heat of the hot bath we were in. He leaned in and teased me back. It turned me on so much, feeling my sexy man mimicking my actions. I loved when Colt became the aggressor. His once gentle kisses started to become untamed. I could feel his teeth against my own as I increased my seductiveness, by moving my body like I was jumping up and down. I could hear little sounds escaping him the faster I moved. When his nails dug into my ass and steadied my pace, I knew he was about to finish. I could feel him releasing as it pumped inside the walls of my pussy. I matched his moment of euphoria, throwing my head back and letting my wet breasts rub against his chest.

Finally, I collapsed over him, letting my head fall onto his broad shoulder. He turned his head and kissed my forehead. It was easy to close my eyes and finally relax when I knew I was in his arms.

After our bath, we put on pajamas before climbing into bed. There was no telling when a child was going to come sneaking into bed with us. Colt took my Kindle and put it on his night stand. He shook his head and pulled me into his arms. "Not tonight, darlin'."

I didn't argue, because I was exactly where I needed to be.

For the next week, Noah avoided being around as much as possible. He'd do his chores and whatever we asked of him, but there was no other type of communication between us. I think Colt just didn't know what to do with him.

Zeke called that next Monday, which was also the day of my mammogram. Since I hadn't told the family that I needed to get the test done, I had to go all by myself. My doctor had, pretty much, assured me that it was just a routine double check, so I felt as if it was just a waste of time to get done. Still, I knew that my health was important so I went through with it.

That test sucked. My boob was smashed into a pancake. No, it was like a waffle machine. I wanted to cry, but bit down on my lip and took the pain instead of looking like a sissy.

Once I had my clothes back on, they told me I could leave and my doctor would call me with the results in a couple of days. Why couldn't they just tell me? I hated that I had to wait.

It was after noon when I got home and Colt was watching the sports channel, eating a piece of pizza. He nodded when I walked by, but kept his attention glued to that bottom line running across the screen.

Since he was obviously preoccupied, I headed into the kitchen to make myself something to eat. I'd no sooner sat down at the table to eat my sandwich, when he came into the kitchen and sat down across from me. "I heard from Zeke today."

I stopped chewing for a second and looked right at him. "And?"

"His tour ends in a week. He said he's shootin' a video in Puerto Rico next month, so he wanted us to come before that."

I sat my sandwich down and swallowed what was in my mouth. "So, when are you leaving?"

He cleared his voice and hesitated. I knew I wasn't going to like what he said. "I found a flight for Friday."

"So, you're leaving the day that Noah gets out for summer break?"

He reached his hands across the table and grabbed mine. "It's the best time, Savanna. It's in between chicken deliveries and I have to attend that Cattle auction next month."

"It's just so soon. I guess I thought that I would have some time to prepare. Things are so broken between Noah and me, right now."

He squeezed my hand. "He'll come around, darlin'."

I pulled away and stood up, letting my body lean against the countertop. "When, Colt? After he's lived the cool life with his uncle? Do you really think a week with memories of Krista are going to bring him back to me?"

He put his hands over his face, like it was all too frustrating to talk about. I could feel the tears forming in my eyes.

It wasn't just that I was jealous.

I was scared.

If Noah ended up resenting me, I didn't know how I would get through that kind of heartbreak.

"Savanna, please just trust me on this."

I walked over and leaned on the table top. He finally looked up at me. "You want me to trust you when you have no control over what the outcome of all this will be. Did it ever occur to you that he might really hate me?"

The tears had broken out and they were falling down my cheeks.

"You're bein' ridiculous. How could you even think somethin' like that? I get that he's goin' through somethin', but you need to understand that it ain't goin' to last forever."

I held up my hand. "I can't talk about this with you, right now. Do what you feel is right for your son, Colt. I'll be here when you get back."

I walked into the living room and started straightening up. He followed me. "Don't you think you are bein' just a little irrational here? I'm takin' Noah. It ain't like I'm dropping him off with the guy. He's goin' to be with me the whole damn time, Savanna."

"You don't get it, because he's always going to be your son. Nothing can ever change that for you. I don't have that convenience. The only ties that I share with Noah is our last name. The older he gets, the more apparent that is. This shit with Zeke just reminded me of what little say I have in his life. I can only be his mother if he lets me. The older he gets the more apparent it is that we don't share a blood connection."

"You're bein' unreasonable?"

"Am I, Colt? How would you feel if you were in my shoes? How would it make you feel if the child you raised as your own told you they hated you. He resents me. Do you get that?"

Colt threw his hands in the air, like he did every time we fought. "I'm not even goin' to talk to you about this anymore. I already booked the flight, so we're goin'."

"Obviously, I wasn't important enough to include in your planning. Why bother to tell me at all?"

I headed up the stairs, because I hated fighting with him. When I heard the front door slam, I knew he'd left me to sulk alone. Colt didn't get it and getting him to understand was just too much work.

Colt was taking Noah to see his uncle and all I could do about it was cry. On top of all of that, I had to spend the weekend alone with the girls, worrying about the damn lump that may or not be in my breast.

Chapter 14

Colt

She was being so irrational. It was just a trip to visit someone. I could hardly imagine my son not loving her anymore, just because he had a rockstar uncle.

When she got herself upset like that, there was no making things better. Walking away was the best thing I could do.

It was going to be a long week, dealing with an excited kid and a pissed off wife. Plus, I had to make sure the ranch was in order for me to be able to leave for a week. It wasn't like I could ask Conner to come stay and fill in for me. Amy was due any day and I'd never want him to miss that.

My only other option would be to ask Ty to come.

Now, obviously, I knew that Savanna and Ty were close. I wasn't stupid though. They shared a past and when things were bad between her and I, it was hard not to picture her wondering if she should have stayed with him.

With the wedge between us, Savanna kept her distance. She went as far as taking the girls to her parents one night for dinner, leaving me and Noah to eat leftovers. At night, she read her stories and acted like I wasn't even in the room.

It wasn't how I wanted to leave things.

Finally, the night before our flight, I climbed into bed and refused to get the cold shoulder. I grabbed her Kindle and put it on my bedside table. "Darlin', we need to talk."

She crossed her arms in front of her chest. "I have nothing to say. It hurts too much and you don't get it."

"I do get it."

She turned and gave me a dirty look. "You have no idea what it's like to go day in and day out knowing he doesn't want to be near me. I pass him in the hallway and he treats me like I have the plague."

"You're exaggeratin'."

She held up her hands. "Colt, please just go to bed. It's obvious that we aren't going to agree and I'd rather say nothing then cause a huge blowout before you leave tomorrow."

"Fine!" I rolled over in bed and said nothing else for the rest of the night. The sleep didn't come for at least an hour later. I was too angry to relax.

Savanna's mother came over in the morning to watch the girls while she drove us to the airport. Noah spoke directly to me about the trip, but said less than three words to Savanna.

When we got out of the car, she walked around and hugged me goodbye. Noah didn't respond when she put her arms around him. I could tell right away it hurt her feelings.

"We'll miss you, darlin'. Give the girls a kiss every day from me. I love you."

She waved as we walked away. "I will. I love you too!"

We had a six hour flight and during that time, it was too congested to have a serious talk with Noah. He was too busy listening to his iPod. When he finally fell asleep, I took the thing and went through his songs. Sure enough, he had downloaded all of Zeke's songs. I was so angry about it, that I woke the kid up. "What is this?"

He shrugged.

"Noah, I told you that these songs were not appropriate."

"I wanted to know about Zeke and his band, Dad. I won't sing the words out loud." He was acting like it wasn't a big deal.

"You have one week to straighten your little butt up, son. I'm not having you disobey me and your mother like this. What gave you the right to go behind our backs?"

He just shrugged again.

I kept the iPod in my hand for the rest of the flight. I could tell he was pissed about it, but he wouldn't dare argue with me over it.

A limousine was waiting for us, which excited Noah. Suddenly, he no longer cared about being in trouble with me. His whole focus turned to living the life of a rockstar.

I was on edge. After sending Savanna a text, I was too stressed to consider how much of a mistake this could turn out to be. The limousine driver looked like a lumber jack. He was gigantic and reminded me of the Jolly Green Giant from the vegetable cans.

Noah was blown away by the size of the vehicle. It was full of sodas, and I grabbed two once we pulled away from the curb. "This is awesome, Dad!"

"You think we could have one of these on the ranch?"

"We could fit lots of chickens in it." I knew it was a joke, but raised my eyebrow at him anyway.

"Very funny."

Since it had been a while since I had visited California, and I knew Noah had never been there before, I figured that we could make this a vacation for the both of us, even aside from having to visit Zeke. It was cool to see Noah reacting to the big city. He pointed to all types of places as we drove past them.

I knew we were probably getting close when the city turned into large hills overlooking valleys. Once you got out of the city, it was a nice place to drive through.

We came to a gated entrance about ten minutes outside of town. The limo driver held up a key card and the gate opened. We started to pull down a driveway as long as the dirt road at home. The house was enormous and bigger than I originally expected.

As the driver walked to the rear of the car to let us out, Zeke came walking out of his front door in a robe. His tattooed chest was exposed. "How was the flight, guys?"

I reluctantly shook his hand. "It was fine. This place is tremendous."

"I know, right? I wanted the best house that money could buy." He waved his hands. "Come on inside. Cal will grab your bags and take them to your rooms."

We walked into to an extremely large foyer. The floor shined like it was glass. The walls were red and the floors were all a white marble. Black and white décor followed through to each room. Zeke walked us around, showing us his home theater room, his large master bedroom with a rotating round bed and a bowling alley in the basement. The house also included an indoor and outdoor pool and a recording studio. I was taken aback by all of the things that one person had put in this single family mansion. Aside from the insane amount of extras, the house had seven bedrooms and eight bathrooms.

Piper, Zeke's wife, was out lounging by the pool. She was wearing a very skimpy bathing suit and huge sunglasses. When she heard her husband talking, she sat up. "I didn't know you were here already. Did you bring your suits?"

Noah was in awe. I think he was literally speechless. As cool as it all was, I could see how it was overwhelming.

Zeke patted me on the back. "You like what you see?"

"You've done well for yourself, Zeke."

"My chef is making us dinner. He's preparing you and Noah separate entrée's so you don't have to eat what we have. I'm pretty sure he can make anything you guys want. A little later I can take you into the kitchen so you can tell him the things you like. I want you both to make yourselves at home. I need to run out for a little bit, but I will be back for dinner."

Noah didn't waste any time getting his trunks on and jumping in the pool. The kid had forgotten about being in trouble and was only focused on living the high life at his uncle's pad. It was hard to feel protective when it felt like we were in a family resort, instead of someone's house that posed a threat to our family.

After watching Noah swim outside and go down the slide at least twenty times, I retreated into the house to check on Savanna and the girls. I plopped down on the extra soft king size bed in my room and dialed her number.

Hello.

Hey darlin'.

How is it going?

It's good. Noah has been swimming all day. Zeke had somethin' to do this afternoon, so we've just been hangin' around. He said somethin' about takin' Noah to the beach tomorrow. Noah asked him if Jaws was going to be in the water.

I'm not surprised. So what's it like there? Are their pictures of skulls all over the place?

No. Not at all. It's pretty fancy. The whole house is red and white with black accents. You wouldn't believe what this guy has in his house. He's got a bowling alley, a home theater room and recording studio.

You sound like it's amazing.

How are the girls? I miss you already.

I miss you too. It's good you're there with Noah. He needs this, I guess.

I'm sorry for how we left things. You know I hate fightin' with you.

I know. Me too. I'm going to let the girls sleep in our bed tonight. They're all excited about it.

Give them kisses. I will call you tomorrow, darlin'.

Okay, babe. Goodnight.

We ate outside, once Zeke got back from wherever he had to go. While they enjoyed eating their health food, Noah and I chowed down on barbeque ribs and French fries covered in cheese and bacon. We'd only been there for a few hours and I could already tell that my son was in love with the place.

I was happy that he was having a good time, but it meant that he wasn't going to be thrilled about going home. I had a feeling that this trip was going to hurt Savanna more than she already was and I didn't know what the hell I could do to fix it.

After dinner, we watched a movie in the home theater room. Noah sat next to Zeke, while Piper and I sat behind them. They seemed to be getting along good. Noah, who was all smiles, kept laughing at things that his uncle was saying to him. I was too far back to hear what it was, but the kid felt comfortable, that was for sure.

After the movie, I was beat. Since they'd been fine this whole time, I felt like it was okay to go up to my room, while Noah stayed with Zeke and Piper.

Savanna wouldn't have agreed with my decision. If she'd known that I done it, she'd be on a plane to come kick my ass and take her son home.

I had one week to figure out how to fix this mess; one week to come up with a solution to get Noah and Savanna back to normal.

I'm not real sure what time my son went to bed, but before the sun came up the next morning, he was standing over my bed waiting for me to wake up. I wiped the sleep out of my eyes. "Noah, why are you just standin' there?"

"Nobody is awake yet. Uncle Zeke said we could go to the beach today. When do you think he will get up? Why is it still dark out?"

I sat up and looked over at the clock. It was six in the morning. I scratched my head and thought about how to explain to my over excited child that normal people liked to sleep in on the weekends and it was actually three hours earlier than it was at home. "Noah, remember how you learned about the different time zones? Well it's actually three hours earlier than it is at home. Go back to bed for three more hours, kid."

"I'm not tired, Dad. Let's watch a movie. He's got that robot movie in 3D."

Since we were guests, I didn't want my son waking up the whole house. As much as I didn't want to, I climbed out of bed and followed Noah down to the basement, so that we could watch a movie. It was going to be a very long day and I hoped to hell that Zeke had enough sense to install a fancy coffee maker somewhere in the house. I was going to need it.

Chapter 15

Savanna

The weekend went by so slow. My parents had me and the girls over for dinner Saturday and we all went to church on Sunday. Colt called as often as he could, but it seemed like Zeke was keeping them busy. I'd hoped that Noah would want to talk to me, but Colt never mentioned it, so neither did I.

When the girls would fall asleep, I cried until I couldn't stay awake any longer. As hard as it was for me to accept, I knew that I was losing what we once shared. Our bond had been broken by something so small. It made me wonder if he ever truly loved me.

I thought back to that day when he came into our life. I could have walked away, but my heart told me to stay. I was feeling like this was so much worse than any kind of breakup with a lover. This was a deeper kind of heartbreak; the kind you never got over.

When Monday morning came around, I was physically and mentally exhausted. It was a good thing that Colt's mom offered to take them on a girl's day. She picked them up at nine and the house was finally quiet.

I started straightening up when I heard my phone ringing. The number on the caller ID said it was my doctor's office. Immediately, my stomach started to hurt. I picked up the phone with shaky hands.

Hello?

Is this Savanna Mitchell?

Yes, it is.

This is Kay from Doctor Wellington's office. He'd like you to come in to talk about the results of your mammogram. Are you available tomorrow morning at nine?

Yes.

I will pencil you in. We'll see you tomorrow at nine.

When I hung up the phone, I kept telling myself not to panic, but I wasn't an idiot. Doctors only called you back into the office when the news was bad. My hand went straight to my breast in question. I still felt nothing.

My body sank down on my couch and I just started bawling. A month ago I would have thought that my family could get through anything. Now, with these new developments, I wondered if that was actually possible.

I looked around at the pictures of our family. The one on the coffee table was of the five of us. The kids were all smiling and Colt was looking down at me with a grin on his face. I traced over him.

I didn't want to think about what the doctor was going to say. I knew what it meant to have a lump in the breast. I also knew that it was a fifty-fifty chance that the results could mean cancer.

I held onto that picture while I continued to cry in the quiet, dark house. It was a good thing that Colt's mother had the girls, because there just wasn't anyway I would have been able to keep them occupied without losing it.

I wanted to call Colt, but he already had enough on his plate. Surely my news could wait until he got back. I still didn't know anything.

I considered calling my mother, but I couldn't let myself worry her. This was something that I was just going to have to suck up and handle myself until I knew more.

With the exception of the two hours I got after I had taken a valium, I didn't sleep at all. How could I, when my life could be on the line? I prayed to God for it to be a mistake in the test. It happens all the time. Surely, I could be the one that it happened to. I was a good wife and mother, and a devoted Christian. Not that anyone deserved to have something wrong with them, but hadn't I been dealt with enough in my young life already?

I arrived at the doctor's office an hour before my appointment. My palms were sweaty and I hated that I was going in all alone. Wasn't this the type of thing you had a support group for?

The front desk lady must have sensed my eagerness. She went in the back and had the doctor come out to greet me.

He opened the door for me to enter into the back. "Savanna. You're early."

I felt embarrassed. Didn't anyone else feel nervous like I did? "Is that a problem?"

"Of course not. We can meet before the first appointment arrives. Come in and sit down." He walked out of his office and came back in with my chart. Once he sat down in front of me, he opened up the large envelope that contained my mammogram results. While he pointed to a certain area with his pen, he looked up at me. "This is the lump that I felt during your examination. I was thinking that it was going to be just a pocket of collected tissue. The mammogram shows that it is in fact a mass. It isn't very big, but any mass can be a concern. I'd like to get you in to have it biopsied this week."

My mouth just dropped. I got that he was a professional and he did these sorts of things all day, but he did it without emotion. "So, how serious is it? Should I be worried, because I have to tell you, I am scared to death."

He fidgeted with his pen. Maybe it was how he separated himself from his patient's emotional breakdowns. "I can tell you it's nothing, but right now, we just don't know. It's located in a difficult area of the breast and until we get in there and can test it properly, we just don't know what we are dealing with."

"Is it too soon to talk about outcomes? Maybe I am jumping the gun, but if it's...if it's cancer, what are my options?"

He held both hands up and lifted his brows. "We don't want to jump the gun here, Savanna. This could be just a growth that won't put you in any danger. Talking about options before we know anything will only make you worry more. Thousands of women get biopsies and half of them turn out to be nothing."

I stared down at my shaking hands. "So how do we find out?" My eyes were starting to water. I got that his job was to be informative and he was used to giving people bad news, but it didn't make it any easier for me. I was going through this without my husband and dealing with a step-son that may or may not even care if I lived or died.

"I can see if I can get you in to see the oncologist this week. He may just go ahead and do the biopsy without a first appointment. Did you want me to go ahead with that?"

I was too shaken up to answer, so I just nodded and put my head down.

The doctor got up and walked out of the office for a second. I pulled my knees into my chest and the tears started to fall down my face. I thought about my family, in fact, it was all I could think about.

What would happen if I died?

How hard would it be for them to get by without me?

How long would I have to live?

Would they be scared if I lost my hair?

I thought about my girls growing up without a mother.

I was overwhelmed with hopeless fear.

The doctor came back into the office to find me an emotional wreck. He sat down and cleared his throat. "Savanna, I realize this is scary. You aren't alone. Take it day by day until we figure out what's going on." He wrote something down in his laptop. "They are going to squeeze you in on Thursday. Can you be there at seven in the morning?"

It was early, but nothing that I wasn't used to. "Yes."

"When you walk out stop by the front desk. Kay will give you paperwork that their office faxed over to us. Just take that with you. They're located in the building behind this one. He knows that I want a rush on the labs. I can't guarantee that we will have them before the weekend. It usually takes seven days, so I imagine four is a rushed order. If you don't hear anything before Wednesday next week, just give us a call."

"Sounds good," I sniffled through my words.

"Try to not get yourself too upset until we have the next results. This could still be nothing to worry about."

We said our goodbyes and I grabbed the paperwork, while still crying.

Once I got to the car is when my bawling became uncontrolled. I was petrified. Everyone thinks that it can't happen to them. The truth is, it could happen to any of us.

I needed to call Colt, but he was with Noah, who would never forgive me if I ruined their trip. Colt would want to come home and be with me through all of this.

I had to do it alone.

I don't remember dialing the number, but Miranda's name filled my screen.

The voice on the other line was not the person I wanted to talk to.

Cocksucker's Anonymous, how may I direct your call?

Ty, can I talk to Miranda?

Are you crying?

No!

Stop lying. I can hear it in your voice.

Is she there or not?

She left her phone home. Stop changing the subject. Did Colt hook up with a groupie? He did, didn't he?"

No! I have to go.

I hung up the phone before he could say anything else. The last thing I needed was Ty's two cents.

The phone rang again, but I hit the silent button. By the time I got a mile down the road, he'd rang my phone constantly.

What?

Do you really think that I'm just going to be okay with you hanging up on me when clearly you need to talk to someone?

You are the last person on the earth that I can talk to this about.

You got warts?

I hung up on him again.

He called my phone non-stop the entire ride home. The worst part was that once I got driving, my Bluetooth connected to my SUV and it rang louder than a regular phone. At least I could hit ignore from my steering wheel.

When I pulled down our long dirt driveway, he was still calling. I'd realized that his shenanigans had actually forced me to stop crying, since I was so annoyed.

I picked up the phone one last time to tell him where he could stick it.

If you don't stop calling me..

How long have we known each other?

Since we were kids, why?

Talk to me, Van. I'll listen, I promise.

I can't talk about this, Ty. It's personal.

I know you. What gives? What could be that bad that you don't want anyone to know? Are you having an affair?

No! Oh my God, you would think that!

Are you pregnant?

I wish it was something like that, Ty.

Is it your health?

I shouldn't have even called Miranda. I don't want the family knowing this. Please just forget I called. Don't tell your wife, Ty. It's best if I keep this to myself.

If you hang up on me, I'm driving out there. You're making me worry, now. Please, Van, just tell me you're going to be alright?

Don't come here, Ty. I'm going to be fine.

Except, I wasn't going to be fine.

Once I got back in the house, I crawled into bed and had a sob fest. It wasn't unusual for me to get emotional about things. It was how I was wired, I guess. The unusual part was this was legitimately a good reason to be breaking down.

A little while later my mother in-law called and asked if she could take my mother and the girls to some doll convention that was a few towns over. Since she was footing the bill and already had them excited, I knew I had to say yes.

I lied and told her I wasn't home, so that they could come and pack some clothes. Without even putting shoes on, I grabbed my keys and moved my SUV into the garage so they wouldn't see my car. Like a little kid, I hid in the office with the door locked, so they wouldn't find me.

I knew that if I saw my two beautiful little girls and my two mothers, I would lose it and the cat would be out of the bag.

They took forever getting their things together for the overnight trip. I could hear the excitement in their voices and I wished that I hadn't been so selfish so that I could kiss them each goodbye. I love my little princesses so much. Family was always the most important thing in my life.

When the house got quiet, I knew I was in the clear. They had turned on every single light, even though it was daytime. While walking through the house, turning them all back out, I stopped and looked at the pictures on the wall. They were all such happy times that we'd shared together. I imagined them all getting on without me and it crushed my heart even more.

Without considering the time of the day, I put on one of Colt's t-shirts and climbed into my bed, alone.

After being overwhelmed with anxiety, sleep came fast and I didn't fight it. I woke to knocking on the front door and looked over at the clock. It said that it was after ten. I'd been asleep for a good eight hours. Just to be proper, I threw on a pair of shorts before walking downstairs.

When I opened up the door and saw who was standing there, I couldn't believe it was real. I had to be dreaming.

Chapter 16

Colt

I missed my wife and girls, but I had to admit that I was having a pretty darn good time. Noah was in heaven. After we'd spent the weekend sightseeing and visiting all of Zeke's favorite places, we spent the next two days lounging around the house.

Zeke and Noah were getting to know each other and it wasn't half as bad as Savanna and I had imagined.

He and his wife really did live pretty normal lives. Sure, they were filthy rich and surrounded by an entourage of very emo folk, but when we were all alone they were as normal as you could get.

Zeke had told me ahead of time that they were having a get together to celebrate the end of his tour. His other band mate's wives were taking all the kids to an amusement park and Piper had offered to take Noah. This was another thing that Savanna would have frowned upon, but the last thing I wanted to do was hang out with a bunch of women and kids all day. I just figured I could have the night off from being a guard dog to my son. I'd planned on relaxing for the night, possibly catching a game on television or having a beer by the pool. I never expected to be thrown into a party that could possibly cause me to be a divorced man.

The people didn't start showing up until after dinner. By that time, the caterers had already set up everything on the first floor and out in the pool area. Alcoholic beverages could be found every ten feet and I appreciated that Zeke and Piper had the decency to make sure my son wasn't in the house.

After at least fifty people had showed up, I was starting to realize that the party list didn't just include band members. Another dead ringer was the fact that slews of half dressed females were pouring in by the minute.

I grabbed a six pack of beer and several mini-sandwiches and found my way through the crowds, up to my room. The last thing I wanted to do was party with these people. I didn't even understand how Zeke was doing it, considering he was a recovering addict himself. No wonder it was so difficult for celebrities to kick the habit for good.

Once I got up to my room, I took my shirt off and got comfortable on the bed, knowing I was going to fall asleep there for the night. I flipped through the channels until I came across the basketball championship game. The series was tied and this game would determine the winner.

I'd watched the whole game, while listening to the crowd of people and music coming from the lower level, but when there was only two minutes left, two giggling broads came barging into my room. I sat up in the bed, looking at them paying me no mind at all. "Hey, this room is taken!"

They looked at each other and giggled. "The more the merrier, right?" They approached me from either side of the bed. I looked down and remembered that I wasn't wearing a shirt. This was not an invitation like they thought it was. "Seriously, I'm a married man." I backed myself as far as I could on the bed. They climbed on either side.

"Every man in this house is married. That means nothing, honey." In one instant the girl was whipping off her top and kneeling in front of me shirtless.

I wasn't sure what her friend was doing since I closed my eyes. "You got the wrong idea. I ain't interested in this type of thing."

When I felt one of them grabbing my arm, I pushed her away and jumped off the bed. The half naked one just sat there with her hands on her thighs. "Are you gay? The hot ones always are."

"No! What the hell? I ain't interested in you because I got a family back home and I don't think my wife would appreciate me shackin' up with other women."

They looked at each other and smiled.

I shook my head and walked out of the room. There was no way I was going to be caught in that type of predicament.

It took a while to find Zeke. He was laying under a canopy with three topless girls around him. "Colt! Did you decide to join the party?"

The naked girls were groping each other, paying me no mind.

"No! I didn't decide to join in on this nonsense. I was tryin' to relax in my room when two crazy women busted in. Who has a million dollar home with no locks on the bedroom doors?"

Zeke laughed at me. "Look around you, Colt. This is the high life, man. For once why don't you sit back and enjoy yourself. Nobody will know!"

I was obviously not getting anywhere with this guy. Apparently, his wife was fine was him being around naked women. I guess that was why he was in those magazines with other women.

"When are the kids gettin' back? I don't want my son seein' this!"

He ran his hands through one of the blonde girl's hair. "In the morning. Piper knows to stay away until everyone is gone."

"You didn't ask to keep him overnight. Savanna ain't goin' to like this."

"She's not here, Colt. Come on, dude. Just let yourself unwind. You don't have to cheat to have a good time with these ladies."

"Just give me Piper's number so I can call my son." I waited for him to write it down, before walking away from

Zeke so I didn't put my fist into his face. I couldn't call Savanna and tell her any of this. She was going to kill me. This was what she'd warned me about.

I got to the far side of the pool area and sat down on a large lounge chair. The party was completely out of hand. Topless women were running all around the pool area and jumping in the water. Guys were getting loud, like they'd had way too much to drink. There was some kind of platform in the center of the pool that some girl was dancing around on. Of course she was topless. Male and females in the pool were cheering her on to remove her shorts. I shook my head when I watched her shimmy out of them.

I wasn't a pussy. I'd been to strip clubs and had exotic dancers all over me before. This was different. Once I met Savanna, those days were over for me. I had no interest in being turned on by another woman. She gave me everything I needed.

Knowing that every corner of the house was filled with these types of women, I figured there was no way around it. I grabbed a beer and sat back down in the far corner lounge chair. The dancer danced and the other women ran around naked and fondled each other. It was like every teenage boys wet dream.

I thought about my cousins Ty and Conner and what they would be doing if they were sitting where I was. Without thinking about what I was doing, I pulled out my phone and took a picture of the madness. I sent them both the photo, with the caption of 'wish you were here'.

While I was hating it, they'd be so jealous.

The party lasted until five in the morning. The crazy females that had been dancing around and giving the shows, were all passed out around the house. They still weren't covered up. All I wanted to do was get to my bed and go to sleep. When I got to my room I found the two girls, completely naked, asleep.

"What the fuck?"

It only took me a second to turn back around and look for another place to lay my head. Seemingly, though, everywhere I turned, there were people. Trashy women were sprawled all over the place. I'd even found a couple having sex in the garage.

This was not the kind of thing that I ever wanted my son to know about. If I would have found out that Noah came to visit and was exposed to this kind of nonsense, someone would have been put in a grave.

After exhausting all other sleeping options, I headed back to my room to kick the girls out.

I looked around the large bedroom. Then I thought about what these women had been doing for all this time. Suddenly, the urge to kick them out of my room was gone. My bed had been soiled by some freaky sex-fest. Back in college, I would have loved to see what had happened.

After walking over and covering up the girls, I grabbed a throw and two pillows and went to sleep on a fancy rug in the bathroom. It was extra plush and felt like it may have been real fur. Another thing I liked was that this particular room did have a lock on the door.

I didn't want any naked girls thinking they could creep on my shit while I was trying to sleep. I also didn't want anyone walking in the room and assuming that I'd been involved with them. All I needed was to go home and be kicked out of my own house. Living with my mother was never going to be an option. I had to do my best to make it out of this damn trip with my dignity and marriage intact.

Chapter 17

Savanna

I stood in the doorway staring at Ty. He had his hands crossed against his chest.

"What are you doing here?" I repeated.

He looked back and I noticed a cab was sitting with the engine running. "You got any cash? This dude says his credit card machine ain't working."

I rummaged through my purse and handed him my whole wallet to go through. I think I was just so shocked that he was standing in front of me that I couldn't comprehend what I was actually doing.

When he came back inside, he had a small book bag on his back. He sat it down on the chair and walked over to me. Before I could say anything, Ty pulled me into a tight hug. "I got here as soon as I could."

"What are you doing here?"

"I'm taking care of my best friend, like I said I would. Geesh, do I have to spell it out?"

I plopped down on the couch and watched him sit next to me. "You shouldn't have come. What did you tell Miranda? She must think you're up to something."

"Miranda is fine. I would have brought her with me if Amy wasn't due to pop a baby out of her vagina any day now. Besides, she thinks I'm here to help out while Colt is gone."

I didn't want Ty holding information from his wife. This was just a big fat mess. "You should go home, Ty. I will pay for the ticket. I'm fine. It was just a false alarm."

I went to stand up and he grabbed my arm, pulling me back down on the couch. "Not so fast, Wonder Woman. Look me in the eye and tell me that nothing is wrong."

I opened my eyes wide and looked at him, but the words wouldn't come out. I could deny it all I wanted, but I knew that he would see right through my lies. I covered my face with my hands. "I can't talk about this with you, Ty."

He pulled one of my hands down and held it. "I'm here because you need me to be, whether you will admit it or not. I have no hidden agenda and I sure as hell don't want your money. Like it or not, you're going to tell me."

I could have sat there and beat around the bush until he gave up, but I knew that come morning, he would be hounding me for answers again. I had to face the fact that he was the only person around who was supporting me. I wished it was Colt, although, I knew he was where he needed to be. Life went on, even if I ended up having cancer or not.

"Do you promise not to tell anyone, especially Colt?"

He nodded. "Yeah. Now just spit it out. I haven't pissed since I left the airport and the three beers I had before I got on the plane are ready to come back out."

"Just forget it! This is hopeless. You can't even be serious for three seconds."

I was getting so frustrated with him. For Ty to hop on a plane to come to my rescue was just surreal. I knew he cared about me. We were family and that's how it should be, but I just couldn't believe that he would drop everything to make sure I was alright.

"Go to the bathroom and we can talk when you get back."

Ty got up and headed down the hall. Since I'd slept for so long, it felt like morning for me. I grabbed a bottle of wine and a beer out of the refrigerator. After I had a glass, I met Ty back in the living room.

"Ugh, oh! We need alcohol for this discussion?" He seemed as worried to hear my news as I was to say it out loud.

I poured the red wine into my glass and drank half of it before answering him. "My doctor found a lump in my breast."

He said nothing.

I couldn't look at him. I was so afraid of what he was thinking. Ty look a long drink of his beer and shook his head like it was hard to swallow. "Van, you have to tell Colt."

I put my hands over my face. "I can't tell him yet. I have to know how bad it is first."

He reached over and pulled me into his chest. "Please don't cry. Dammit, woman! I knew it was something like this. Why do you think I got here so fast?"

I let Ty continue to comfort me. "I didn't want everyone knowing. Right now, I don't know how serious it is. How can I explain things when I don't even know what to do myself?"

"When does Colt get home?" He asked.

"He won't be home until Saturday," I cried. I just wanted him to be holding me and doing what Ty was trying to do. I appreciated it so much, but it wasn't his job.

"I'll stay until Colt gets home. Miranda is fine with it. I sat her down and told her how upset you were and how you had called for her. She wanted to call you right away, but thought you'd get pissed at me for telling her that something was wrong. With Amy on the verge of popping out another little kid, she didn't want to leave. She sends her love and said that when you're ready to talk, you know how to find her."

Miranda and Ty had always been there for me. Their love continued to grow, as well as the trust that they shared. No matter how much the man joked, she knew he was always just going to love her.

"I kind of figured you would tell her."

He rubbed my shoulder and made me look up at him. "What's the next step?"

I shrugged. "They are doing a biopsy on Thursday."

"I'm going with you." He was adamant.

I shook my head. "You can't! Colt will kill you!"

"Van, here's the way I see it. You haven't told Colt anything. He's busy protecting your son and you don't want to interrupt that. I get it. The thing is, you can't go through this alone. Maybe I was the last person on earth that you wanted to know this information, but I do know. Now, it would be impossible for me to let you go through it alone."

This was the side of Ty that not many people got to see. His emotional side was usually camouflaged by humor. "What if I don't want your support?"

He cocked his eyebrow and laughed at me. "Of course you do." He reached over and grabbed both of my hands, then pulled them up to his lips and kissed them. "Everything is going to be okay, Van. Just pretend I'm Colt."

I pulled away. "You're nothing like him."

"You're right! I still have a set of balls, where Colt lost his man card years ago."

"You just went from hero to asshole in ten seconds flat."

He patted my leg. "I'm going up to the guest room to get some sleep. Just as a precaution, I'm locking the door. I know it's going to be hard for you to resist the real man sleeping a few rooms down." He winked and got up off the couch.

"Eh, how does Miranda put up with you?"

He was halfway up the stairs. "Be nice or I will do an upper decker in all of your toilets!"

I threw my hands in the air. "Oh my God! Go home!"

"See you in the morning!" He yelled.

When I finally got up to my room, and locked my own door, I thought about having to call Colt and let him know that Ty was at the ranch. Since he hadn't been in a good mood for weeks, I couldn't imagine him being happy about it.

Knowing that I wasn't going to get much sleep, since I'd already slept so long earlier, I grabbed my Kindle and started on a book that I had on my to-be-read list.

I finished the whole thing before sleep came again, and when it did, I kind of wished it hadn't.

I had horrible nightmares of being dead and watching my kids grow up without me. I saw my daughters grow up without a mother and Colt becoming so old and lonely. I dreamed of Noah being a rockstar and getting emancipated from his father.

Each dream was worse than the one before it.

By seven in the morning, I'd had about enough of them, so I went downstairs to make some coffee. Once I had my cup, I went into the living room to relax before Ty woke up and started getting on my nerves.

A vibration caught my attention and I noticed that Ty must have left his cell phone downstairs when he went up to bed. After it buzzed so much that it got on my nerves, I grabbed it just to turn off the notification.

Seeing that the message was from Colt, made me want to know if Ty had told him he was coming. Curiosity got the best of me, as I opened up the message.

I couldn't believe my eyes.

It had to have been some kind of joke.

There was no way my husband was around naked women and sharing the pictures with his cousin.

I couldn't stop looking at it.

The caption...that caption said it all.

I was hurt, jealous, mad and a bunch of other things all in one. Colt was going to hear me loud and clear when he picked up the phone. While still holding the phone with the incriminating message, I ran toward my bedroom to grab my phone.

Ty stopped me in the hallway. "I was looking for that."

I put it behind my back. "I need it for a minute."

"Did you lose yours?"

"No! Just...I need it, okay?"

I no sooner spun around, when I felt him grabbing my arm. "Hold on! What could be so important that you have to use my phone?" He snatched it out of my hand and looked down at the opened screen. A huge grin formed on his face.

"Holy shit! This is awes…err, it's terrible. It must be just a joke. I send him naked pictures all the time. He probably Googled it."

"You are doing that thing you do!"

He looked all innocent. "What thing?"

"The thing where you take up for each other, so us women don't find out you really did something wrong!"

"Bullshit!"

I pushed Ty and went running into my room, locking the door, so he couldn't follow me. "When I get done with his ass, he may not have balls left!"

"Van! Open the door. He doesn't know I'm here. Just wait until he calls you. I'm sure there is an explanation. Do you really think he'd let Noah around that kind of thing?"

I stopped punching in Colt's number and thought about what Ty was saying. There was no way Colt would have allowed our son to be near anything like that. As mad as I was about the picture, I wondered if I was freaking out over something that never happened.

Reluctantly, I opened the door and saw Ty standing there. "You're telling him a different reason for coming here, Ty. I'll talk to him about the picture later."

Little voices filled the foyer and I found myself almost running downstairs to greet the girls. They both had new dolls in their hands that were wearing outfits that matched their own.

Addy held her doll up. "Mommy, look what Grandma got me."

"That's so cute! You girls look like you had a great time."

Colt's mom smiled. I could tell how much she loved being a grandmother. "They were angels. I told them we could go next year if they wanted to."

"There's my pretty nieces!" Ty came running down the stairs.

I could see the curious look he was getting from his aunt. "Ty got here late last night to help out when the alarm company comes to fix the chicken houses. Since Colt isn't here, him or Conner had to be here. I told him there was plenty of room at your house."

"I guess you're better company than me and Lucy. We tend to get boring nowadays."

Ty hugged his aunt. "You're never too old to have a good time. Maybe you could cook me some of your fried chicken while I'm here."

She shook her head. "Sometimes, I think all he loves me for is that darn chicken." She patted him on the shoulder. "Didn't Miranda and the kids come?"

He held up his arms. "I wanted her to, but with Amy being due, she didn't want to leave. That's why I'm here and Conner stayed."

"Of course. Amy would kill him if he wasn't there for this one. They claim this is the last one they're having, but we all know how the two of them are." Colt's mom gave Ty the look like she knew what they did in their spare time.

We all three laughed.

Addy and Christian had run upstairs and finally came back down. Addy looked sad. "Where's Daddy and Noah?"

"They're still in California. They'll be back this weekend." I tried to reassure her.

"Can you ask him to come home now? I want to show him my doll."

I bent down and kissed her little forehead. "They will be home in a couple of days."

"How about, after Uncle Ty gets done with the alarm guy, we go out for ice cream?" He always talked to the kids like he was one himself.

She started getting all excited. "Mommy, can we? Can we please?"

"Of course."

Colt's mom leaned down to talk to Addy. "How about Grandma makes fried chicken for dinner and then you can go have ice cream afterwards?"

"Yay!"

"That sounds great, Mom. I will bring a side dish."

She started to walk toward the door. "See you all at six, then. Savanna, don't you let him get on your nerves too much."

Her reference to Ty must have hit a nerve. "I'm not that bad, am I?"

We both looked at each other and ignored his comment.

Once she was gone, Ty turned to me. "You came up with a story fast."

"It's not a story. I was going to have to call Colt and give him the bad news about it. They were fitting us into their schedule. Anyway, they'll be here around ten. It's the first four chicken houses. You just need to be there to sign and answer any questions that he might have." I had almost forgot about them coming. I would have had no clue what to tell the men.

"I guess it's time to call Colt!"

I smiled. "Yeah, I guess it is."

I walked out on the porch with my phone and dialed my husband. The vision of the naked girls was still fresh in my mind, but I was truly believing that it was just a joke he was playing on the guys.

The phone rang four times before someone picked up.

And it wasn't Colt.

Chapter 18

Colt

I woke up on the bathroom floor, looking around and trying remember why the hell I was where I was. Once I was in the sitting position, it all came back to me.

Without my phone, or a clock in the bathroom, I had no idea what time it was. All I knew was that it was daylight out.

I could hear my phone's ringtone, but it wasn't in the bathroom, so I jumped up and headed out into the bedroom to find it.

I stopped in my tracks when I saw one of the blondes from the night before holding it in her hand and talking to whoever had called. I said a little prayer, hoping to God that it wasn't my wife. I'd never hear the end of it, if it was.

"Hold on, he's right here!" She handed me my phone.

Hello?

The line was already dead.

I looked up at the girl. "Who was it?"

She giggled. "I think it was your wife. She thought she dialed the wrong number, I guess."

"Shit!" I started pacing around the room. "You two need to get your shit and get out of here, now!"

Her smiled dissipated as she gathered the rest of her clothes and her sleeping girlfriend and ran out of my room.

I sat down on the bed and stared at my phone. Without giving myself time to rethink things, I dialed Savanna.

I don't want to talk to you right now, Colt!

Just hear me out, would ya?

I think I've heard about enough!

Savanna, it ain't what you think. That was just Pi...

Don't you dare lie to me, Colt Mitchell. So help me God.

You're this mad over someone answering my phone?

No! I'm not just mad about that. I'm mad about something else, too.

Well, I ain't done nothin' else.

Bullshit!

Savanna, I don't know what you're talkin' about.

For someone that sent the message himself, I'm finding it hard to believe that you can't remember. I mean, if I took a picture of a bunch of naked men, I think I'd remember it.

What the hell? Let me guess, Ty sent you that shit?

No! I saw it on his phone this morning. He's here to help the alarm company install a new system.

He ain't stayin' at our house.

Don't you dare go there with me! Until you can explain to me what you were doing and what you were thinking, I don't want to talk to you, Colt. You've hurt me and you're acting like you did nothing wrong. You have no idea what I'm going through. Do you know how it made me feel to see you sending a picture like that. You better not wish I was there, because right now I'd cut off your testicles and feed them to Sam!"

I tossed the phone on the bed and laid down next to it. I was in the dog house, when it came to my wife. A little while later, Noah came barging into my room. "Dad, you're never goin' to believe it. I got to meet some of the players from the Raiders. They own the restaurant that we ate at last night. Piper got them to autograph some things for you."

I sat up and took in just how excited my son was. "Sounds like a good time. I figured you'd call last night before you went to bed."

"Sorry! Me and Johnny stayed up playing his Xbox." Noah was oblivious to what had went down at the house the night before.

Well, he didn't know until the screaming began.

Piper and Zeke were really having it out. I could tell that it bothered Noah. We weren't a loud kind of family. Sure, we had typical redneck arguments, but we didn't get loud and we surely didn't do it in front of the children.

"What's goin' on?"

I patted him on the back. "I reckon they're havin' it out about somethin'. It ain't none of our business though. Did you eat breakfast?"

"I had a doughnut. I'm still hungry." The screaming was getting to him. He started fidgeting.

"How about you and me head out and get something to eat. I'm sure that limo driver can take us somewhere."

His eyes lit up. "Cool. I want pancakes with whip cream and strawberries."

I shook my head. He was a chip off the old block. I finished putting on my shoes. "Let's go find us some pancakes then."

It was easy to slip out of the house unnoticed and luckily we found the limo driver outside, talking on his cell phone. Noah seemed so excited that we didn't have to pull the guy's leg to get him to take us somewhere.

He drove us to a corner diner and assured us that the appearance on the outside had nothing to do with the quality of food on the inside. It was what he called a 'gem'.

We invited him to join us, but he instantly declined. Noah and I found a booth seat against a window and started looking over the menu. "Dad, they have the pancakes, with any kind of fruit you could ever want. This place is awesome!"

I looked over at him while I sat down my menu. "I'll just have what you're gettin' then."

Noah told the waitress what we wanted and I added a coffee before she walked away. He was looking all around outside the window. "So, Noah, are you havin' a nice visit?"

"Yeah. I can't wait to come again. Piper said Uncle Zeke has a surprise for me. Do you know what it is?"

This was news to me. I didn't know anything about a surprise and the thought of it made me leery. In fact, everything about Zeke made me leery after last night. He was trying to make himself out to be this normal guy, but behind closed doors, he was anything but that. What worried me more was that Noah was oblivious to any of the bad stuff. He only saw the cool and amazing things that Zeke wanted him to see. He was wooing him into acceptance and that wasn't alright, in my book. It was downright wrong!

Our pancakes came with a mountain of whipped cream, strawberries and blueberries. Noah dug in right away, after pouring a giant cup of maple syrup all over his plate.

We spent a lot of time together on the farm, but most of the time, it was because he was helping me with something. It had never been because we were on a trip together. As angry as I was at how he was treating Savanna, I had to appreciate being able to have this time with him.

Still, in the back of my mind, I worried about Savanna being so mad at me. I also had a problem with Ty being the shoulder she was going to cry on. Don't get me wrong, I loved my cousin and his quirky ways, albeit he was Savanna's first love, and that was hard to let go of. I'd be a fool if I didn't worry about the two of them.

I didn't have Miranda on my side when it came to my feelings about the two of them. Ever since the mess that Heather put them through, she'd been sure that he would never stray from their marriage. All I could do was hope that she was right.

I think I'd been on edge for so long that everything Ty said was just getting to me more than it ever had before. My relationship with Savanna felt different, somehow. Being away just wasn't helping things in that department. It was hard, having to choose between your child and your wife, when they both seemed to need me equally.

When we were just about finished eating, the limousine driver came in and said that Zeke had requested that he bring us to where he was shooting his new music video. He said that Noah's surprise was going to be there, so naturally, Noah got all excited.

We paid for our food and got back in the limousine to start on a long drive. Our destination was not what I would have pictured for a music video being shot. It was located at a dilapidated house. Outside of the house, several work vans were parked with media logos printed on the sides. A few people stood on the porch talking to one another.

When Zeke didn't come outside, we started to walk in to look for him. This crazy women, probably in her late fifties, came running toward Noah. She grabbed him by the arm and started pulling him further inside of the house. "It's about time you got here. We've been waiting thirty minutes to get this scene in. Time is money, child."

I grabbed his other arm, causing them to stop. "Just hold on a minute, lady. Who are you and what the heck are you talkin' about?"

She shook her head, like she was dealing with a couple of idiots. "The video, of course..."

"I think I can explain." Zeke came out of a room. He was wearing jeans, for a change. His hair was more tame and his shirt covered up almost all of his tattoos. "This is Ramona. She's my manager. Just ignore her forwardness. Anywhoo, I brought you guys here today to give Noah a big surprise." He looked down at Noah. "How would you like to be in my rock video?"

While my son jumped up and down like a monkey, I crossed my arms over my chest. "We need to talk. In private! Now!" There was no way in hell this guy was going to do something so bold without mine and Savanna's written permission. This wasn't a surprise for Noah, at all. He was exposing him to something that I wasn't about to be okay with.

He turned to Ramona. "Watch the kid. Be nice!"

Zeke led me to an empty bedroom. He shut the door behind us and finally gave me his attention. "What's up, Colt?"

I pointed at his face. "I'll tell you what's wrong! You got no right to make decisions regardin' my son without my permission. Me and his mother are the only ones to decide what's best for him."

"Look, man, it's a fucking video, not a surgical procedure. I ain't asking you for a kidney. I thought you would feel honored."

I ran my hands through my hair and just shook my head trying to control myself before I threw this asshole up against the wall. "I did you a favor by lettin' my son come to stay with you. It's nice that you want to get to know Noah, but I can't let him do somethin' like this without talkin' to his mother."

He chuckled. "It's funny that you keep calling her that, considering we both know she ain't his real mother."

"She's been his REAL mother since the day he came into our lives. You can say and think whatever you want. Savanna and I have given that kid more than your sister ever could. I won't stand here and hear you say shit like that. Got it?"

He put his hands up. "Okay, okay! I get it. Look, I want Noah to do this with me. It would mean a lot. If you need to make some calls and talk it over with Savanna, go ahead. I can let everyone know that we need to shoot a different scene until I know what to do."

It was weird that he calmed down so quickly. I didn't doubt that he was afraid of me, but it seemed like he just agreed to make me happy. "Fine. I'll call his mother and let you know."

"What do I tell the kid in the meantime?"

"You tell him that minors need permission from their parents to participate, because it's the damn truth." I walked out of the house, still feeling like I wanted to bust him up. Savanna was definitely going to flip with this one.

Chapter 19

Savanna

I hated fighting with Colt, especially when he was so far away. Honestly, I think I missed him so much that my frustration was making things ten times worse. Ty being here just added fuel to the already burning fire.

After our heated argument, I put my phone in my purse and promised myself that I wasn't going to answer it again until I calmed down. My mother always said never to say anything to people you love when you're mad. Some things, you just can't take back.

Since I had a full day to wait for my biopsy, I was full of worry. The only thing that kept my mind off of the test was scrubbing everything within reach. The girls were occupied in the playroom, planning the wedding of Barbie and Joe. I could hear them making decisions and discussing how they wanted to decorate the room for the event.

After getting the bathrooms done, I started on the bedrooms, even organizing the girl's dresser drawers. When I got to Noah's room, I was finally getting tired of cleaning. Deciding that his dresser drawers where the way to go, I pulled one out at a time and sat it down on the bed next to me. I folded all of his t-shirts and placed them back into the drawer, before pulling out the next one. When I dumped out the mess of clothing, I noticed a pair of dress pants that needed to be hung up. The closet was a mess, but I was determined that I wasn't going to work on it, too. Once I got the pants hung up, I noticed a couple large folded papers on the shelf above. Since I'd put them up there myself, I remembered what they were.

On the first day of kindergarten, Noah came home with a poster size piece of paper. The assignment was to draw a picture of someone that you love. In multi-colored finger paint, he had drawn a picture of him and I. We were holding hands. Above it, the teacher had wrote what the picture meant.

I love my Mommy because she makes the best grilled cheese and she lets me ride horses. My Mom is my best friend.

I traced the words with my fingers and got teary eyed just reading it. Noah was such a special little piece of my life. I believed with all my heart that he was sent to me from heaven to take away all of the pain in the past that I had been dealt with. Not only had he healed my heart, but he filled it with a love that I could have never imagined existed. That little boy was my hero. There was a time when I was the most important thing in his little life. For a long time, I had assumed that nothing could ever tear our bond apart.

When I heard someone clearing their throat, I looked up to see Ty standing in the doorway. "Hey, you alright?"

I nodded and wiped the tears away. "Yeah, I was just looking at something Noah made me a long time ago."

Ty picked up the paper and smiled. "This must have been back when grilled cheese was the only thing that mattered in life besides shitting in his pants."

I pushed him. "He was such a good little boy. Think about it. Not only did he lose his mother tragically, but he was in the car when she died. Then he's delivered to a father who never even knew he existed."

"And he turned to you, Van," he interrupted. "He loved you from the first moment he saw you. Who wouldn't? You're like a damn saint when it comes to kids."

"I just longed to be a mother so badly. It was all I could think about. We'd tried so hard to get pregnant and when I lost the baby, I felt like maybe I wasn't supposed to have children. I just wanted to feel that unconditional love."

He put his arm around me. "Can you not be so damn gloom? I am ready to go draw wedding flowers with the girls, just to avoid your sad ass."

"Shut up!"

"Dinner is going to be ready soon. I thought we could just all four ride up to the main house together. It will give those two old women something to gossip about when we leave. They'll think it's scandalous and we're having a heated affair right under everyone's noses. It will be fantastic!"

I stood up and put Noah's drawer back in his dresser. "You seriously have issues. First off, I would never, in a million years, cheat on my husband. Secondly, you are the last person on earth I would do it with and third…"

He threw his arms up in the air. "Save me the excuses. I've already been there and done that, so to speak. Well, actually, I really have had that. Anyway, I know it isn't going to happen. You ain't my sexual cup of tea either. I mean, have you seen how flexible my wife is?"

I shook my head as I walked out of the room. He was still talking when I started to walk down the hall.

"She can put her legs behind her head and crawl around on the floor, Van. It's awesome!"

The girls were still in the playroom and had done quite a job at decorating everything. They had cut out, well they'd tried to cut out, flowers with construction paper.

"Mommy, you're just in time! How do you spell, just married?" Christian had a marker in her hand.

I told her and watched her writing down the letters in her neatest first grader handwriting. Addy leaned over the table and watched her sister, like she wanted to know how to spell it herself.

"So, when is the big day?"

She stuck out her tongue when she tried to make little hearts on the corner of the paper. "It's Saturday night. Daddy and Noah have to be home for it."

"Are we having it in here?" I looked around the room full of toys.

"Yes. Can we bring up some chairs?" Obviously this event was really going to happen. I wanted to laugh at how serious they both were about it.

Then it hit me.

I needed to prepare myself for not being able to be around for these kind of things. Even if the test was negative for cancer, I still needed to live each day as if it were my last, incase there was no tomorrow. I just wanted to surround myself with the family that I adored so much.

I could feel myself getting upset as I stood thinking about my girls being without me. Before I could let them see me, I ducked out of the room.

Ty was standing outside the door and without even saying anything, he opened his arms up for me. After I had sniffled back my emotional breakdown, he pulled away. "God isn't going to take you from them, Van."

For him to say something so serious like that, just reminded me of how real the situation was. "You don't know that. It happens all the time, Ty. We can't change our fate."

"Would you please stop being so negative? I get that you're scared. Hell, I'm scared for you, but we have to have hope, because without that, we have nothing." He rubbed his face. "Let's just...We need a beer!"

He pulled me down the stairs like he used to when we were kids. I followed behind him and didn't argue or fight. He was here to be supportive and I needed it, now more than ever. In fact, aside from Colt, Ty knew me better than anyone, even the girls. Colt wouldn't have agreed with me, but it felt normal for him to fill in.

He pulled out a bottle of wine from the refrigerator and smelled it. "This shit is rank. You got anything harder?"

"We have beer in the garage." Colt drank on weekends or if we had company, but it wasn't like we did it every night. Surely, I hadn't planned on Ty coming to visit, so I had no reason to go out and buy it.

"No! I'm talking about the shit that puts hair on your ass." He opened the pantry and looked around. "Hey, remember when you and Colt were in here getting it on? That was awesome!"

"Colt keeps that stuff locked in his office. He didn't want the kids getting into it."

Ty popped out of the pantry. "What are they, five and six year old alcoholics?"

"It was a precautionary measure for the future. Noah will be curious in a couple years." Ty's sons were going to be trouble. I could just see it in his future. He'd be gray in the next ten years, for sure.

"It takes one time and he'll change his mind. That little peck will sneak a few shots and it will knock him on his ass. After he pukes it up, he'll put off drinking for a few more years."

I started to laugh. "Where did you learn that, because I'm sure it wasn't from a professional."

"It doesn't matter. I'm a guy and it's the truth. Just face it, I'm awesome!"

No matter what I could say to him, he was going to turn it around and make a joke out of it. I grabbed the bottle of wine and drank right from it. "It's going to be a long night."

He grabbed a large cucumber off the kitchen table. "If you're planning on taking this up to your room tonight, can you at least take a picture?" He was laughing before he even finished the sentence.

"You're sick. Besides, I bought it for you. I thought I heard you tell me that you liked them big." I smacked him and walked out of the kitchen.

As gross and perverted as Ty was, he was offering me little distractions and it was working. Even if Colt was around, we would have been dwelling on the negatives together.

Realizing that it was almost time for dinner, I left Ty in the kitchen and ran up to get changed. I checked on the girls before getting a quick shower. When I was ready, I found the girls downstairs playing with their uncle. He had Addy on his back and was crawling around the couch, chasing Christian. She was giggling so hard that they were gaining space on her. When he caught her, they all tumbled on top of each other and laughed.

"Are you three children ready to go?"

They all stood up and said, 'yes', at the same time.

When I checked my phone, I'd had several missed calls from Colt and even a voice message. I excused myself from the living room and went to listen to it.

Darlin' it's me. Look I get that you're angry, but there's somethin' important that I need to talk to you about. Can you give me a call, please? I love you.

I listened to the message twice just so I could hear his voice. Sure, I was angry at him, but I missed him terribly and the distance between us wasn't helping with any of our problems. Plus, it was really bothering me that Ty knew my secret and Colt didn't.

I decided to text him, instead of calling. The reasoning behind that being that I just didn't have the energy to get myself all upset in front of the girls. They didn't need to know anything was out of the ordinary.

Headed to dinner at your mother's house. I will call you later when the girls are in bed. I love you, too. -S

Colt was rough around the edges, but he was born to be a family man and I believed in the bottom of my heart that it was never going to change. I could only hope that the doubts I was having were just my imagination playing tricks on me. Losing him would kill me before any ailment could.

Dinner at my mother-in-laws was always a good time. We drank wine and talked about all sorts of things. Ty was like the eighth man out, never really getting into our social life talk. Lucy made the best dessert and while scrubbing the house, I'd steamed some vegetables. It wasn't anything fancy, but it was enough.

We played cards for a little while, but the girls were getting too tired and whiney for us to stay any longer. While Ty carried a sleepy Addy to the golf cart, and Christian followed behind them, my mother-in-law pulled me to the side. "Is everything okay, Savanna?"

"Are you asking because Colt is away, or because Ty is staying at the house?" I didn't mean it to come out defensive, but I guess she took it that way.

"You just seemed off, that's all. I know real love when I see it and you and Ty both have that with other people. If I was afraid of that, I would have just come out and asked you."

I hugged her. "Mom, I'm sorry. I guess I'm just not used to Colt being gone. We've always traveled together. Plus, this problem that I'm having with Noah is just driving me crazy inside. Just tell me it will all get better?"

She kissed my cheek. "Oh, honey, it will. You just have to take it one day at a time. Boys will be boys."

"Thanks for having us over, Mom."

"If my nephew gets on your nerves too much, you know where to send him," she teased.

"Yes, I have a couple good ideas where to send him."

We both laughed as I exited the house and joined the crew on the golf cart.

When we got home and tucked both of my girls into my bed, I knew I had to make that phone call that I had procrastinated about. Ty was busy watching basketball on television, so I snuck out onto the porch and called Colt.

Darlin', I was startin' to wonder if I'd have to hop on a plane for you to talk to me.

It might of helped.

Listen, you got the wrong idea about them girls.

Is that what you're calling me about?

No. I'm callin' you because somethin's happened and I wanted you to be a part of the decision, but since you didn't call me back, I had to make it on my own.

What kind of decision? Don't tell me you're leaving Noah there with them.

Of course not, Savanna. What kind of parent would I be to do that. At this point, I don't even want to be here, but the kid is having a good time. That's what I needed to talk to you about. Zeke is puttin' Noah in his next music video and…

He what? How could you allow something like this, Colt? How could you subject our son like this? We said we didn't want him in the spotlight. You promised everything was going to be okay!

It is. I'll be with him the whole time. He's so darn excited about it that I didn't want to disappoint him.

Well, you've sure disappointed me. I thought we were a team, Colt. If it was that important you could have called Ty or your mother to get in touch with me. Instead you just went ahead and signed him over to the devil himself.

Savanna, stop being so dramatic. He's goin' to be fine.

He will never be the same innocent kid again. Don't you get that? You put him right into the spotlight and I don't know if I can forgive you for that. I don't know if I can forgive you for making me feel like I have no say in his life. He's my son too, you know.

I never said he wasn't! Damn, would you just calm dow…

I hung up the phone and turned the damn thing off. The last thing I wanted to do was talk to the man who had put my baby out there for the whole world to see. He was no longer my sweet, protected little boy. I was more than angry.

Ty looked over at me when I walked back into the house. "Don't plan on going to sleep anytime soon. We're getting drunk!"

Chapter 20

Colt

I tried to call her throughout the day and she just wouldn't answer the phone. Yeah, I probably could have called Ty's phone, but I hated that he was even there.

Why was he really there, anyway?

I appreciated his help on the ranch, albeit I feared something bad was going to happen. In all the years that I'd been with my wife, they'd never stayed together alone. Was I wrong for thinking that something could happen? Being so far away was making me doubt my wife. I hated feeling that way about her and about our love for each other.

When I couldn't get ahold of Savanna, Zeke worked things out so that Noah didn't have to shoot his scenes until Friday. When we arrived back at his place, everything seemed to go back to normal. Piper was lounging out by the pool and the chef was preparing dinner. The house had been cleaned, even all the bedding. To anyone just walking in, it would seem as if nothing had ever happened.

After my heated argument with my wife, I laid in bed and stared at the ceiling for a good while. My wife was furious with me and that was never a good thing. She could be moody and hardheaded, but she was usually right when we fought. Savanna had a way of working situations out in her head and being able to come up with practical solutions that work out for everyone involved.

If Noah hadn't been so darn adamant about the video, I would have had time to reach out and get her opinion. I was digging myself into a deeper hole. It all started with Zeke and now I was on a downhill spiral.

I heard a knock on my door and in came my son. He was wearing his pajama shorts and a new t-shirt that we'd picked up when we were out. I sat up right away. "What's up, buddy?"

"I heard you yellin' on the phone. Were you talking to Mom?"

I patted the spot next to me and waited for him to sit down. I couldn't tell the kid that his mother was completely against him being in the video. He didn't need another reason to put that wall up. "She's havin' a hard time bein' away from us."

"She's mad at me, isn't she?"

She was, but I couldn't tell him that. "No. Your mom is just feelin' like we're leavin' her out. She misses us."

I thought he was about to say that he missed her too. Instead he turned around and got an excited look on his face. "Why ain't you havin' fun here, Dad? This is the coolest place I've ever been."

"I've had fun this week, but I miss your mom and your sisters. One day you'll see how our life ain't so bad."

"When I grow up, I want to live in a place just like this." Yep, he said it. As much as I wished that I'd never heard it, I think it will be etched into my mind for the rest of my life.

I patted him on the leg. "Son, I hope one day you can appreciated the real meanin' of home. It ain't about appearances, it's what fills it that counts the most."

He look around the room. "You mean the furniture?"

"No! I mean the people. A house is not a home until it's filled with real whole-hearted love. It can't be bought with any kind of money."

He shook his head and let out an air filled laugh. "Yeah, I think I'd rather have this."

I was disappointed in him, but he wasn't even eleven years old yet. How could I expect him to know the things that I'd learned through growing up?

"I hope you change your mind, Noah. One day I'm goin' to need someone to take over for me. I'd like it to be you, but it's your choice in the end."

I think the conversation was just getting to deep for Noah. He told me goodnight and went back to his room. Fear overwhelmed me when I thought about my son wanting this type of lifestyle. I knew he was a child and this was probably the greatest place he could have imagined being in, but the walls were empty. Instead of family photos, they were filled with band pictures and decorated records. The house lacked a heart, and for me, that was sad.

I fell asleep thinking about my son, so it was only natural for me to dream about him. I dreamed that he'd somehow taken over for his uncle. A very grownup version of Noah was surrounded by beautiful soulless women, that were willing to do anything to get a hand in his pot of wealth. While he was surrounded by people who only loved his name, he'd lost touch with us, his real family.

I shot out of bed and looked around the room. If this was how my wife had been feeling, then I finally understood completely.

I had to find a way out of the contract. There had to be some way to free Noah from his obligation and get the kid where he belonged.

It was easier said than done. After calling my attorney, who informed me that it wasn't exactly his field, I was left feeling like there was no way out. Noah would have to be in the video and thus he would be exposed to the whole world.

Zeke had planned a whole day of places to take us. We started out going to the Hollywood Walk of Fame, followed by a few hours at some exclusive beach attached to a private club that he was obviously a member of. We were waited on hand and foot and even had this hut looking thing that had rooms in it.. It seemed that Noah's obsession with Jaws had him petrified to go into the water. After standing in knee deep for over an hour, he played catch with some kids instead. When it was time to leave, we were able to get cleaned up and head on our way without being sandy.

For dinner, he took us to his friend's restaurant. Zeke ate another weird concoction, while Noah and I had big, fat, juicy steaks. Noah ordered a dessert bigger than his head. Once he finished, we headed to a wax museum that had life sized statues of famous people. I took lots of pictures to show Savanna, especially the ones where Noah stood next to superheroes.

It was absurd to me how Zeke could be normal one minute and a complete asshole the next. Of course, Noah never saw that side of him.

Our day was long and exhausting and after everything we'd done, we were both ready to go home and go to bed. Zeke had his driver drop him off at some club on the way home. I didn't get how he could go to clubs and be around all the drugs and booze and still have a good time.

Upon our arrival back at the mansion, Noah went right up to his room. I pulled out my phone to call Savanna, but overheard someone crying. I pulled back the curtain to see Piper sitting outside under a cabana. I could see someone's legs sitting across from her, but their face was blocked. I should have just walked away, but curiosity killed the cat.

I stood there listening.

"You don't know what it's like, Pete. I try to be happy and I know someone in my position shouldn't complain, but he's never home. When he is, he's throwing crazy parties. I can't deal with it anymore. I know he does things behind my back. I know he sleeps with other women. It's practically broadcasted to every media site daily. Does he just expect me to sit around and deal with that?"

"I don't know what to tell you. You know how I feel about you, Piper. I've loved you for two years and hoped that one day you would feel the same about me. You think it's easy for me to just sit here and watch you go through this. He's a prick for taking you for granted."

She started to sob loudly. "I just thought that if we had a child, things would be better. I thought he would want to change. It was all he used to talk about."

"Do you honestly want to raise a child with someone like Zeke?"

"I don't know."

"Piper, I will give you what you want, but I'm not going to sit back and let him raise my child. I don't want any child of mine growing up with this life."

"You promised. You said it was a gift to me. Please don't do this now." She was begging him.

"You expect me to just sit back and watch you carry my child and say nothing? You expect me to be okay with you laying in a bed next to that piece of shit, when all I want to do is have you for myself?"

"Pete, I can't leave him."

"Don't make me go public, Piper."

"You would threaten me with that? After all that Zeke has done for you, how can you hurt him like that?"

"It's simple! He's hurt you, time and time again, while I had to sit and watch. I was the one who picked up the pieces each and every time that son of a bitch fucked up. It was me who took you to the fertility doctor and it was my sperm they used to make that baby you're carrying. What's your husband going to do when he finds out he's been sterile this whole time? How do you know he didn't see those results himself? All he had to do was call."

"He doesn't know! He won't find out! If you love me, you won't tell him."

The man stood up and I recognized him as one of Zeke's bodyguards. "Piper, I do love you, but I'm not letting you do this any longer. If I can't raise my own child, then neither will he."

He walked away and left her crying. I didn't know what disturbed me more; the crying or the affair. My phone started to ring and I knew I'd been exposed. Piper jumped and came running in the house. "Colt? That wasn't what you think it was."

"It's none of my business."

"You hate me don't you?" She plopped down on a chair.

I sat across from her and folded my hands. "I don't hate you. It seems like you're hatin' yourself."

"Everyone thinks this life is so amazing. They have no idea how horrible it can be. Between the media and the fans, we never catch a break. Zeke can be a great guy. I know somewhere inside of him there is a good man. It's just, he can't get away from who he is."

"I'm seein' that."

"I love my husband, but you see how he is. He doesn't have time to be married. All we share right now is a house and a piece of paper. I don't even know if he loves me anymore. Pete's been there for me, every time something has happened between me and Zeke. When he told me he had feelings for me, I assured him that nothing would ever happen. Then I found out Zeke was sterile. You have to understand, I wanted a baby more than anything and I couldn't get pregnant. Zeke wouldn't have understood. He didn't want to start a family, at first. That's when Pete offered me a solution. He donated his sperm and we did in-vitro-fertilization. I never cheated on Zeke. I swear!"

As she continued crying, I cleared my throat, getting her to look at me. "My wife and I had a lot of problems conceiving. When she finally did get pregnant, she was kidnapped and held by a criminal. While tryin' to get free, she was injured and lost the baby. We were devastated. Noah came into our life right after that happened. He was the miracle that Savanna needed to move forward. Children are a great gift, but bein' a parent is the greatest gift of all. Listen, Piper, I don't know how you feel about Pete. It's obvious that he cares deeply for you. Zeke doesn't seem like the kind of guy who is ready to just give up his life and start raisin' a family. Do you really want your child subjected to this kind of lifestyle?"

She shrugged and wiped away the tears on her face. "I love Zeke, but he loves himself. As much as I want him to change, I don't see it happening."

"What are you goin' to do?"

She looked worried. "Are you going to tell him?"

"It ain't my place."

She covered her face. "I feel so ashamed. No one was supposed to know."

"Where I come from, marriage is sacred. I promised to love and be faithful to my wife and I meant that shit. I think you need to be honest with yourself before you can make decisions for other people."

She nodded, while still crying. "You're right. I know that's what I have to do. It's just so hard. Every move I make is plastered in the magazines. I feel like I can't breathe. If this comes out, it could be career ending for Zeke. Right now, he has to have good media. He's dug himself so deep into a hole that he may not be able to crawl out with dignity." She grabbed a pack of cigarettes and lit one up. "I guess I need to quit these."

"Piper, I ain't sayin' nothin' to Zeke or the media, but I need to know somethin' from you in return."

"Sure. Anything."

"What does Zeke really want from my son? It's obvious that he wouldn't just come around without a reason. I just don't buy what he's been telling me. If my son is in some kind of danger, I need to know the truth, so I can protect him."

She took another drag of her cigarette and then put it out in an ashtray. "All I know is that Zeke came to me and told me he had a nephew he wanted me to meet. As you can probably tell, we aren't exactly Fred and Wilma. Zeke goes weeks without even calling. Most of the time, I don't even know where he is."

I felt sorry for this girl and I couldn't help but wonder if it applied to the lifestyle that they were involved in. It made me appreciate my life back in Kentucky even more. "I hope you get things worked out. If you'll excuse me, I need to call my wife."

One thing that I hated more than drama, was knowing secrets. They always had a way to come back around and bite you in the ass.

I found a quiet spot on the outside patio and dialed my wife's number. Hearing her voice was going to make everything better.

Except, she didn't answer.

She was spending time with Tyler and couldn't even take my calls. If he laid one hand on her I was going to kill him.

Chapter 21

Savanna

Getting drunk with Ty was never a good idea, especially when there wasn't any other adults around us. I never thought that it would become romantic. We were best friends and he was being my shoulder to cry to on.

We'd had a couple of shots and both of us were starting to feel giddy. Ty was determined to keep my mind off of the procedure that I was having done the next morning. He told dirty jokes and made fun of everyone that we knew.

As the night progressed, my mind never venture far from my husband and son. As angry as I was at Colt, I still wished that I was there with them. Maybe the decisions would have ended up the same. I just wanted the opportunity to have a say.

Ty got this bright idea that he wanted to Ding Dong Ditch my parents. I went up and checked on the girls. Unless they got sick, they wouldn't wake up until the next morning. Just to be safe, I called over to the main house and asked Lucy if she could sit with them for ten minutes.

Ten minutes later, her and Colt's mom came walking through the door. They were both in their pajamas. "What's wrong?"

I walked up to my mother-in-law, but couldn't stop giggling. "Nothing is wrong. We want to play a joke on my parents."

She put her hands on her hips. "What kind of joke?"

"I want to Ding Dong Ditch them. You want to come?" I couldn't believe that Ty asked her.

A huge smile formed across her face. "It's been a long time since I had a good laugh."

Just like that, we left Lucy to listen for the kids and headed out on the golf cart. It was so dark on the ranch, especially when you drove to areas that were off the beaten path. It just so happened that my parents were way off it.

We turned off our headlights when we got close enough to see their house. The bedroom light was on and we could see the television flashing. Suddenly, I became the quiet one, while I listened to Ty and his aunt discussing their strategy.

Colt wouldn't have believed me if I told him that this was happening.

Since the golf cart was extremely quiet, we were able to pull up on the side of their house without making a sound.

"Okay, this is what's going to happen. You two are going to drop me here. Go park in the front yard, facing the house. I'm going to knock and run out to you. When they open the door, we will all three yell it. Are you ready?"

We both nodded and watched Ty jump off the cart. While I drove and parked where he told me to, he was running up to the door. Not only did he beat on it, but he was screaming and making crazy sounds. Then, just as fast as he'd knocked, he came running back to the cart.

We were laughing so hard that we almost didn't see my father opening the door. He had a fireplace poker in his hand. I flipped on the lights, blinding him so he couldn't see us.

"DING DONG DITCH!"

I spun us around in the grass and we flew down the lane as fast as the little golf cart could go. The whole while we were laughing so hard at what we'd done.

She and Lucy ended up staying for anther hour before they went back to their place. Colt's mom was always surprising me. One day she could be the most sophisticated women I'd ever met. Another day, she was just as comical as Ty. It was pretty cool.

Before they left, she asked me again if there was something wrong. It brought me back to reality when I had to think of my procedure and how I was hiding it from everyone that cared about me.

I think Ty read my mind. He handed me another shot before I could ask for one. "Last one and then we need to get some sleep."

"I won't be able to sleep tonight. I'm too scared. My life is riding on this test, Ty."

"Van, you can't think of it like that. Even if it is cancer, that doesn't mean your life is over. Medicine has come a hell of a long way. They have treatment facilities and state of the art equipment to do it with. No matter what the outcome is, you'll be in good hands."

I started to cry and with the alcohol that I'd consumed, I was a mess. "I'm afraid of dying. What if I'm one of the ones that can't be treated? What if my babies grow up without a mother? How can I look at them and know that my days are limited? I can't do it, Ty. Some things I just don't want to know."

Ty pulled the shot glass out of my hand and sat it down on the table next to his. He grabbed both of my hands with his. "No matter what happens, you're a fighter. You won't give up, because I won't let you. Do you remember when we were kids and you came out to the hole for the first time? Remember how scared you were to go on the rope swing? Colt was making fun of you and calling you a sissy little boy and it was making you cry."

"I remember," I whined.

"What happened that day, Van?"

I remembered that day vividly, probably because it was the day that I fell in love with Tyler Mitchell. He was my hero that day. "You took my hands and kissed them, and then you told me that I could do anything that I wanted to. You showed me how to hold the rope to get the most air, so that when I finally did it, I went the farthest."

He smiled, hearing me tell the story. "I knew you could do it. I will never forget the look on their faces when you almost made it clear across that water. It was badass."

"You were so sweet to me back then." I think I was blushing thinking about it.

"I had to make you my girl, so I didn't have to act that way around anyone else. Besides, I knew you'd turn out to be beautiful. Even an ugly duck can be a beautiful swan."

He was showing me that side again, which meant that he was concerned about me. I squeezed his hand. "Aside from the cheating, you always took care of me. You may have been a terrible boyfriend, but you were an amazing best friend. I can't imagine my life without you in it." I reached over and kissed him on the cheek. " I know I said I was mad, but I'm glad you're here, Ty. I don't think anyone could get me through this the way that you can."

Ty smiled. He leaned his head back on the couch. "You're going to be okay, Van. No matter what, I just know you are."

I leaned my head against Ty's side and closed my eyes. Sure, I wished Colt was here to comfort me, but it felt good to not be alone. Besides, if Colt were around, Ty wouldn't have come. The last couple days with him had really helped me. Maybe it was just supposed to happen the way it was.

I woke up to someone poking me in the leg. When I opened my eyes I saw Christian standing in front of me. I shot off the couch and realized that I was sleeping against Ty's arm. His head was even leaning on mine. I was appalled to think of what my daughter had running through her mind. "Mommy, why are you sleeping down here with Uncle Ty?"

"I must have fallen asleep when we were watching television."

She handed me my cell phone. "Daddy's on the phone for you. I told him you and uncle Ty were asleep, but he said that I needed to wake you up, right now."

"Thanks, honey."

Ty yawned and stretched, paying what happened no mind. I frantically took the phone out on the front porch.

Hello

What the hell is goin' on Savanna. Is this your way of gettin' back at me for the photo?

What? No! I just...

Save it. When I get home in Saturday, we are sitting down and having a talk.

Fine by me. I have a lot I want to say to you.

I bet you do. I'm goin' to tell you one thing, Savanna. Ty better be gone when I get there.

Why is that?

Don't you play stupid with me. I know what's goin' on. I'm surprised it took you this long. I just can't believe you did it with our girls in the house. How could you disrespect me like that?

Colt, you really have the wrong idea. There is nothing going on between me and Ty. I swear. We stayed up late talking and both fell asleep sitting up on the couch. That's all there is to tell. Honestly, I can't believe you don't trust me.

Trust you? Darlin' I can't even talk to you right now. I'll see you Saturday.

I couldn't believe this was happening. How had things gotten so bad between us? Before I could get upset, I noticed that I had a half hour to be at my appointment and I still had to take the girls to my mother's.

Ty must have noticed the time as well, he was carrying both girls down the stairs. They were still in their pajamas, but he had clothes in his hand. "Did you see what time it is?"

"Yes." I started running up the stairs.

"I'll run them over to your parents." I heard the door shutting as I made it to my bedroom and started looking for clothes to wear.

By the time I was dressed and had brushed my hair and teeth, Ty had my SUV parked out front with the motor running.

We got halfway down the road when it hit me where we were actually headed. Driving somewhere that could determine my fate wasn't exactly exciting. I was petrified. I stared out the window, trying not to lose it. I felt a hand reaching out and holding mine. He squeezed it and smiled when I looked his way. "Deep breaths, Van. I got your back, I promise. If you need me to hold your hand the whole time. If you need me to watch the doctor and make sure he isn't copping a feel, I can be that man."

I took our hands and slapped him. "You just want to see my tits."

We both started laughing.

"I just wanted to protect the goods."

"My husband wants to kick your ass and you're joking about seeing my tits. You really know how to push his buttons. He says you have better be gone before he gets home."

Ty turned to look at me with his eyebrow cocked. "Is that so? Van, be honest, do you still say my name in your sleep? Is that why he's so uptight?"

"Would you stop it." I laughed again. "I don't dream about you that way and you know it. I honestly don't get why he's freaking out. Maybe he feels guilty about something he's done. It isn't like we just became friends again. You've been my best friend since we were kids."

"Are we back to the picture again?"

I shook my head. "No! when I called the other day, a female answered. He's been weird when we talk and I feel like he isn't including me in important decisions. God, how did things get so messed up?"

We pulled up to the doctor's office and Ty turned off the ignition. "You're going to go in here and rip open your shirt and tell them be gentle."

I climbed out of the vehicle. "I'm going to go in there and put on a gown and wait for the doctor to stick a giant needle in my tit." When Ty kept following me, I turned around. "What are you doing?"

"I'm coming with you." He looked away for a second and went from joking to serious. "Look Van, this doesn't have to be weird. All fun aside, this is important and I want to do this for you. I owe you so much for always being my friend and I love you. I can't imagine my life without you. Whatever it takes, Van, I'm going to be here."

I wrapped my arms around Ty and just hugged him so hard. "Thank you."

When we finally pulled away, he held out his arm and I put mine inside. He led me into the doctor's office and even though I felt like everything was going wrong, I knew I had my best friend by my side. When Colt got home everything would work itself out and he would be glad I wasn't alone.

I hoped.

Chapter 22

Colt

Noah woke me up bright and early, due to his excitement about starring in the music video. After having a heart to heart with Piper, being around Zeke was the last thing I wanted to do. We only had one more day until we could go home, and I couldn't wait, because things were worse than when I had left.

Once he knew I was awake, Noah went downstairs to eat breakfast. I looked over on the nightstand and saw my phone. There was nothing that I wanted more than to be able to figure out what was going on with my wife. It wasn't that I thought she was having an affair, but there was something going on. I couldn't see Ty just going to the ranch to be there for the alarm company. They'd been gone for days and he was still there.

As much as I told Piper that I didn't like meddling in other people's business, I found myself calling my cousin.

I was wondering when you were going to call.

Just tell me what's goin' on, Ty. I know you're keepin' somethin' from me.

It's not what you're thinking, Colt. You have it all wrong.

So, you're tellin' me that you aren't there, in my house, comforting my wife?

You need to talk to her. I'm not comfortable talking about something that's between the two of you.

If you're fuckin' my wife, I will kill you.

Just talk to your wife, dude.

I'm askin' you.

Do you know how hurt she is? Have you even considered what all of this is doing to her? She needed to be included. She needed to feel like she'd always be Noah's mother. Why do you keep shutting her out? Stop being such a stubborn ass.

Stay away from my wife, Ty. I'm not kidding.

I'm sorry, Colt, but I can't do that. I made a promise to her and I won't break it. You can be pissed at me all you want. She's my best friend.

She's MY best friend. Go home to your own wife.

My own wife is who sent me here, you jackass!

We'll see about that!

I hung up the phone and started looking for Miranda's number. I didn't call her much and I wasn't sure how I had programmed it. Before I could finish hitting send, my phone rang. Miranda was calling me.

I was just callin' y...

Colt, you need to stop it.

Stop what?

Look, I don't know what's goin' on with Savanna, but Ty is there because I can't be. Stop bein' such a dick and get over yourself.

How can you just sit there and be okay with them bein' alone?

Honestly, Colt, I trust them. For the past nine years, Ty has been completely devoted to me and our family. That man would die before he let anything break us apart.

Things happen, Miranda.

Do you even hear yourself? You're talking about our family. We are in this together, all of us. For years, we've all been the best of friends. The only problem that I'm seein' in this family is you. Leave Ty out of it, Colt. He's doin' you a favor.

Then she hung up on me.

I was so damn confused. What the hell was going on?

Noah came up to tell me that we had twenty minutes before we had to leave, so instead of trying to call Savanna, I hurried up and got changed.

On the way to the shoot, I sent Savanna a message.

I love you – C

Figuring that I would get a reply right back, I held on to my phone while I sat there watching them get Noah ready. After about twenty minutes, I still had no reply back from

Savanna. Something was just off and I couldn't stand being so far away that I wasn't able to fix things.

She's always been so organized and fixed to her daily routine. Something had to be wrong for her to change it all of the sudden.

I heard commotion coming from inside of the house, so I put my phone in my pocket and headed inside. Zeke was arguing with his manager, Ramona.

"I told you that this was what had to be done. One more day and we can send the kid back to Kentucky. Why is this so hard for you to understand, Zeke?"

"I just want to play music. I don't give a shit what everyone thinks about me."

"When you stop selling albums, your ass is going to care! Now get in there and act like you love the kid. Your future depends on this video."

"Do you really think this is going to work?"

"Yes, of course it will. They want to see emotions. Get your ass in there and pretend to have a relationship with the kid for one more day. We'll get some pictures and sell them to the papers. Once the world sees you bonding with the kid, all of the bad shit will just go away."

I saw Noah coming around the corner. He'd finally finished getting his hair and makeup done. I could see the excitement in his eyes, but all of that vanished when he heard his uncle's next words.

"The sooner this little brat gets out of my life the better. God, I can't stand kids. Why I let you talk me into this, I will never know!"

Noah's face turned white and I saw that little lost kid that was once standing on my porch looking for a home. Tears fell down his cheeks as he approached me. "Dad, can you please take me home?"

"It's goin' to be alright, son." I hugged him.

"I just want my mom," he cried.

I kissed him on the top of the head. "Yeah, I want to see her, too. Just give me a minute and we can get the hell out of here."

I walked right up to Zeke, grabbed him by the collar and slammed him against the wall. "What are you doing, Colt?" He backed away from me.

I got right up in his face. "This thing with my son is done! I heard everything. Did you think you could just use him and toss him out like he wasn't blood? So help me God, you are so lucky that my son is standin' here, because I would like nothin' more than to tear your ass apart. Find another kid to play the part, because my son is done with you! If you come near me or my family again, you'll be sorry!"

"He's under contract!" Ramona got between us.

I realized that I would have to lie to get us out of it. "I just recorded your entire conversation, lady. There is no more contract. The way I see it, that thing is null and void! Take that piece of paper and shove it up your ass! We're done here!"

Noah and I had been walking for about ten minutes before a car pulled over and offered us a ride. It took me a second to realize that it was Pete, Zeke's bodyguard.

"Get in. I can take you to get your bags and drive you to the airport."

"Did Zeke send you?" I didn't want his handouts.

"No! I just quit. His wife is carrying my baby and I let him know it. Between what happened with you guys and my news, I'm sure his manager will be doing damage control for the next year." He laughed, like he'd accomplished a goal.

"I hope you get to raise your child." I put my arm around my son. "Nothing beats having a family."

Noah and I got our things together, while Pete helped Piper pack up some things. I wasn't sure what they were going to do and I really didn't care. I just wanted to never have to come back to the place again.

We said our goodbyes at the airport and waved at the expectant couple as they drove away. Then I had to go inside and try to change our flight to an earlier time.

After three hours we were boarding a plane and heading home.

Noah hadn't said much ever since we'd left the shoot location. He had his ear buds in his ears and once in a while I would catch him crying. I felt so bad for the little guy. For a short time, he truly believed that he had the coolest uncle in the world. I felt so bad for him and blamed myself for letting it all happen. If I'd just put my foot down, maybe I could have avoided it all.

Now, our family was strained. Savanna and I were struggling and I'd never felt so separated from her before. How was I supposed to make things right again, when I couldn't even begin to understand how they'd gotten to be so bad?

Not only was my wife upset with me, but I'd managed to piss off my cousins.

Instead of calling Savanna to come pick me up, I took a cab. It wasn't because I was trying to be sneaky. Noah was tired and it was right around the time that Savanna would be making dinner. I didn't want to have to wait for her to get finished to come and get us. He was too upset and I could tell that he just wanted to be home.

When I walked into the house and didn't see anyone, I looked out back and noticed that our SUV was missing. If Savanna were anywhere on the ranch, she would have driven the golf cart.

Noah seemed so relieved to be home that I sent him up to his room to get some, much needed, rest. I walked upstairs and looked around. The futon in the playroom had been pulled out and Ty's stuff was still in it.

I pulled out my phone and tried to call Savanna again but it continued to go right to voicemail, like it wasn't even turned on.

I didn't get it.

I was also starting to think that maybe something was wrong. With a quick call to my mother-in-law, things got even more confusing.

Hello?

Mom, it's me, Colt. Have you heard from Savanna? Noah and I just got home early and she's not here.

I have the girls. Tyler dropped them off this morning and said that Van was running late for a doctor's appointment. I don't know what doctor, but that's where she is.

So, Ty went with her?

I really don't know. He just said she overslept and he was doing her a favor by bringing the girls.

Alright. Thanks.

Did you have a good trip?

No! It was terrible and I should have just listened to Savanna when she told me it was a bad idea. I'm goin' to come get the girls now.

Addy is taking a nap. How about I bring them when she wakes up?

Sounds good. Thanks, Mom.

I was stumped. Ty wasn't anywhere on the ranch, so clearly he was with my wife, who was supposedly at the doctors. Why would he have to go with her?

Again, nothing made sense.

When I heard a vehicle pulling down the driveway, I instinctively looked outside. Our SUV was pulling up out front, instead of out back where we normally parked.

Instead of walking outside, I stood at the window, watching.

Ty jumped out of the driver's seat and ran around to the passenger side of the vehicle. He opened the door for Savanna and wrapped his arm around her as they walked up the porch steps.

That was enough for me to become irate. I rushed through the front door. When they saw me, they both just stood there, amazed that I was home already.

"I caught you, you lyin' son of a bitch!" I threw myself at Ty, causing us to tumble to the ground. I got one punch in before I felt Savanna trying to rip me off of him.

"Colt! Please stop! Oh my God! You have the wrong idea!" She pulled and pulled, while screaming at me at the top of her lungs.

I sat up straight and just stared at Ty, who covered his face with is hands. "Dude, it's not what you think. Get the fuck off of me and let your wife explain."

I climbed off of Ty, but pointed right at him. "Get your shit out of my house and go the hell home. You make me sick."

Ty rolled over and got into a standing position. He was brushing off clothes, before he walked into the house. As he passed by Savanna, he grabbed her arm. "I'm sorry, Van."

She was crying. "Me, too."

Once he was out of my sight, I looked over at my wife. With tears running down her face, she said nothing.

"Are you goin' to start explainin' what's goin' on?"

She shook her head. "I don't want to talk to you right now, Colt." She ran inside after Ty. I sat down on my front porch, trying really hard to keep from going in there and killing him. Was she really choosing him over me?

In a matter of minutes, they both came out of the house. I stood up and turned to look at them. Savanna moved her body in front of my cousin. "Don't you touch him, Colt!"

I shook my head. It was more than just feeling disgusted, I wanted to put my fist to his face again. "What is this? Are you choosin' him over me?"

My heart was being ripped apart with jealousy. I clenched my fists and waited for that little bastard to say something smart.

Savanna put her hands on her hips. "There's something you need to know." She started sobbing and I watched Ty touch her shoulder. It made me so mad and when he saw the look on my face, he removed it.

"You better start talkin' fast, darlin."

"Or what, Colt?" She was challenging me. "What is it that you think is going on here? You really think that we waited all these years to have a week alone so that we could be together again? Is that what you think?"

"Maybe it is!" I was standing my ground. If this was how I was going to lose her, I wasn't just going to let her go without a fight. "He probably did this shit just to spite me for takin' you away from him. That little prick probably…"

"Shut up, Colt! Just shut up! I can't take this anymore. How could you think that about us?"

"Tell me you don't love him, Savanna." I needed to get away from them. She was protecting him and I couldn't stand being around it. I felt like I was back under that tent hearing her accept his proposal, so long ago. It made me want to be sick.

"You know how I feel about, Ty and you know how I feel about you."

"So we're back to that? After all this time, we're back to that?"

Ty moved to the front of Savanna and I was ready to battle. He put his hands up. "Before you go and ruin your marriage, I think you need to know something." He looked back at Savanna. "He needs to know the truth, Van. Please don't hate me."

I prepared myself for the worst, but never expected what came out of his mouth.

"While you were out dealing with Noah, your wife got bad news. She called Miranda crying, but she left her phone home that day and I intercepted the call. I made her tell me what was wrong. Maybe it was wrong of me, but I knew she was alone and she's my best friend. When I told Miranda, she made me come here to be with Van. I didn't do shit with your wife except support her. Fuck you, Colt! Fuck you for thinking that after all this time, I would destroy our whole family like that." He turned around and kissed Savanna on the cheek. "I'll call you when my flight gets in. John's picking me up from your parent's house."

He pushed past me, knocking his shoulder into mine. I was so worried about Savanna that I paid him no attention.

"What's he talkin' about?"

She sank down on the porch steps and cried harder. Instinctively, I sat down beside her and tried to put my arm around her. She moved her body when my hands touched her. It was clear that she was furious with me.

I sat there waiting for her to be able to tell me what was going on. I'd never considered that it could be something bad. I just assumed they were sneaking around behind my back.

"Savanna, please talk to me."

She was still sobbing, but managed to get out one sentence. "The doctor found a lump in my breast."

A knot formed in my throat and I could hear the severity in her voice. While I was away with our son, she had been going through hell. Every one of our phone calls had ended badly when she needed my support the most. How would I ever be able to make this up to her?

As angry as I was at Colt for what' he'd done to Ty, a part of me was so relieved to have him sitting there next to me. I'd wanted his support since this had all begun. He should have been there for me instead of his cousin. Now, poor Ty was going home with a black eye and hard feelings.

Colt put his head down when I told him what the doctor had found. I think the shock of what I'd said had finally calmed him down and brought the man back to reality. God knows, he had been way off base.

As I continued to try to calm myself down, Colt tried once again to put his arm around me. Sometimes actions speak louder than words, and in this case, it was true. I leaned my head against him. "How bad is it darlin'? When are they goin' to do a biopsy?"

"I had it done this morning. That's why Ty was here. He took me to the doctors."

"Oh, hell, Savanna. I didn't know. I just thought he was tryin' to take you from me." I could tell he felt terrible and there was a part of me that wanted him to. He should have just talked to me, instead of losing his temper. No matter how old he got, some things just didn't change.

"He was being there for me because he knew you couldn't be, but it wasn't because he wanted me for himself. Colt, I've known him practically my whole life. He's my best friend."

"He was your first love, darlin'. It's hard for me to not think about that. It's hard for me to know you still love him." Colt looked in another direction. "It kills me to know he was here for you. I should have been here. Why didn't you call me, Savanna? I never would have gone if I'd known."

"You were taking care of our son, Colt. Just because something bad was happening to me, doesn't mean we can just give up on our kids. I knew it was important to Noah and with the wedge between us, I couldn't be the person to ruin it for him." I wiped my face and took a few deep breaths. "I was just going to go through the tests alone. If it was nothing, than I didn't want anyone else to have to worry about me. When I left the office and called Miranda, I was just so scared. Ty sensed it right away and wouldn't leave me alone until I told him what was going on. Colt, I swear to you that there is nothing going on between us, but I don't know how I would have gotten through this week without him. That's why I didn't ask him to leave."

Colt's phone started vibrating in his pants. He pulled it out and hit the ignore button. "It's Miranda. I know she's going to tear me a new ass. I don't have time for that, right now. I can't believe this is happenin'. You know I would have been here for you, Savanna. I can't understand why you thought it was necessary to keep it from me. I don't even care what I had goin' on. This was more important than anything." He covered his face with his hands for a second and then looked over at me. Those beautiful green eyes were watered up. "I'm so sorry, Savanna. I'd fall apart without you, darlin'. Nothin' makes sense in my life if you're not in it." He grabbed my hand and kissed it. "What's the doctor sayin'? How long until we get the results?"

"My doctor said that he would call me as soon as he gets them." I'm so sorry I didn't tell you. I wanted to call you and tell you every day. I was just so upset and I don't want the kids to know. I don't want anyone to know that there's a possibility that I might not be around much longer." I could barely get out the last words.

Colt held me tight. I could hear him sniffling, but refused to look up at his face. "Please don't talk like that. I don't care what it costs, or what we have to do. If the results are positive for cancer, we'll beat it together. Never talk about it bein' the end, darlin'. Please don't ever do that." Colt was starting to lose it. The sniffling was becoming more frequent and I knew that he wasn't going to leave my side.

"I'm so scared, Colt. I know I should be optimistic, but I can't stop thinking about the bad. I just want to be prepared for the worst possible result, so that if it's any better, I can at least be happy about that."

He brushed the hair away from my face. "Have you done any research?"

I shook my head. "No. I was too afraid. My doctor said it was a bad idea."

He stood up and reached out for my hand. "Let's go inside. I had to wait hours for a flight at the airport. We were so damn tired that Noah came right in and went to sleep."

I realized that I hadn't even asked why he was home a day early. "What happened? I thought you told me you weren't coming home until tomorrow."

We went into the kitchen. I sat down at the table while he leaned against the countertop. "It seems Zeke wasn't as forward for information as we thought. At first, everything was great. His house was unbelievable and Noah was spoiled with attention. I was startin' to think I wouldn't be able to get him to leave."

I got up and poured us both some tea. "So what changed?"

"First, Piper took Noah overnight with the other band member's wives and their kids, so that Zeke could throw a crazy party. I thought Noah was comin' home, but I'm glad he didn't. I had to sleep on my bathroom rug to get away from the madness."

"I take it that's the night the picture was taken?"

He started laughing and shaking his head. "Savanna, I went into my room to be alone and two naked chicks were in my bed. Honest to God, they wouldn't leave. Everywhere I went in the house, there were people havin' sex with each other. You need to understand that I took that picture to get a rouse out my cousins. I never intended for you to see it."

I cocked my eyebrow. "That doesn't make me feel any better."

"It ain't like that and you know it. Darlin', I was missin' you too much to pay any attention to other women."

I walked up close to him and pressed my hands against his chest. Sure, I was still mad at him, but I also needed him. Colt made everything seem easier. "Right answer, Mr. Mitchell."

He ran his hands up and down the top of my arms. "Piper is pregnant by the bodyguard and Zeke only wanted Noah to visit so it could help his troubled image. Anyway, Noah overheard Zeke admitting that he was just using him. Before, I could rip him a new ass, Noah came runnin' out askin' to go home. It turns out, all he wanted was his mother."

I think my mouth hit the floor. Noah had made it clear that he wanted nothing to do with me before he left and now I was who he was asking for. "You're kidding?"

"Nope! He got all upset and said he wanted you. We high tailed out of there and didn't stop until we walked in the front door. Savanna, I told you he'd come around. You're his mother and he knows it. That kid will never stop lovin' you. He couldn't survive without your love. None of us could."

He hugged me close, but I pulled away and looked up at him. "What about the lawyers?"

"That's easy. I told them I recorded their conversation. I don't think we'll be hearin' from Zeke or his lawyer. Plus, I told him I'd kill him if he came near my family again."

I felt Colt's arms around me, but then I felt another set of hands wrapping around the front of me. I turned around to see Noah standing there. "Hi, Mom."

"Hi, babe. I'm so sorry you had to come home early." I really wasn't, but I wanted him to feel better.

"I'm not. Zeke is a jerk. He never even cared about me at all."

I wrapped my arms around him. "He's a fool."

Noah looked up at me. "I was a jerk, too. I'm sorry, Mom. I didn't mean what I said to you."

I started crying again. "It's okay. No matter what happens, I'm always going to love you with all of my heart. Nobody can ever change that. You'll always be my son."

He smiled and hugged me tighter. With all of the worry that filled my mind, nothing could have soothed me more than having my son in my arms. Feeling his love was just what the doctor ordered.

He pulled away and looked up at me. "Can I go outside and play with Sam?"

"Of course, as soon as you unpack your things." His father had spoken and a reluctant kid went stomping up the stairs to do what he was told.

I found my place back in Colt's arms. "You know you're going to have to apologize to Ty."

He patted my back. "Yeah, I know. I'm goin' to let him sweat for a little while though. He still got to spend entirely too much time with you." He lifted my chin and kissed me on my lips. "Can we go get our girls? I told your mom I'd wait, but I want to see them."

I found it to be so sweet that Colt missed his girls. I'm sure they'd missed them because I hadn't exactly been a fun person to be around. "I just want to warn you that the wedding of Joe and Barbie is in full swing. They were just waiting for you to get home."

"Great. Should we call a pastor over?" He was teasing and I knew it when he winked at me. "If Christian and Addy have anything to do with it, the whole family will be invited."

"Probably."

"Poor Joe!" He shook his head.

"Poor Barbie, you mean?"

Colt smiled. "Yeah, whatever you say."

He took my hand and led me to the front porch, then called back into the house to let Noah know where we were going. We heard him running down the steps. "Can I go too? I want to tell Grandpa about our trip."

Colt looked at him like he was crazy. "It was your idea to come home early."

"Yeah, but we had a good time, didn't we, dad? I mean, when it was just us?"

Colt put his hands on the back of Noah's shoulders and guided him off the porch. "Yeah, buddy, we did."

The three of us climbed on the golf cart, while good ole Sam followed beside us. For the first time in a week, I felt like things were getting back to normal. Now, all I needed were my results to be in my favor and everything would be back to perfect again.

Chapter 24

Colt

It was great to see the smiles of both of our girls. I'd missed them all more than I even knew possible. Our life may have seemed boring to others, but it meant everything to us. Being away, and seeing how some people live, made me appreciate just what I had at home. I think it did the same for Noah.

When we got home, we were all too tired to go to my mother's for dinner. The little one's were wide awake, but they were too busy making more wedding plans. I had no idea what that actually entailed, but they were quiet and it wasn't because they were doing something bad.

Noah sat next to his mother on the couch and they started watching some crazy show about a man from Kentucky that caught wild animals with his bare hands. The one thing I hated about the show was that it made Kentucky seem like none of us had any teeth. Since not one person in my family was missing any teeth, I knew it didn't apply to everyone. Sure, I knew a couple farmers that had let their mouths go to shit. We took care of our teeth.

As much as I hated his hygiene, the show was catchy and I found myself cuddling next to my wife watching it.

Before we knew it, the sun was setting and we hadn't had anything to eat. As a treat, I decided to take out the family to our favorite steak house. Nothing felt better than to walk into a public establishment with my wife and kids at my side.

When we all got seated in an extra large booth, I looked around the table at them and thought about how precious they were to me. I loved my life and imagining spending a second without my wife was enough to rip my heart straight out of my chest.

While everyone enjoyed their food, I found myself dwelling on Savanna. It pained me that she'd left me out, but I understood why she had. Our children were always her first priority, even when it put her needs on the backburner.

I think she knew what I was doing. She looked right at me and gave me one of her looks. If she could be strong, than I was going to have to do the same. The next few days of not knowing were going to be the hardest. With optimism running in the opposite direction, we needed to find a light at the end of the tunnel. I couldn't let myself think about a life that didn't include my beautiful wife.

Suddenly, being out in public wasn't where I wanted to be. I wanted to be home, with my wife and kids. I wanted to have her in my arms, holding her tight. She needed to know that I wasn't going to give up, no matter what those results said.

I held Savanna's hand on the ride home, while listening to three kids argue about what movie they wanted to watch during the ride. She kept looking at me as I drove and I would squeeze her hand so she knew I was paying attention.

By the time we got home it was around nine. The girls were yawning and even Noah seemed like he was tired. Since it was a Friday night, they didn't have a bedtime. After the girls got a bath, they both settled in and went to sleep in their beds. They'd be in our bed at some point, but for the time being, our king size bed was free.

Noah came downstairs after getting his shower. He handed his mother his IPod. "Mom, I can't figure out to remove songs. Can you do it for me?"

She grabbed the device and started looking through the songs. "When did you put these on here?"

His face turned red. "I did it before we went to California. Dad already punished me."

"This is what you want removed?" She asked.

"Yeah. Just take them all off. I didn't like them anyway."

Savanna smiled and looked over at me. "Son, I'm sorry we wasted our time goin' to California. I know you had high hopes of knowin' your uncle. It's a shame he turned out to be such a turd, but you need to know it had nothin' to do with the type of boy you are. Some people can't see a good thing even when it bites them in the tail."

"Uncle Zeke was cool at first. I thought I wanted to be like him. He lived in a house bigger than Grandma's. But...he was a jerk. I saw him kissin' a lady that wasn't Piper. I didn't want to tell you because I knew you would hate him. I hate him, though. I hope I never have to go back there again."

Savanna reached out and grabbed his arm. "Noah, you don't ever have to go there again. If someone tries to make you, I will bust them up."

Noah's eyes got huge. He looked at me and we both started laughing, because the idea of Savanna beating someone up was just absurd. She couldn't hurt a fly.

"Keep laughing you two. I'll show you how tough I can be when it comes to my kids."

Savanna grabbed Noah and pulled him down on the couch. She started tickling him. He was screaming and laughing at the same time. Finally, when he pulled the 'I can't breathe' card, she settled down. "I missed you, Mom."

Savanna hugged him again. "I missed you too, buddy.

"As much as I love to see you two happy again, I think it's time for us old folks to get to bed. I mean, if you want your mom to still look pretty, she really needs that beauty rest."

Savanna pushed me. "That's so wrong!"

"Can we have pancakes tomorrow morning?" Noah didn't even get my joke.

"Of course we can." Savanna poked him in his nose. "You have to set the table."

He started walking up the stairs. "I will. Goodnight!"

I reached out for Savanna. "Come with me."

She grabbed my hand and let me pull her up off the couch. I pulled her closer, forcing her body against my hard chest. Her hands slid up to my shoulders. My hands ran down her little waist and got comfortable on that fine ass. I squeezed her cheeks, pulling her into me more. Then I kissed the side of her face. "I want to take you upstairs." I teased her lips with mine "I want to undress you, slowly." I kissed her gently, letting my tongue drag over her bottom lip. "Then I want to be inside of you, darlin'."

I licked my lips, imagining what it felt like to make love to my wife. I needed to get her up to our room, before the couch became where we ended up.

We separated, but only to be able to walk up the stairs without tripping. Our kissing continued down the hallway until we made it inside our room. That's when we paused while I pulled off her shirt. I kissed on the skin of her neck, letting my lips drag across her smooth skin. She moaned when I kissed her this way and it turned me on every time I heard it.

Savanna didn't waste anytime either. Her nails tickled me as her hands lifted my shirt up and over my head. She ran her fingers over my naked chest and leaned in to kiss around one of my nipples. I reached behind her back and removed her bra, pulling the cups away from her nipples slowly.

Savanna pulled at the button to my jeans. When they started to come down, I took it upon myself to pull down her cotton pants. As soon as I had her naked, I picked Savanna up and carried her over to our bed. Her kisses became savage, like there was no place else she wanted to be than right there with me. Her fingers explored my skin as if it were our first time together.

When I touched her, she began to tremble. Her lips opened slowly and I watched her tongue wetting them. I couldn't help but reach in and kiss them. Her taste was so familiar and I couldn't get enough of her sweet lips.

Her back was laying flat on our bed and my body was lingering over hers. My hands explored every inch of her body, finally coming to the hot spot between her legs. I ran the palm of my hand over her pussy, using the friction to drive her wild. She moaned and moved her body as I continued to tease her with my hand.

I could feel my hard erection pressing against her skin. She was fully aware of what I wanted from her and she wasn't about to stop me from taking it. Two fingers slid between her moist folds. As her natural essence lubricated my fingers, I let them penetrate into her most treasured place. She cried out as I started a rhythm with my fingers.

When I knew she was about to explode, I pulled them out of her and brought them up to my mouth. The look on her face was more than I could handle. I dove down between her legs, tasting her sweet juice with my tongue. Her little bud was calling my name and I gave it all my attention. The more I savored, the more she cried out. Her legs tightened and her body bucked against my face.

When she finally stilled, I kissed my way back up her body. Her legs wrapped around me before I could grab them myself. She knew what I wanted and as I entered my wife, it felt like it had been forever, but it was as perfect as I remembered. Her warmth welcomed me and her sexy body did the rest. I leaned down to kiss her and once we started, we couldn't stop. Her lips were like candy and I wanted to suck the flavor right off of them.

The slower I tried to go, the faster Savanna grinded against me. She was forcing me to keep going, even though I didn't have much left before I couldn't go anymore.

It felt so good, not just to be making love to my wife, but to be home with her. For the short period that I felt like I'd lost her, it was hard to imagine moving on. Savanna was everything to me. She was the rock that kept our family glued together.

Her long nails dug into my back as she arched her own. I ran my nose over one of her breasts, finally letting my tongue reach out and lick her hard nipple. I sucked it into my mouth, hard, changing the natural shape of it. I mimicked my movements on the other side, kissing my way back up to her lips.

Savanna knew I was close. She used her legs to flip herself on top of me. I watched her dark hair fall down over her tits. She was driving me crazy, even before she straddled herself over my erection to perfectly slide me back in. Her body moved up and down, but all I could focus on was her perfect breasts. I reached up and pinched both of her nipples, sending her into a frenzy.

Watching her letting go was hot as hell. I couldn't hold it much longer after that. I stilled my wife's body, while my pent up anxiety was released from me. Savanna finally collapsed on top of me. I wrapped my arms around her and kissed the top of her head. "It's good to be home, darlin'."

She kissed my shoulder. "It's good to have you home, babe."

"Savanna?"

"Yes."

"Everything's goin' to be okay. Nothin's goin' to take you away from us."

I felt her fingers sliding inside of mine. "I hope you're right, Colt, because I can't imagine not being able to be like this with you for the next fifty years."

I wasn't a doctor. I couldn't guarantee her health, but I believed that God wouldn't ever take away something that was so precious to all of us.

I wasn't even willing to accept that I would ever have to spend one day out of my life without Savanna in it.

Chapter 25

Savanna

Ever since Colt had come home, everything seemed a little easier. Sure, we were both worried about the results of the biopsy. Who wouldn't be.

Colt had been researching everything he could find about breast lumps and even cancer. He was my rock and although I knew he was scared, he was always there when I had emotional breakdowns. I knew he'd be there for me no matter what the outcome.

He still hadn't called to apologize to Ty, but I'd talked to him since then. I couldn't be too angry with Colt. If the roles were reversed, I knew I would be jealous of him having a relationship with an ex, like I had with Ty.

I think even if we weren't related, he would still be in my life. As children, he had always taken up for me and protected me. We had this connection that seemed to be eternal. Did I want to be with Ty? Of course not. Still, I couldn't get by without his friendship.

Ty took Colt's attack as the start to a new battle. Just as I would have suspected, by the time the family got wind of it, Colt was the bad guy. Even his mother had issues with Colt blowing up. Obviously, she'd been around me and Ty when Colt and Noah were in California. She was a keen woman who could see beyond what was on the outside. Even with her being able to sense that we were close, I think she knew that neither of us would ever cross those boundaries.

With a wedge formed between my two favorite guys, Miranda and Amy didn't talk to me as much. It was weird considering Ty called me everyday. At first, I thought it was because he was the only one who knew about my medical issue. I thought maybe they were offended, even though it wasn't meant to be that way, at all.

Colt never said a word about me talking to Ty every day. He usually called in the mornings when he knew Colt wasn't at the house. Since the whole family now knew about my predicament, they bombarded me with attention. Sometimes it was just too overwhelming. It only reminded me that I had a serious matter to worry about.

Life became hard to focus on that next week. If it weren't for the kids, I think I would have gone crazy.

Colt said that things wouldn't change between us, but already I could see him doing extra things to appease me. Not that I didn't appreciate it, because I most certainly did. I just hated that he was doing it because he felt sorry for what I was going through. All in all, I knew he was going through it as well. I had to keep reminding myself that I wasn't in this mess alone.

The doctor's office called on Thursday. I was sitting down matching socks when the phone rang. I think I just knew it was them calling. After a minute, I had an appointment to go in and talk to the doctor that afternoon. I sat there with that phone in my hand just staring at it for at least twenty minutes. I wasn't shaking or crying. No, I was perfectly still, realizing that this was really happening.

Finally, when I noticed how long I'd been frozen in place, I called Colt and told him that he needed to come home. I didn't have to tell him why. I think he was expecting the phone call to come when he wasn't home.

The second he walked in the door, I broke down. We didn't even know the extent of the results. All we knew was that if it were nothing, they would have told us. We needed to prepare for the worst and just pray it wasn't that bad.

Colt called my mother to let her know, since I wasn't in any condition to talk to anyone. By noon, we were on our way to learn my fate.

I was more than petrified. I didn't know how to feel or act. I knew the risks and the statistics. I knew there was a chance that my life was going to be cut short. I thought about my beautiful babies again. How was I going to be able to look them in the eyes if I found out I wasn't going to live much longer.

Colt patted me on the leg when we'd arrived and I hadn't noticed.

We walked into the office holding hands. I was happy about that, considering at any moment I felt like I was going to pass out. I tried to think of all the women and men before me that had come into this office for the same reason. It sickened me to think that it happens so often.

The front desk lady took us right back into the doctor's office. While waiting for him to come in, Colt reached his hand over and grabbed mine. "I love you, darlin'."

"I'm so scared, Colt." I could feel myself shaking in the seat.

The doctor came in catching our attention. Colt cleared his throat and reached over to shake hands with the man.

He sat down across the desk from us and opened up my chart. "Sorry it took so long getting these results. I know it's hard playing the waiting game." He pulled out a couple pictures and pointed to certain areas. "This was the spot in question. On this imagine it looks a lot bigger than it actually is." He read something and then looked up at me. "The good news is that this was detected very early."

"What's the bad news?" I couldn't wait for him to give me the run around. If I was going to die, I wanted to know immediately. I couldn't take it anymore.

"The area that we biopsied came back malignant."

Colt squeezed my hand, but said nothing. I could barely get the words out. "So, I have cancer? Am I going to die?"

He put his hands up. "Let's not get ahead of ourselves, Mrs. Mitchell. The first thing I would recommend doing is a surgical procedure to remove the mass. If we act now, we can stop the spreading to surrounding areas."

"So, you can just remove it and I'll be cancer free?"

"Not exactly. Removing the mass is just the first step. Once we remove the malignant tumor, we can then do a thorough check to make sure that your body is cancer free. Unfortunately, once you have this, is more likely to come back. Many women end up getting mastectomies as a preventative procedure."

I was crying, but still able to talk. "You want me to cut off my breasts?"

"I usually give my patients the option upon early detection. Listen Mrs. Mitchell, one in eight women will experience what you're going through right now. Even men can get breast cancer. Early detection, as is your case, is the best result. We are able to attack the cells before they can broadcast themselves to other organs. It is impertinent that we remove it as soon as possible. However, I would recommend one round of radiation and then we will retest after that."

"Is there a chance that I could die?"

He took a deep breath. "Cancer is ugly. It takes lives and I'm not going to sugar coat things for you. Right now, where we stand, I have no reason to believe that you can't beat this.

However, you're going to have to be monitored for the rest of your life. If or when it does come back, we'll catch it early enough to treat. I tell all of my patients the same thing. You need to take it one day at a time. You absolutely can not dwell on the negative aspects of this. I realize you have a million emotions rolling through your mind, but I do think we can get you through this."

He was right about the emotions. I felt like I was going to be sick. As the vomit reached my mouth, I ran out in search of a toilet.

Even after I'd finished getting sick, I slouched down on the cold tile floor and lost control. How could this be happening to me? I was always so healthy. I went to church, said my prayers, and tried to be the best person I could be. What did I ever do to deserve this kind of punishment?

A knock on the bathroom door startled me. "Savanna, darlin', are you alright?"

I stood up and unlocked the door. Colt came in while I was wiping off my face. "I'm not okay. It's never going to be okay again." I cried so hard that I know everyone in that office could hear me. I didn't even care. The doctor's words continued to repeat in my mind. Over and over I heard him telling me that I had cancer.

"He said we can beat this."

"He doesn't know for sure. What if it's already spread through my body? What am I going to do? How are we going to tell the kids?"

He held me close and rubbed my back. "I ain't goin' to lose you, Savanna."

He could say that as many times as he wanted. It wouldn't change the fact that I could be dying.

Once he talked me out of the bathroom, the doctor was already with other patients. He had given Colt a bunch of information to take home and go over. The front desk clerk scheduled my first surgery in one week's time. It was all just happening so fast that I felt like my life was spinning out of control.

Colt was quiet as he drove us home. I leaned my head against the glass window and sobbed. He could have been crying too, but I didn't have the strength to look his way to see. I just couldn't handle it.

When we got home, he came around to my side of the vehicle and helped me out of the car. He kept his arm around me until I was laying down on the couch, but still said nothing. Maybe he knew I couldn't deal with talking about it, or maybe he was just as broken up as I was about it.

After he got me some tea, he went into his office and closed the door. I could hear the murmurs of him talking on the phone. I knew he was calling the family. He was trying to be respectful, but just knowing he was in there telling everyone I loved my bad news, was difficult. I almost felt like I just wanted to get through it all by myself, instead of them worrying about me.

I could hear my cell phone vibrating in my purse. It had been doing it for a while and I couldn't handle talking to anyone.

When Colt came out of the office, he heard it and pulled it out. I could see the look on his face and knew who had called. He pushed the blanket to the side and sat down on the edge of the couch. "How are you doin'?"

I shrugged. "Not good. When do the kids get home?"

"Your parents are keepin' them. I think your dad said they are going to take them to bible school tonight, so they won't think anything of it."

"How did they take the news?" Right away, my eyes began to burn.

He took his hat off and tossed it on the table, then wiped his face with one of his hands. "They're upset. They kept askin' me a bunch of questions."

"I can only imagine what they must be feeling. I'm their only child. They moved here to be close to me. What will happen if this takes my life?"

He turned and looked me right in the eyes. I could see the pain that he was carrying. His eyes were red and I knew he'd gotten emotional in his office. "It ain't goin' to. Savanna, please stop talkin' like that. You've got so much to live for, darlin'. I don't think I could live a single day without you. We all need you. I don't care how hard it gets. You're goin' to fight this. You hear me?"

I nodded but continued to cry. I hated this so much. It was so difficult.

"When you went into the bathroom, the doctor told me that he thinks you have a good chance at beatin' this. Darlin', I know you can. I've seen you fight for what you want."

With every feeling playing heavy on my mind, there was one thing that I knew for certain. "I won't give up! I promise."

He leaned over and kissed me. "That's my girl." He smiled, just enough to show me he was proud. Then he reached over and handed me my phone. "You better call Ty. He's sent you several messages and I know he's worried."

I didn't feel like talking, but I certainly didn't want him jumping on a plane again, so I called Ty.

It's about time.

I didn't feel like talking.

Well, you can't just leave me hanging. I knew Colt wasn't going to call. I had to hear it from Conner. Do you know how sucky that was for me?

Can you not make this about you? I have bigger problems than wondering who knows my business.

So, now what happens?

They are going to go in and remove it.

Then you're out of the woods?

No. I have to do one round of radiation.

Will you lose your hair? I bet you'd be hot bald.

I couldn't believe he was joking around, but it did make me laugh.

Stop joking around.

If I were you, I'd wear a clown wig. That would be fucking funny.

I'm going to hang up on you, if you don't stop.

I'm sorry. I went online and did some research. Did you know that if you get a double mastectomy, it decreases your chances of it coming back by a lot.

I can't believe I am talking to you about this, but my doctor told me that as well.

So, are you going to do it?

I don't know! I'm scared.

Colt will still love you, Van. If that's what's keeping you from doing it, you need to rethink that decision. He wants you healthy. It's all that matters to him.

I know.

Did you know they can tattoo nipples back on the skin? I've been looking at nipple tattoos for the past hour. I tried to show Miranda how cool it was. She smacked the shit out of me and called me an insensitive asshole.

I burst into laughter. I just couldn't help it. The day had been so horrible and only Ty could make a joke out of something so serious. I didn't know if I was just being ridiculous, or I really found him funny. He wasn't trying to be a jerk. He wanted me to have a reason to smile. Ty wanted me to be able to see something funny out of what I feared. He wanted to know that every single time I thought about that surgery, I thought about the funny things he'd said. I loved him for that.

You are disgusting and definitely an asshole!

I can't help myself. You know I can't do serious. Whoever created sadness is an asshole!

Yeah, you got that right.

Where's your hubby? Is he still planning my demise?

No! he's right here.

He still doesn't want to talk to me?

Not yet.

What a douche. Is he treating you good? Do I need to come out there and knock him around?

I started laughing again. Ty had never been able to take on Colt and he knew it. *He's being wonderful.*

Miranda said to tell you she loves you. She also said that if you don't call her, she's going to send the boys to live with you and Colt.

I laughed again. *Okay, I promise I will call her. Just give me some time. I need to get my feelings in order first.*

I get it. Listen, if you need to smile, you know where to find me. I'm only a phone call away. I'd do anything to take this pain away from you, Van. You're the best person that I've ever known. We all love you so much.

I started to sob. *I love you all, too.*

Colt took the phone and put it back in my purse. He sat back down and gave me all of his attention. "We don't have to talk about anything until you're ready.

"I know."

"Savanna, do you even know how my people love you? Do you get how many hearts you reached out and touched? You don't have to go through this alone, darlin'. You will never be alone. I promise."

I don't know if it was that exact moment, but I became determined to do whatever I needed to do to get through this. I had children to raise and a family to grow old with. I wasn't going to let some little mass in my breast end my life. Not when I had a million reasons to live.

Chapter 26

Colt

I think hearing someone has cancer is hard for anyone to handle, but hearing it about your own wife is indescribably hard. This was the woman that I promised to love for the rest of my life. If she was taken from me prematurely, I didn't know how I would survive. I'd always considered myself a good father, but I couldn't be the parent that she was. She was the rock of our family and without her we would crumble.

Savanna took the news as I would have expected her to. She shut down, and in between bouts of crying, she just laid around. Nobody could blame her. It was her only coping mechanism. Even I couldn't imagine everything she was going through.

With her surgery being nearly a week away, she did her best to pretend things were okay when the kids were around. We'd made the decision to keep it from them. Children worried and didn't understand things like that anyway. She didn't want to burden them with that.

By the end of the week, she had thrown herself into a wedding for Joe and Barbie. She and the girls had gone out and picked real flowers and they'd turned our dining room into a place fit for a proper wedding. She'd even gone out and bought the girls matching dresses and Barbie a wedding gown. They made invitations and invited their grandparents. It was cute and it kept her mind off of things just enough that she could get by.

She didn't know it, but I was so proud of her. Even at her worst, she was still one hell of a mother. It just reminded me of what would happen if we ever lost her. I hated thinking about it, but with everything going on, it still popped in my head all too frequently.

The wedding of Joe and Barbie was commenced by Savanna's father after we'd all returned from church. Both my mom and Savanna's had brought a spread of food. We spent that Sunday celebrating as if they were real people. To the kids, it was for fun, but I think in some ways Savanna just wanted a reason to have the family around without having to talk to them about her health. While us guys, including Noah, settled in the living room to watch basketball, Savanna and our mother's stayed in the kitchen. I wasn't sure what they talked about, but she seemed to be in a good mood after everyone left.

After the kids were asleep, I found her soaking in the bathtub. It was full of bubbles and her head was laying against a towel. She saw me come in the bathroom and smiled. "Hey."

"Today was fun."

"Thanks for going along with it. The girls will never forget it."

I sat down on the edge of the tub and ran my fingers in the water. "Is that why you did it? Savanna, please don't tell me you went all out because you are afraid your time is limited. You promised me you wouldn't be like that."

She looked sad. "I just want them to have good memories, no matter what happens. Is that so bad?"

"It is when you're doin' it because you think you're not goin' to be around." I hated even saying it out loud.

She shook her head and got tears in her eyes. "You're right. I guess I'm just scared. There are so many 'what ifs'."

I didn't know what to say to that, so instead of using any words at all, I started taking off my clothes. Savanna gave me that look and I knew that she was okay with my actions. She scooted over to allow me room to slide in behind her. I reached forward and pulled her body back against mine. The soapy water made it easy to slide my hands down her arms and then back up again. Savanna laid her head back against my chest. She lifted one of her arms and reached it back behind my neck to pull my head down to kiss her. Our lips lingered, like they didn't want to separate. She even spun her body around and wrapped her slippery legs around my waist. The tub made sounds as our bodies became pretzeled together. With her sitting on top of me, I couldn't help but become instantly hard. Her wet hair was stuck to the sides of her arms. I moved it out of the way and kissed over her neck. She turned so I could have an open area to caress. Her body was hot from the temperature of the water. Sweat was already starting to form on my forehead.

She found my lips again, this time kissing me more forcefully. Her desperation was hot and I didn't want her to stop. I reached my hand down and got a hold of her ass. With her being in the water, it was simple to move her up and down over my throbbing hard cock. I wanted her to know that I was ready whenever she was. Our tongues played games with one another outside of our mouths. She bit my bottom lip and pulled it back, while making this growling sound that drove me wild. It was rare that she got this way and it was always because she was taking out stress. My dick didn't care what the reason was. I wanted more.

We made out like kids at a drive-in. Our hands explored the most sensitive areas of each other until we were both panting and out of breath. I reached my hand between her legs while we continued kissing. Her body was grinding into mine, so I stuck my thumb over her sensitive clit and rubbed hard. The more I rubbed, the harder she grinded. I wasn't just pleasing her. In turn, she was pleasing me.

Her breasts were bobbing up and down out of the bubbles. I could feel them rubbing against my own chest. I pulled away and kissed down to them, taking one of her wet nipples into my mouth. I kept it there until she screamed out in pleasure. The combination of my thumbs and lips had given her a fantastic orgasm. When her moans began to settle, I ran my hands up both of her breasts. Her eyes opened wide and my wife just froze. She took my hands and moved them. "Please don't!"

She slid off of me and sat across the tub.

"Don't what? What's wrong?"

She started to cry. "How will you even be able to look at me?"

I was rock hard and had no idea what she was talking about. "Darlin', what just happened?"

"How will you be able to look at me after they take away my breasts?" She covered her face and started to cry. I felt so defeated, like no matter what I tried to do, I always ended up in the same place.

"Jesus, Savanna. You think I won't love you anymore because you're having skin removed?"

She still wouldn't look up. "I just feel like you're going to want to find someone else. What if I can't turn you on anymore?"

I ran my hands through my hair, considering what I could say to get myself out of this mess. The last thing I wanted was to fight with her. "Do you have any idea how crazy you sound? Do you think I married you for your tits?"

She shook her head. "No!"

I grabbed her chin and looked into her eyes. "Savanna, I don't care what you look like. I will never stop lovin' you. Now get your ass back over here and love me."

I pulled her back on top of me. Our lips were almost touching. I leaned in just enough to brush mine against hers. She closed her eyes and finally kissed me back. I could feel her crying, but I wasn't going to let her become upset when we were in the middle of making love. Her legs were easy to wrap back around me and the water eased the way to guide my erection right inside of her. She bit down on my shoulder as I filled her with my length. Her tears dissipated as our bodies began to get a rhythm.

Savanna grabbed my throat and pushed me back against the edge of the tub. The harder she pushed, the more turned on I got. I grabbed her little waist and shoved her up and down, almost letting my length out before slamming it back in. She threw her head back and cried out again and again. It was too much to handle. I felt myself erupting and it was exactly what she wanted to happen. She let go of my throat and pressed her lips against mine. I closed my eyes and held her body as still as I could, considering she was fighting me. Her fine ass grinded just enough to give me the shivers.

Finally, when the tingling subsided, I held her naked body against mine and kissed down her shoulder. "Don't doubt my love, Savanna."

"I'm sorry."

It was hard to get mad at her knowing she was struggling to accept it herself. I think she was more worried about loving her body than she was about me having issues with it. I was a man and maybe it was hard for me to express myself the way she needed me to. I always just assumed that she knew what I was thinking.

That night, Savanna cuddled up close to me and slept better than she had in days. I stayed awake listening to her breathing. It was hard to pretend to be tough when I was petrified of losing her. I couldn't admit it to anyone.

Well, there was one person that I knew I could talk to, but I wasn't willing to admit I was wrong. Tyler loved Savanna in a way that I may never understand. He didn't want to be with her, but he cared for her like she was blood. Instead of being jealous, I should have appreciated that she had someone that loved her enough to drop everything and be by her side. That's the kind of person she was, though. She made everyone love her and she never even had to try.

As if he could feel me thinking about him, my phone rang and Ty's picture popped up on the screen.

I considered hitting ignore.

Hello? Do you have ESP?

Yeah, I'm the Wizard of Fucking OZ!

What do you want, Ty?

I know you're a mess, man.

Yeah, do you blame me?

Nope. I don't.

It's hard. I'm tryin' my best to be strong for her.

Look, I know you're mad at me. I get it. Maybe I overstepped some cousin boundaries when I stepped in. I just couldn't let her deal with it by herself.

I get it now.

Colt, none of us want you to go through this alone.

I appreciate that.

She's going to be okay, you know.

I hope you're right, Ty.

I'm always right, fucker. Call if you need anything.

I shook my head when I heard the line go dead. It was weird that he'd called when I needed him to. Ty had a way of always being there when someone needed something. He had a weird way of doing things, but he was a good guy.

Savanna's father offered to manage things on the ranch, so I could stay home with her. We still hadn't told the kids, but I think Noah knew something was going on. He'd asked several times if Savanna was still mad at him. It was hard for me to not tell him the truth, when I worried their relationship depended on it.

The boy had already lost one mother. I couldn't let him fear losing another.

While the kids were at school, Savanna and I would sit down and read up on everything we could about cancer. There were so many questions to be answered.

I think as the days went by, she was finally starting to be able to act more like herself. There was nothing we could do but move forward.

On the morning of her surgery, I saw her standing in front of the mirror without clothes on. She cupped one of her hands over her breast. "How would you feel if I had them both removed?"

I leaned against the counter. "How would you feel?"

She shrugged but kept looking at herself. "It would be weird at first, but I could always get implants. The one website said I wouldn't even have to wait that long to get them."

I stood behind her and reached my arms around her waist. "No matter what you decide, you'll still be beautiful."

She let go of her breast and turned around to look at me. "I couldn't do this without you, Colt."

"You don't have to. You never have to."

I kissed her forehead and held my lips there. It was just a small moment that meant the world to her.

Chapter 27

Savanna

I'd be lying if I said I wasn't petrified. This life changing surgery was almost more than I could handle. I tried not to dwell on the negative. They were removing the cancer from my body, and for that, I had to be content.

Colt was a champ as far as being there or me, but I could tell that it was weighing heavily on him. The more he tried to hide it, the more I knew just how affected he was.

When we got into the hospital, I was taken to a preoperative room with other patients that were also having some kind of surgery. A nurse allowed Colt and my mother come in with me. She gave me a gown, cap and booties to change into. We sat there for a while waiting for my doctor to arrive. In the meantime, the nurse came in and got my IV ready.

Once the doctor arrived, he pulled down my gown and drew markings over the breast to show where his incision would be made. The marker tickled, and even though he was performing surgery, I felt weird about him drawing on my boob.

Before Colt and my mother had to leave, the doctor gave us a couple minutes alone. My mom kissed me and left Colt and me alone in the room.

I was fine until it was time to say goodbye to Colt. He was holding my hand and I refused to let it go. The more he attempted to pull away, the more I fought him. "Darlin' you're goin' to be fine."

"I'm so scared. I don't want you to go."

"The sooner I go, the faster they can get done. I love you with my whole heart, Savanna." He was getting choked up and I needed to let him go. Our fingers parted and I felt alone.

I was still crying when the anesthesiologist came into the room. It was a middle aged man, who obviously knew what I was in the operating room for. My doctor came in right after him. He was filling out something on his laptop, before turning his attention to me. "How are we doing?"

"Not good!"

He patted my arm. "My friend here is going to make you more comfortable. When you wake up, I'll be all done." He looked at my vitals on the monitor for a second. "Today we're going to remove the mass in your left breast. As far as the double mastectomy goes, I think we'll wait until next month. If you want to have reconstructive implants, we can do them at the same time."

"So I won't be without breasts?"

He chuckled. "Not unless you want to be. Listen, if you want to read a good story, a movie star just had this same surgery done a few months ago. Until she came forward, nobody even knew it had happened. I just want you to be sure about what you want once we do this. Our main priority is removing the malignant cells today."

"I'm ready." Getting new breasts would take some of the worry off of me. I didn't want to feel different. I certainly didn't want my children looking at me like my body was falling apart. Being treated for cancer was going to be hard enough. I was going to get sick and possibly lose my hair. If there was anything that could help, I wanted to take it.

"You're most likely going to have drains put in. It will help the access fluid leave your body to prevent infection. In the next couple days your nurse will keep checking and making sure they are doing their job. If it goes as I plan, we may be able to remove the drain before you leave the hospital. If you're ready, I'd like to get started."

"Let's do this!" I put on a fake smile and watched the anesthesiologist come over and stick a needle into my IV. Before I could count to five, I was out.

I woke up in a recovery room. Colt was sitting across from me, reading a magazine. When he saw that I was awake, he came rushing over to the bed. "Hey. Are you in any pain?"

My mouth was dry, so I shook my head.

He brushed the hair away from my face. I was still hooked up to an IV for pain and even though I couldn't feel pain, I was still irritated by the tubes. "The doctor said that everything went as planned. He said you'll be able to go home in two days."

I smiled, thinking about being home. I couldn't wait to see the kids. They knew I had to have surgery, but they didn't know what for.

He grabbed my hand and kissed it, like he always did. "Your mom went home, but she said she'd be back later tonight. Ty and Miranda called several times. They said they love you. Oh and I just want to warn you, my mom called the florist. Be prepared for flowers to be delivered."

Colt continued to talk, but I was still so drugged that I lost track of what he was talking about. I could feel my eyes closing and I couldn't seem to fight it.

I woke up a while later and saw the nurse checking my vitals. "How are you feelin'?"

"I'm thirsty," I whispered.

"I will get you some ice water."

When I didn't see Colt, I started to get upset. "He's outside in the hallway. He got a call and didn't want to wake you." She finished what she was doing. "I'll be right back with that water."

As she walked out, Colt walked in. He stayed with me for the next two days. In fact, the only time he left was to shower and eat. By the first evening, I was sitting up and feeling like myself again. The pain medication was through a button, and even though it was there for me to use, I tried to go without it as much as I could.

The girls were too young to visit, but Noah was old enough. I was so excited to see him walking in the room the next morning. My father had brought him after I'd talk to him on the phone. I could tell that he was a little scared to see me lying in the hospital bed. I reached out my hand and he walked right up to it. "Hi, sweetie."

He put a vase full of flowers on the table beside me. "Hi, Mom. Does it hurt?"

"Not really bad. It's just really tight right now. The flowers are beautiful."

He couldn't see where I was wrapped up since I was wearing a gown and I had a blanket over me. " We got them on the way here. Christian and Addy were crying because they couldn't come in. Grandma had to take them to get ice cream."

I played with his hand. "Are you being helpful?"

"Yeah. When are you comin' home? I don't want to stay at their house anymore. Can't we take care of you?"

I felt so appreciated. "I'm coming home tomorrow and Dad's going to need your help. I'm going to be sore for a while."

"Mom, why did they have to operate on you?" The concern in his eyes broke my heart. He just stood there waiting for me to reply.

"I had a little growth inside of my body and the doctors cut it out, so it wouldn't make me sick."

"Are you goin' to be alright?" He was worried about me.

I squeezed his hand. "I am, now that you came to visit."

He finally smiled. "I cleaned my room. Dad said we need to pitch in more. Christian cleaned hers too. We're making a chore list to do."

Colt winked at me. I was impressed that he was already on top of things. "Thank you for doing that. I'm sure your grandparents are going to help Dad out. Plus, you know Lucy. She won't let you go hungry."

"Yeah." Noah looked around the hospital room. I knew he was uncomfortable.

I handed him the remote control. "Want to watch something with me?"

He flipped on the television. As slowly as possible, I moved over and patted the small spot beside me. "Will it hurt you?"

I knew it would hurt a little bit, but nothing was going to stop me from cuddling with my son. Since he was on my right side, it wasn't so bad. He put on a superhero hero movie and wrapped one arm around me. "I love you, Noah. Thanks for coming to see me. I hate it here."

"Do they feed you?"

It hurt to laugh and as I much as I tried to hold it in, I just couldn't. "Of course they feed me. I had cereal for breakfast and a salad for lunch. They give a menu and you pick what you want."

"Is it good?"

"No! Its horrible. Maybe next time you can bring me a chicken sandwich."

"When Dad brings you home tomorrow he can stop and get you one, right Dad?" Noah looked to Colt.

"If she wants me to." He pointed towards the door. "I'm going to walk down to the cafeteria with your dad. I'll check on you both later."

We waved as Colt left the room with my dad. Noah was already occupied in the television, while I focused on him being so close. I'd been through something so traumatic just one day before. Noah being in my arms made me realize just how grateful I was for my life. I wanted to live every single day for my children and my family. They needed me as much as I needed them, and together, we could get through anything.

Noah stayed until visiting hours were over. My father took him home, while Colt stayed the night. We went to bed early, in hopes of being released as soon as the sun came up. We ended up having to wait until ten the next morning. I refused to eat another hospital meal, so once we left the hospital, we stopped and got something to eat, while we waited for my prescriptions to be filled. I was given antibiotics to fight off infections, pain medication, and some kind of hormone replacement. My radiation wasn't going to start for a couple of weeks, to give my body the full time to recuperate.

I should have known that our Kentucky family would be at my house to welcome me home. The house smelled like a bakery and signs were hung all over the living room. My girls both ran up and hugged me around the waist. I pulled them into my body, appreciating that they missed me as much as I missed them.

My parents sat with Colt's mom and Lucy, while I was overwhelmed with hugs from my children. Noah was gentle with me, where the girls didn't know any better.

We spent the better part of the afternoon with the family. They left just before dinner, so that I could go upstairs and get some rest. Taking a nap had never been so eventful. All four of them walked me up to my room. Colt pulled down the covers and the kids all climbed in the bed. I got in slowly and felt Colt lifted the covers over me. He leaned down and kissed me on the lips. "Welcome home, darlin'."

I smiled and looked around at the kids. They were all three smiling. "It's great to be home."

Chapter 28

Colt

It was so good to have my wife home. She was still weak, even after a couple of days. The doctor said it would take her weeks to get back to her normal self. The kids had been so happy to have her home that they all wanted to sleep with her that first night. I wouldn't have minded if they didn't kick and roll around all night. It was too much of a risk for one of them to accidentally rip her drain or her sutures. Since Savanna went to bed at dinner time, it was easy to get the kids to come downstairs. For once, they didn't complain.

The girls stayed up for another couple of hours, while Noah stayed up watching the game with me.

"Dad, can I ask you a question?"

I looked away from the game and gave him my attention. "What's up?"

"It's cancer, isn't it?"

I was so shocked that I didn't know how to answer. We'd never mentioned that word to him. "Why would you think that?"

"Well, I didn't know what Oncologist meant, so I looked it up. It said that it's a cancer doctor. So, I'm askin' you man to man. Does mom have it?"

How was I supposed to answer him. If he was old enough to go looking for answers, he was old enough to handle the truth. Savanna was going to be upset, but I couldn't lie to my son. "That's why she had surgery. The doctor went in and removed the cancer."

He started to sniffle and I watched him wipe his face. "Is she goin' to die?"

It hit me hard. I'd prayed to God every single night, begging him to save her. How was I supposed to put Noah's mind at ease, when I feared the same fate? "No!"

He shook his head and started crying louder. "This is all my fault. I made her sad and she got sick."

I reached over and shook him gently. "Noah, this had nothin' to do with you. People don't get cancer because they're sad. You didn't do this, son. I promise you that."

"So it's gone? They took it out and she's goin' to be okay?"

I turned down the volume to the game to give Noah my full attention. "They removed the mass that contained the cancer, yes. Your mom will still need to receive a special treatment to be sure they got everything out. She might get sick and we're goin' to need to make sure we do everything we can to help her out."

He looked down at his hands. "Is she goin' to be okay?"

"Yeah, buddy. I think she's goin' to be fine."

Noah smiled. "I don't want to lose her, Dad."

I put my arm around Noah. "You're not! It's our love that's goin' to help her get better. As long as she knows she has us, she'll be alright."

"I'll do whatever it takes. I'll help wash clothes and do the dishes. I'll feed the horses and do all my chores."

"I know you will."

Noah was a good boy and I was proud that he wanted to do whatever it took to help out his mother. I never doubted the way he felt about her. "We can't tell your sisters."

He nodded. "I know. They won't understand."

After a few moments of silence, I turned back on the game like our conversation hadn't even happened. Noah sat back against the couch and did the same. My son was more and more like me every day.

When I finally climbed into bed, Savanna was nestled in between a bunch of pillows. I'd waited days to be able to sleep in the same bed as her, so I removed the ones that were separating us and cuddled up against her. Her body was so warm and I was careful not to touch her near the bandage.

She stirred, but didn't wake up like she normally would have. Her pain medication was strong and it was exactly what she needed to let her body recover.

Savanna was always hardheaded when she was injured or sick. She'd push herself until she made things worse. This surgery was serious and we couldn't take the chance of making her go back into the hospital. Her safety was up to me to control, so it was necessary for me to be there for her until she was able to take care of herself.

I was trying to be everything that she needed, even without her asking.

While she slept so soundly, I laid there next to her watching. She was so beautiful to me. I didn't care about a scar, or the way she would look with a double mastectomy. She was my everything and nothing could ever taint the way I felt about her. If anything, I loved her more for being so strong.

Savanna had been home for four days when we got the call that Amy was in labor. As excited as we were to have a new addition to our family, I knew we weren't going to be able to go to North Carolina with the rest of the family. The drive would be too long for Savanna to handle. She needed to be able to readjust herself frequently.

She cried and pleaded with me to take her, but at the end of the day, I was in charge.

To make things easier, my mother took the girls with her to visit the new baby. For the first time ever, Noah declined on his invitation to go see Bella. Ever since that day in the hospital, he'd never left her side. I think he believed that if he was with her all of the time, nothing bad could happen. It was both sweet and alarming. I worried that he really feared if he turned his back for a second, she'd be gone. I didn't want him living his life like that.

Savanna wasn't exactly thrilled that I'd told him the truth about her condition. She worried that he wouldn't understand, but from what I could see, he understood completely.

Cassandra Elizabeth Healy was born at five o'clock in the morning on a warm summer day. The whole family had gone to welcome the new baby, which they were already calling Cassie. Yeah, I know what you're thinking. Conner and Amy had named three of their four children Cammie, Callie, and Cassie. How they would keep that straight was beyond my understanding. I got my kids mixed up and none of their names even started with the same letter.

Anyway, when my mother got back in town, not only did she bring pictures, but she brought Bella as well. Noah was so happy to have his cousin come and stay with us, that I figured he would forget about helping out. Instead, he surprised me even more. Every morning, he would enlist his cousin to help out with chores. Before they disappeared to play together, he would make sure everything was taken care of.

He was a blessing and without him, I think I would have set myself crazy.

Bella was great to have around. The girls thought she was the best thing since sweet tea. They followed her around and begged her to play with them instead of Noah.

Ty and Miranda called every night to talk to their daughter. Savanna would stay on the phone with them catching up each time. She was getting bored and I knew she would be itching to go somewhere as soon as she got the okay from her doctor. We'd been going out to the grocery store and other local places, but she wanted to get to North Carolina to see her new niece. Pictures were never enough for my wife. Besides, she wanted to take her own.

On the day she got the go-ahead, we made plans to go out of town. Her radiation was set to begin that next week and it was important for her to travel when she wasn't feeling ill. The doctor had informed us that her treatment was more for a preventative and it would be 'low-grade', as opposed to the intense treatment that other people require. He informed her that she probably wouldn't lose her hair and that she may only have flu like symptoms.

We knew that every person handles things differently, so we packed up the kids, including Bella and made the long drive to North Carolina.

Our first stop was Conner and Amy's house. Noah unhooked his sister and before Savanna and I could get out of the truck, the kids were running into the house. Amy was sitting in the rocking chair feeding the new baby when we walked in. Savanna rushed over and hugged her and then took a peek at our newest cousin. "Oh my goodness, she's so pretty!" Savanna was all smiles and I loved seeing her that way.

Since Amy was breastfeeding, I opted to wait until she was back to decent. I waved from afar. "Where's Conner?"

"They're out at the barn working on some engine." She whispered.

"I reckon I'll just go look for them." I walked out of the house and noticed that my kids had already found their cousins. They were out back playing in the fort Conner and Ty had built for them. The girls were on the swings, while Josh and Noah were up high looking through a scope. Noah was showing him something.

Conner and Ty were both on the ground out in front of the barn. They were covered in dirt and grease. "What the hell are you two doin'?"

"What does it look like, you old cocksucker?" Conner stood up and brushed off his pants.

Ty stayed on the ground. This was the first time I'd seen him since we'd fought in my front yard. We'd spoken, but it wasn't the same as being in the same space. I nodded to him and he gave me a flip look and kept at what he was doing. "How'd she do on the ride?"

I should have known that the first words out of his mouth would be about my wife. "She's good. I think she's stiff, but it ain't like she'd admit it."

Finally Ty stood up and held out his hand to shake mine. "Are we good?"

I shook his hand. "Yeah, we're good."

Conner stood between us and put a hand on both of our shoulders. "Now that we got that settled, let's go have a beer."

We walked into the old barn, where we played pool and cards with the family. Ty pulled three beers out of the refrigerator. We all popped the tops and took a drink of the cold goodness. "Is she upset about the radiation?"

"I think she's more anxious." I leaned against the pool table. "I can't blame her. We all just want to put this shit behind us. It's been so hard."

"She told me you hate being Mr. Mom." Ty started laughing. "Do you wear an apron while you vacuum?"

Conner chimed in. "He only wears an apron. Can you see him with a feather duster?" They both started laughing at me.

I shook my head and took another swig of beer. "I just got here! Can't you act right for ten minutes?"

They looked at each other and answered at the same time. "No!"

I just shook my head. There was no changing them and since they spent all of their time together, they even thought alike. It was disturbing.

We spent the next hour shooting the shit and talking about the new baby. Since neither of them could be serious for more than five minutes, I felt like I was babysitting, instead of hanging out.

In some ways I was jealous that the two of them had fun all of the time. I took my life and my family serious. I didn't have time to fool around. Somehow, they managed to make it work.

In celebration of our visit, we barbequed at Conner's house. After stuffing our faces with fried chicken, steaks and every kind of side item that the girls could think of, we sat around a campfire out back. The kids had long sticks for roasting marshmallows. I held Addy on my lap, while Christian and Noah managed their own sticks. Every one of those kids caught their marshmallow on fire except Christian. She took her time, browning it to a perfect hue. Jax and Jake took their first ones and caught them on fire just to be able to fling them in the field. Of course, where they fell was dry and soon caught fire. It wouldn't have been so bad if Conner hadn't sat bales of hay on the field edge. Once it reached one of the bales, we had a huge bonfire. While the women frantically counted the kids, we managed to wet the entire surrounding area. Ty and Conner got a great idea to keep the fire going. They threw wood on it and soon we were further away from the house with flames that were higher than the house.

Ty's mother called to check on us. She told him they could see the flames from their house. My two dingbat cousins then let the kids come over to the new fire and roast more marshmallows. However, Jake and Jax were not allowed to have their own sticks. While pouting over it, they decided to start fighting with each other. Soon they were wrestling on the ground. Ty grabbed one of them by the back of their shirt, while Miranda ran up and grabbed the other one.

I looked over at my wife and saw her smiling back at me. If I knew one thing for sure, it was that she loved this family that we belonged to. She loved all of their crazy quirks and how we were bound by blood and friendship.

Then I looked up at the night sky and thanked the Lord again for protecting her for me. We were on the road to recovery and I planned on sticking by her until it was over. No matter how long it took, or what we had to go through, she was never going to be doing it alone.

Chapter 29
Savanna

I had been itching to get to North Carolina since before Amy went into labor. Colt had become so protective that he followed every rule by the book. If I had to be stuck in my house for one more day, I was going to have myself committed. I was recovering from the successful removal of a mass, not battling leprosy. Not that body parts actually fall off when you get it, but history does portray it that way.

Anyway, it was about time the doctor said I could finally travel.

Amy and Conner's newest daughter was as pretty as sunshine. She looked just like her other two sisters. Poor Josh was outnumbered and I wouldn't have recommended him hanging out with Jake and Jax. Those two were Hell on wheels. Ty and Miranda really had their hands full. After they set fire to a hay bale, they managed to catch a baby bunny and tie a piece of thread to it's tail. How in the world did two five years olds come up with these ideas?

Conner had invited us to stay at their house, and I think Colt was all for it, considering that our other option was staying with Ty and Miranda. I think he didn't want the boys anywhere near our girls. It wasn't that I thought they'd hurt the girls. Christian was a force to be reckoned with when someone made her mad. I was certain she could handle both of them with no problem. Addy was the sensitive one. Everything hurt her feelings and she loved getting people in trouble. Since she'd be sleeping with us anyway, Colt and I agreed to stay with Ty and Miranda. Conner's house sometimes seemed like a daycare and I didn't have enough energy yet to deal with it constantly.

It was getting late and the kids were becoming whiney. Amy took the baby and the little ones in the house and turned on a movie. They'd probably all fall asleep on the floor and we could let them spend the night.

Noah and Bella were making smores. I looked over and saw them giggling. All of the suddenly, Noah got up and ran into the house like his pants were on fire. Bella giggled again and kept looking at me.

A few minutes later, Noah came outside carrying a guitar. He handed it to his father and whispered in his ear. Colt smiled and looked right at me, shooting me a wink before he started playing a cord.

He hadn't played in a really long time, but seemed to have remembered what he was doing. At first, he just hummed to match the tune of the strings. Then he began to sing a special song, while looking right at me.

"This life would kill me If I didn't have you. I couldn't live without you, baby. I wouldn't want to. If you didn't love me so much, I'd never make it through.

'Cuz this life would kill me...This life would kill me if I didn't have you."

It had been so long since Colt sang to me. It literally took my breath away. Noah went over and they started doing medley's together, but all I could hear was him singing those words to me. My eyes filled with tears and they weren't from pain or fear. I was blown away by his devotion to me.

He'd never left my side. When he told me that he wouldn't, I just expected him to go back to his normal routines in life.

Instead, he'd dropped everything to be with me.

I loved being with our family, but after that happened, all I wanted to do was be alone and in his arms. Thunder was rolling across the fields and the sky was flashing with lightning.

I closed my eyes and thought back to that night where I found Colt in the rain. We'd made love in the mud, with the storm surrounding us. Nothing has ever compared to that night. I knew he was who I wanted to spend the rest of my life with. The truth was, Colt had always taken care of me.

When the guitar playing stopped, I looked over at Colt. He was giving me that half smile where he knew exactly what I was up to. I blushed and even in the dark I think he knew it.

My heart was beating fast and I had butterflies in my stomach. Ever since my surgery, I hadn't been in any kind of mood or condition to be intimate. The closest that we'd come was when he was giving me sponge baths.

We were focused on each other and it was like the rest of the family disappeared. Colt stood up and sat the guitar down. "If you'll excuse us, I think I'm goin' to take my wife on a little walk."

"But it's goin' to rain." Noah was concerned. He didn't understand that we really needed to be alone.

"I'll keep your mom dry, son. Go on home with your cousin and we'll meet you there." Colt took his arm and put it around my shoulder.

We started walking away and the guys were already saying smart comments. "The combines in the west field this time, losers!" Ty had to be the first to comment. I was glad he could joke about that night. It took me a long time to tell him the details of it, since technically we were engaged to each other, at the time.

"You better hope that lightenin' doesn't bite you in your naked ass!" Conner's deep voice traveled across the field.

"Ignore them, darlin'." Colt leaned over and kissed the top of my head.

Drops of rain were starting to fall as we got further away from the house. "Are you really walking us to the west field?"

He pulled me along. "You're damn right I am. Except this time, I know you belong to me."

As the rain got heavier, my heart beat faster. Suddenly, I wasn't the thirty year old mother of three, battling breast cancer. I was the same young girl in that field so long ago. I was that girl who was so insanely in love with a man that nothing else mattered to me. I would have done anything to taste his skin; to kiss those lips and to be naked in that field making love to him.

I stopped walking, forcing Colt to give me all of his attention. We were now far enough away from the house that only a small light could be seen. I took a couple steps back, leaving Colt watching me. While staring right in his eyes, I started pulling my wet t-shirt off of my body. I held it out in front of me and dropped it on the ground.

Colt took one step forward and I took two back.

I reached behind me and unhooked my bra. I was still a little sensitive, plus this was the first time that I'd undressed outside of our bedroom.

He shook his head as I threw my bra at him. He caught it and watched me take two more steps in the other direction. I think he finally understood what was happening. The more I walked away, the more he followed, picking up my clothes as he moved.

The rain was coming down harder, causing my makeup and hairspray to run down my face. I wiped it away and pushed my hair back off of my face so I could watch my husband decreasing the space between us. "Darlin', you're drivin' me crazy."

I bit down on my lip. "Mmm, that's the point."

He growled and came forward quickly, catching me off guard. I lost my balance and tumbled back onto the wet ground. Colt came down beside me, making sure his weight didn't land on top of me. I backed away, letting my hands fill with mud as I shimmied out of his reach. "Savanna…"

We were acting like teenagers and I loved it. Colt kept laughing, while trying to finally grab me. I managed to stand up and start running away from him. This whole game was about the chase. The closer I got to that west field, the stronger the storm was getting. "Lose the clothes, cowboy!"

The rain was pouring down over us and all I cared about was getting naked and being with my sexy man. I started tugging down my shorts as we walked. I knew he was gaining on me again, in fact, I wanted him to. We were getting closer to the combine. I could see it every time the lightening flashed. I felt my shorts and panties fall down to my ankles and I stepped out of them.

When I turned around to tease him, he stopped dead in his tracks. A large flash of lightening filled the sky. It was now raining so heavy that it was hard to see each other, even though we were only a few feet away. "You're beautiful."

"What?"

This time he yelled. "I said you're beautiful." I watched his shirt come off his body in record time. His cargo shorts followed as I got closer. I wanted to feel his breath on my skin. His lips needed to be on mine.

He grabbed me by the hands and pulled me into his hard chest, wasting no time planting his first kiss over my lips. I could taste the rain on his mouth and tongue. The smell of the fresh tilled dirt filled the air. We crouched down to our knees, letting our bodies sit down on the warm soaked ground. Colt took my legs and pulled them so they straddled where his hard cock sat. He growled when he felt my naked body slap against his. "Say it again." I licked his bottom lip.

He reached his hands up and ran them down my arms. "You're so damn beautiful." I felt his stubby face rubbing against my neck, before his wet tongue slid up to my ear. "We ain't makin' it to the combine."

I swayed my hips, creating the friction against his hard cock to drive him mad. My lips brushed over his. "I know."

He grabbed me from underneath my arms and pulled us both down. I was on top of him, while he lay on the muddy ground. I could feel him kicking his shorts off the rest of way, so it was easier to move his legs.

I sat up, cupping my breasts with my hands, because I just felt uncomfortable. Colt took one hand and pulled my right hand away, then he slowly repeated the process on my injured breast. He fingertips traced over my nipples and with the rain falling down, it was slippery and tantalizing. I leaned my head back, letting it fall down right on my face, while Colt's magic hands took care of my hunger.

I could feel it pressing against my leg, just sitting there ready to enter me. Each time I moved my hips, Colt would move his to let me know he was prepared. I reached down between my legs and took him into my hand. His length still made me tremble when it first penetrated me. This time was no different, except for the fact that we'd gone so long without being intimate.

Colt was fueled by a need and as much as he wanted to be gentle, nothing was gentle about it. Once my hand had him in position, he forcefully thrusted himself inside of me. I gasped and screamed out into the dark night. He thrusted again, this time grunted as he did it. His hands were dug into my arms and he was almost shoving me down to fill me completely. "Is this what you want?" He asked.

I closed my eyes and felt his lips savagely kissing me. Our tongues brushed and our teeth collided, but we were too caught up to feel the pain of it all. It was exactly what I wanted and I wasn't about to let it stop. I gritted my teeth as I answered, "Oh yeah, Colt. I want it like that night."

He pumped harder, sometimes even grunting as he moved up and down. My body was bouncing all around and all I could do was hold on and enjoy the ride. I sat up, and shook out my wet hair, before grabbing it with both hands and moving it out of my face. Colt reached up and grabbed at my shoulders. He pulled down on them, making us almost slap together. I bounced faster, riding him as if he were a mechanical bull. The rougher it was, the more turned on I became. A tingling sensation overwhelmed me and I cried out in ecstasy.

As my pace slowed, Colt picked his up. I dug my nails into the sides of his abdomen, pinching his skin. The more pain I gave the more pleasure he seemed to get. He stopped, but only to flip me around. With my ass in the air, he slapped it before positioning himself right behind me. I was only empty for seconds, but when he went back inside of me, I could feel myself losing control again.

"You like it when I fuck you?" He never talked like that anymore. It was freaking hot. The ground was filthy and starting to get cold. My hands were tangled up in roots and mud and I dug in more, trying to control my being overcome with sexual release. I felt dizzy, like I was literally seeing stars. "Yes!" I screamed and cried at the same time. My body was his and he could do whatever he wanted to it. This was even better than when we were younger. This was fueled by insatiable desire and pent up tension. We both needed to do this, to feel this.

We needed to feel alive.

Colt grabbed my hips and moved quickly. He slapped his body into my wet ass and it was loud, but not as loud as my screams. I wasn't in pain. It was all euphoric. My stomach was filled with butterflies, while my legs felt like butter. I could feel Colt running his hands over the wet skin of my ass. He squeezed one cheek, making sure I could feel his hand sliding around my anus. I pulled away, not willing to let him finish without looking at me. My muddy hands reached around his neck as I sat right over his hard erection, letting it get right back to where it was before I interrupted.

I ran my hands across his cheek, spreading a trail of dirt everywhere I touched. Mud ran down his chest and as the lightning continued to strike, I could see just how dirty he was. I dug into his hair and pulled his lips against mine. We savored another kiss, before I pulled him away from my mouth by his hair. He licked his lips and stared right at me. I grinded myself into him, in a circular motion. My hips were swaying and I leaned back, running my muddy hands over my bouncing breasts. "Look at me, Colt. I want you watching me."

He nodded as I grinded even faster. When his eyes started rolling back, I knew he was losing control. He looked right at me and squinted as his body began to tighten beneath me. "Oh, God!" His body shook a few times before his head fell against my shoulder.

We should have gotten up and found cover.

We really should have.

Except, nothing mattered to us.

We were so caught up in what we'd just experienced that neither of us moved. He held me tight, kissing me frequently.

When the storm finally passed and the night sky cleared, Colt stood up, pulling me with him. He laughed, noticing just how filthy we both were. "What the hell just happened? I mean, did we really just fuck in a damn cornfield, for the second time?"

I laughed with him. "Yeah, we did. Maybe it's our thing."

He grabbed my clothes off the ground. They were too disgusting to put back on, but I at least needed a bra and panties. Colt helped me get them on. "I like it when you get like this."

"Crazy?"

He shook his head. "No! Carefree. I love it when you let go, Savanna. It drives me wild."

We started walking back hand in hand. "You know what I want?"

"Ice cream?"

I shook my head and stood in front of him. "No. I want to make love to you every time it rains."

"I got news for you darlin'. That there had nothin' to do with love and you know it."

I backed away from him and giggled. "Fine. If you want to get all technical on me. I want you to fuck me every time it rains, Colt Mitchell."

His eyes got huge and a wicked smile formed in the corner of his mouth. "I think we can work somethin' out."

Chapter 30

Colt

I think my hands were still shaking when we got back to Ty's house. We were covered from head to toe in mud and had no explanation for our actions.

I had just opened the door, when Miranda and Ty stood in the kitchen with their mouths dropped. "You two should be ashamed of yourselves!" Ty scorned like he was a parent. He held up a finger and ran toward the back of the house. He came back with two towels and a bar of soap. "The pigs bathe out back at the hose!"

He shut the door right in my face.

Savanna started to giggle. "It's better than his official walk of shame."

"Yes, it is."

The hose water came from a well, which meant it was colder than a hairless cat in the snow. Savanna screamed when I squirted her for the first time. After what we'd just done in the field, it sure was a buzz kill. We rinsed off enough mud to be able to walk into the warm house and not track any in. Our first step was to get a real shower. I had dirt in crevices of my body that even I couldn't see.

Ty and Miranda were still in the kitchen when we came

back in. He had her pinned against the counter and they were talking quietly amongst themselves. They turned to see us walking in. "We made up the guest room, but if you'd rather sleep out in the barn, that can be arranged."

I flipped him the middle finger and walked right through the living room, with my wife in tow.

The warm shower was nice, and it was even nicer because I wasn't in it alone. Savanna wrapped her arms around me as I washed her hair and placed kisses on her forehead. We'd just done something so out of our norm, but for some reason, it made me feel closer to her.

We stayed in the shower until the hot water started fading. The best part about that was knowing Ty still had to get a shower and it would be a cold one. After drying us both off, we went into the guest room and put on our pajamas. I had to admit, it was nice of Ty to bring our bags to his house, otherwise, we'd be wearing some crazy ass shit of his. The last time I'd borrowed something, he'd purposely given me all NCU printed clothing to be a prick. For Christmas, Savanna and I had bought him a Kentucky State hoodie. During one of their visits, he conveniently left it at our house.

Ty and Miranda were in the living room when we finally came out. They were staring at the television watching a murder mystery. When the music got intense, he jumped up and shook her, causing her to scream out loud. She smacked him. "Stop it! I hate that!"

Savanna sat down next to Ty and he scooted away from her. "I can still smell the sex on you two."

She patted him on the leg as I sat down beside her. "Are you jealous?"

"Maybe."

Miranda giggled.

"So, how about we talk about somethin' else," I suggested.

"Dude, what else is there to talk about? Our kids aren't bothering us and I can't wait to crawl into bed with her fine ass." He grabbed Miranda's thigh and squeezed it.

"I want to hear about Van's surgery." Miranda turned her attention to my wife. She sat Indian style and leaned back against her annoying husband.

"Well, it isn't happening until after the round of radiation is complete. We wanted to make sure I was perfectly healthy before I underwent another surgical procedure. The doctor is going to remove both breasts and then reconstruct new ones to take their place."

"That's where the tattoos come in, babe." Ty added.

Savanna laughed. "Yeah, my nipples will be removed and so they tattoo new ones on to look like normal ones. Of course they don't have a point to them, but they look real enough. Besides, nobody sees them except Colt."

Ty started waving his hands around. "Hold on, now! I think that I should be allowed a thirty second peek at what the new nipples look like, just because I think they are fucking cool as shit."

I cleared my throat. He was going to shit himself when he heard this. "If Savanna wants to show you, I will allow thirty seconds, from a distance of course."

He got a sad face. "How will I see the detail if I have to be far away?"

Miranda smacked him. "Shut up! This is serious."

"I know. I'm being very serious. It's my life's mission to see Van's new tits. It's only fair since I've seen her current ones."

I cocked an eyebrow. "You know that line that you're always crossin'?"

He chuckled. "Yeah, yeah. I'll shut up."

We started watching the movie and the room got quiet, but every so often Ty would ask some crazy question.

"Are you going to go bigger? If I had a penis replacement, I'd go huge."

Savanna burst into laughter. "You need to!"

"Hey now! Leave my little pecker out of this! Not everyone was born with a trunk like he was." He pointed at me.

"It's not little. It's perfect if you ask me." Miranda was

trying to make him feel better.

Ty pretended to cry. "I'll have you know that the average penis is five inches. I have at least two and a half inches on that. We can't all be born with a horse cock."

"My brother has a horse cock, too. Well, that's what Amy says. It must be from the mother's side of the family." Miranda informed us.

Ty stood up and put his hands on his hips. "That's it! Me and my above average penis are going to bed!"

We all waved as he pouted his way out of the room.

The next morning, we woke up to the smell of breakfast cooking. Noah and Bella were sitting at the kitchen table across from Jake and Jax eating pancakes and bacon. Ty saw me walking in and handed me a plate of food. I looked down at my plate and then back up to Ty, who was all smiles. "Is there a reason all my pancakes look like a penis?"

Ty held up Miranda's plate. She had the same thing. "They're penis cakes, dude. If you don't want them, then I'll feed them to the dog. I worked extra hard on them, you know."

I rolled one up with some butter and shoved it in my mouth. He watched me chew it up and swallow. "As much as I hate sayin' this, I appreciate you takin' care of my wife when I wasn't there."

"So, let me get this straight. You finally realized that I

wasn't trying to sleep with her?"

I looked at Miranda, who had her hands on her hips, waiting for an explanation. "Well?"

"I was wrong, alright. You need to put yourself in my shoes. It looked bad and you know it." I heard the door shut and noticed the kids were gone. "Listen, I may have overreacted, but I had every right to suspect somethin' was goin' on. She was keepin' things from me and ya'll were actin' weird."

Savanna came into the room. "Enough, you two. I haven't had my coffee and we are past this discussion. Let it go."

We both turned and started eating our food.

My wife sat down with Miranda and they planned out the rest of our visit. She had been so excited about coming that she didn't care if we all just sat around and did nothing the whole weekend.

We ended up setting up tents in Conner's yard and letting the kids camp. Of course, us guys were chosen to sleep in the tents with the kids. We had three tents. One for the girls and one for the boys and one for us adults. That lasted a good ten minutes. The girls started crying and the boys started fighting. We ended up taking our own kids in a tent and sleeping that way.

While we babysat, the girls got to stay in the cool house and relax. I would have complained more, but Savanna deserved it.

By the time Sunday night came around, and we'd had another family meal, we hit the road for our long drive home. Savanna finally seemed relaxed. She played with my hand while I drove and gave me looks like she was content with the world. It made me happy to see her so calm.

We still had more ahead of us, but were hopeful that everything was really going to be okay.

The kids were so tired from playing, that they all fell asleep on the way home. Even Noah only lasted the first hour. He was soon asleep with ear buds stuck in his ears.

We didn't get home until midnight that night. Savanna was tired and I was exhausted from driving. I couldn't wait to climb into our soft bed and cuddle up next to her. She knew what my motives were. We helped all three children up to their rooms and got them tucked in before meeting in our room.

Savanna wrapped her arms around me. "Thanks for this weekend."

I kissed her nose. "The trip, or what we did in the field?"

She giggled. "Both."

I wiped her hair away from her face and tucked it

behind her ears. "Are you tired?"

She shrugged. "A little."

I tugged at her shirt and lifted it over her head. She stood there in her bra, looking up at me. I reached down and tugged on her pants, pulling them and her underwear down at the same time. I leaned in and kissed the base of her pussy, while looking up at her watching me. I could tell she was more tired than she was admitting to, so I stood up and removed her bra and then pulled her nightgown over her head.

Savanna looked at me like she was confused.

"Darlin', I just want to hold you in my arms and go to sleep. If that's alright with you, of course. I mean, if you want me to kiss it again, I won't complain."

She placed her hands on my chest and moved them up and down. "I love you."

"And I love you."

Savanna walked toward the bed, leading me by the hand. When we got to her side, she wrapped her arms around me and held me there. "Colt, I'm scared. I don't want to get sick. It's going to scare Noah and the girls and I can't have them fearing me. I don't want them seeing me weak."

"You're goin' to be fine. You heard the doctor. He said that the radiation is going to be mild. You probably won't get sick at all. Darlin' I get that you're worried, but the kids are goin' to want their mother around. They ain't goin' to care if you got sick a couple of days to do it."

She nodded and looked up at me with tears in her eyes. "We're halfway there, ya know."

"We can get through the rest. If I have to, I'll have my mom take the kids to Disney again. By the time they get back, you'll be feelin' better. They'll never know."

"What if something bad happens?"

I got that she was afraid, but she was worrying about things that were set in place to make sure the cancer was gone. It was more important than anything, considering it was life and death. As upset as she was, there was not going to be any backing out. If I had to fight her, I would.

I grabbed her hands and kneeled down in front of her. "Listen to me and hear me good. You are going to get through this."

She nodded. I leaned over and kissed her on the lips. She climbed under the covers and I climbed in behind her, wrapping my arms around her waist. "What would I do without you?"

"You never have to find out, because I ain't goin' anywhere and neither are you."

Chapter 31

Savanna

The next couple of weeks went by too quick, probably because I didn't want to do the radiation treatment. Colt was getting used to taking care of the kids and helping out. I felt fine, but he insisted on keeping with his program until everything was over with. It was summer, so the kids had plenty of time to help him out.

For the most part, they did okay. I found myself sneaking behind them and picking up, or going into the laundry room and switching things over. I think I was so bored that I wanted things to do.

I'd never read so much or watched television, until it was all I had to do. I wasn't surprised when Zeke and Piper were plastered all over the news. When he found out about her being pregnant by another man, he started going crazy. One day while she wasn't at home, the news reported that he had her swimming pool filled with trash. They said he paid someone to drain it and dumb tons of trash in it, including some of her favorite belongings. They talked about how the divorce was going to get ugly. As sad as it was for a marriage to end, I couldn't feel bad for them. He'd tried to drag my son into a publicity scam and left him scarred. If we never saw Zeke again, it would be too soon.

On the day of my first radiation treatment, I was petrified. I thought it was going to make me deathly ill and I'd have to be carried out of the place. It turned out, it was nothing like that at all. My oncologist had to do a couple extra things being that it was my first treatment. They gave me these tiny tattoos that were barely noticeable and went through all of the instructions with me in detail. I had to remain perfectly still and move only when the nurses told me to. The procedure itself only lasted about twenty minutes. The nurses called it baking time. Within an hour of arriving at the place, we were leaving, walking out of there like nothing had happened.

Colt reached over and grabbed my hand while he drove. "What was it like?"

"Actually, it was pretty simple. They said I might get tired, but that's about it. I heard another woman mentioning that she'd done chemo and the radiation was much easier. She said she's never been sick one time from it and this was her thirtieth session."

"Damn, she must have it bad. It's a damn shame they don't have a better cure. You'd think after all these years they'd have found one by now."

It was a shame. So many lives were lost every day to some form of cancer. I had to be glad that mine was detected so early. It had been removed and we were taking all of the precautions to make sure it didn't show it's ugly face ever again.

It took another month after my radiation was over before my doctor would agree to do the mastectomy and reconstruction. They were very kind about the whole process. After measuring the cup size of my real breasts, the doctor told me he would do his best to make my new ones look as natural as possible. For some reason, by the time I got to this step in the process, I was more optimistic, instead of afraid. Sure, there was always going to be a chance that I developed some form of cancer again, but with routines checks and a healthy diet, it was possible to beat the odds.

I had so much to be thankful for in my life and I'd learned to appreciate the little things, because sometimes, they are what matter the most.

I'll never forget the day of my surgery. After the family was sure I was cancer free, Ty had a field day with me getting implants. Even Colt started to joke about it.

They called me Sagfree, whenever they were together. As much as I loved that they were getting along, I didn't appreciate Colt getting on the Ty bandwagon.

Colt drove me to the hospital with a smile on his face. I remember turning and giving him a dirty look. "What are you so happy about?"

He grabbed my hand and kissed it, like he always did. "Well, my wife doesn't have cancer. My kids are healthy and my business is growin'. I'd say that's enough to smile about."

"Colt we're driving to have my breasts removed. I hardly think it's a smile kind of day."

"You do realize that your breasts are going to look like they did when we first got together. Forgive me for bein' an ass, but I'm a little excited about that. I can still picture seeing you naked for the first time. It gets me all kind of crazy."

I could feel myself blushing. "I love how you can be so serious and mature one second and then a normal thinking guy the next."

"What can I say, I'm pretty darn irresistible."

I laughed and nudged his side. "You're lucky you're so damn sexy and you've given me three beautiful children that look just like you. Otherwise, I may have had to slap you around from time to time."

He put his arm around me. "Darlin' you can slap me around whenever you want. I know you like it rough."

"That's our secret!"

"Fine by me."

Since the procedure was more extensive, I had to wait in the pre-surgical unit longer than the last time. Colt stood beside my bed the whole time. He played with my hands or leaned over to kiss me a bunch of times.

I wouldn't say that this all changed him, but it did make

him more in tune with us. Instead of focusing on the ranch and coming home all tired, he spent more time at home. The kids loved him being around and they understood that their dad had obligations. If something happened where he needed to run out, we could always count on him getting back as quickly as possible.

I wasn't nervous until the doctor came in and said they were ready. I started crying for some reason, while Colt held my hand.

The doctor patted me on the arm. "Savanna, this is the easy part."

"It's going to hurt." I'd had enough people tell me that after an implant it was excruciating.

"I will give you something to manage the pain and after a couple weeks you'll be back to your normal self. The good part is that you're not going to be sick. The worst is over." He was reassuring, even if I was being skeptical.

"Darlin', I'll be right here when you get done."

Unlike the last time, when I was put under, during my surgery, I had the most vivid dream. I dreamed that Christian was getting married. She was so grown up and beautiful. Addy was in college. She wanted to be a vet. Noah, who looked identical to his father, worked along side him running the ranch. The wedding was taking place at the barn where her father and I had married. She'd decorated it the same way and even rode in on a horse. It was breathtaking.

Our family had grown, and everyone was older, but yet they were all still around.

When I woke up, I almost wanted to ask to go back to sleep. I wanted to see my babies all grown up again.

Colt was sitting in chair, playing on his phone.

"Hey, you."

He got up and came over to the bed. "Hey. How are you feelin'?"

"I'm not in any pain." He kissed me softly on the head. "I had the best dream. The kids were older. Christian was getting married."

"Who was she marryin'?" Colt cocked his eyebrow and I could tell he was offended.

"Wow, are you going to be one of those dads that doesn't let their daughters out of their sight?" It hurt to laugh at him, but I couldn't help it.

"Let's just say that when the times comes for that, me and Noah will be outside, cleaning our guns as they arrive."

"Our poor girls!"

He chuckled. "I was a young man once. I know how they think."

I just shook my head. It was good thing that I was going to be around for all of this, because those girls were going to need me with a father like Colt. If he had it his way, they'd be wearing purity rings until they were thirty.

Due to the extent of my surgery, I had to stay in the hospital overnight. This time, the kids were all allowed to come visit. By dinner time, my room was filled with flowers and little visitors.

It was the first time that the girls had really been in a hospital, so they were very curious about what machine did what. After sharing my pudding and my bed, I had to hug them goodbye when visiting hours ended.

This time, Colt didn't spend the night. I was fine being alone for one night, while he was home with the kids. Noah offered to stay with me. If he would have been allowed, I probably would have let him. I never should have doubted his devotion to me. His love radiated off of him and we'd never been closer. I could sense that he still felt bad about what happened between us. It seemed like so long ago and we'd all decided to leave the past in the past.

When they got home they all called to say goodnight. Colt wouldn't get much sleep with two kicking girls in bed with him. He said the last time, he woke up and had a foot in his mouth and a knee in his nuts. While I laughed, I think he felt the pain as he talked about it.

Between being uncomfortable and the nurses coming in to check out my drains, I didn't get much sleep either. When morning came and Colt arrived, I was ready to roll out of there. Unfortunately, I didn't get my release papers until later that afternoon.

The kids made signs and the house was sparkling clean when we got home. Colt's mother had made her famous fried chicken. I could smell it as soon as we got out of the truck.

After dinner, the family headed out, leaving us with three wound up kids and a lot of leftovers. Colt and the kids formed an assembly line in the kitchen. One person washed, one dried and the other two put the dishes away. It was actually cute to watch them working together.

I wasn't exactly sore. It was more like I felt tight. My chest was wrapped up and it had to stay that way for a couple of days. I'd never cared much about my breasts until I had the new ones to look at. I didn't know that they swelled up double in size.

Colt and I got the biggest surprise when he unwrapped me to check on my drains. I was huge. His eyes were fixed on them, like he'd never seen boobs before. I actually had to wave my hand in front of him to get his attention. "Hello?"

He grabbed my arms. "You know that I would never ask somethin' like this if it wasn't necessary."

I knew what he wanted and for some reason, I didn't even get offended. "Go get your phone and take the picture." I shook my head and rolled my eyes.

Colt smiled the whole time he was sending Ty the picture. "I told him you went up a couple sizes. He won't know they're just swollen."

"They're more than swollen. I look like I have cantaloupe breasts and they feel like them too." They were hard and tender. "We better get them wrapped back up. I don't want them pointing in opposite directions."

We laughed as Colt put the bandages back on. We'd no sooner finished when his phone started ringing. Colt answered and put it on speaker.

Why didn't you tell me you were going so big? Holy shit you're huge!

I hope you enjoy the picture. This counts as your thirty second show, cuz.

Colt ended the call and ignored it when it rang again. He turned it on vibrate and walked me over to our bed. "He won't stop calling, you know."

"I don't give a shit. I ain't answerin' him. There's more important things to do." He covered me up and kissed me slowly on the lips. "If you weren't so sore, I'd be all over those new titties."

I was a little weirded out by the tattooed nipples. From

afar they looked so real, even three dimensional. To feel them was different. They were flat and it was just going to be something to get used to. It was a good thing that my breast feeding days were over.

"Trust me, as soon as I feel up to it, I'll let you do whatever you want with these new titties." I laughed at myself for using the same word he had used.

He reached his hand between my legs and started rubbing me. "I'm so turned on right now, we may need to think of other ways to solve this problem."

I reached over and stuck my hand down his boxers. "I think I have some ideas."

Chapter 32

Colt

Savanna was sore for a good two weeks. She did her best to try and do as much as she could, no matter how many times I told her I could handle it. I reckon she just had her way of doing things. Try as I might, I couldn't get her system down.

About two months after her mastectomy, and almost four months since her initial lump was removed, we were sitting in her doctor's office waiting on results.

We knew she would have to be tested frequently, but it's hard to prepare when you don't know what will happen.

I held my wife's hand and waited for the doctor to come in the room. She was shaking and maybe I was too. It was scary. Someone can be fine one day and dying the next.

When he came in and told us that she was still cancer free, I think I took the biggest breath of my life. Savanna started to cry tears of joy. Sure, this was just our first of many tests, but so far she was beating it.

I wanted her to be able to live to experience the dream she had of our daughter being married. When I married Savanna, I wanted nothing more than to grow old with her. I would do whatever I had to do, to make that happen.

We took the kids out to celebrate the good news, but only Noah knew why. The look on his face was priceless and I don't think his mother expected him to react the way he did. Noah threw his arms around her and just wouldn't let go.

When things finally settled down again, after a couple of days, I wanted to do something special for my wife. Since I normally worked in the office for a couple hours each day, she never came in to see what I was up to. It was a good thing, because planning a vacation wasn't a fast process.

I wanted it to be perfect, and to do that, I had to make sure every detail was precise.

It was hard waiting until the paperwork was delivered. I had it sent to my mother's house, so Savanna wouldn't open it and get the shock of her life without me.

After letting my mother in on my idea, she agreed to take the kids for the night. It wasn't like I had to beg. The women would have watched them every day if I wanted her to.

I told Savanna that I had to run into town to get supplies for the ranch. Instead, I went to buy flowers and pick up food from her favorite restaurant. She was under the impression that I was bringing home Chinese, so you can imagine the look on her face when I opened up two containers of filet minion.

She put her hands over her mouth. "Oh, wow, what is this?"

"Let's go sit down and I'll tell you."

I could see the burning excitement in her eyes and it was great because she had no idea what was going on.

I ran into the kitchen and grabbed two plates and opened the bottle of wine I'd purchased. Savanna was sitting at the dining room table waiting for me. I was trying to be romantic, but I wasn't exactly good at it. I couldn't find fancy candles, so I lit a scented one. The room filled with the scent of hazelnut coffee. Savanna laughed at my attempts, but anxiously waited for me to spill.

Once I poured our wine, I held up my glass. "I'd like to make a toast."

She put her glass up. "Okay."

"To our future!"

She sipped on her wine, while I put our food on our plates. "Are we celebrating my health, because I feel like you're up to something?"

She knew me too well. "Maybe I am."

She sat her fork down. "Colt Mitchell, you better tell me. You know I hate secrets."

"It's a good one, I teased."

I loved seeing her excited. She'd been through so much. "I was goin' to wait until dessert to tell you. Since you obviously can't wait that long, I guess I have to spill." I walked over to where I had hidden the envelope. She saw me sit back down and looked puzzled. "I was thinking that it would be fun for us to get out of town for a while.""Are we going to

Disney?""This would be without the kids.""Oh."I pushed the

envelope over. "I had this idea. Open it up and see what you think.""Oh my goodness. Are these real tickets? ""Of course they're real." I sorted out the papers and pointed. "I booked the same room we stayed in on our honeymoon. I figured we could make all that happen again."She started to cry. "This is the most perfect idea you've ever had."

"When do we leave?"

"In two weeks. My mom is goin' to take the kids and between her and your parents they will be taken care of. In fact, I doubt they will even miss us."

She got up from her chair and walked over to wrap her arms around me. "I plan on thanking you for this amazing trip the whole time we're away."

I kissed her softly. As she pulled away and opened her eyes, I saw her smiling. "Darlin', you can start thankin' me right now."

She started laughing like I was joking. I shook my head and let out a chuckle. "I ain't kiddin'."

"Yeah, I know you're not." She sat back down at her seat and took another bite. "You can't buy me my favorite food and expect me to abandon it. Don't worry, Colt. I have all night to satisfy your every desire."

I started getting hard just hearing her say it. Every since she's been diagnosed, she'd become freaky. Making love was like a natural nerve pill for her. The more she did it, the less stress she seemed to be under. Far be it from me to stop her. I was loving every minute of it.

We continued celebrating, by taking the bottle of wine upstairs with us. The dishes had to wait until morning, because neither one of us were leaving the bedroom.

Savanna became self conscious about her breasts right after the surgery. I think it was the tattoos that made her feel uncomfortable. To be honest, you couldn't even tell unless you were right up on them. When I licked them, there just wasn't hardness at the ends. It didn't matter to me if she never even had the reconstructive surgery. I would have still been turned on by her simple smile. Her ass was always my favorite thing anyway. That woman could bend over and I'd want to hit it. Still, to this day, she had me begging.

I still had one more surprise up my sleeve and I knew she wasn't expecting it. We were naked, in our bedroom, sprawled across the bed in a heated moment. I pulled my lips away from hers and brushed her cheek with my thumb. "I have to ask you somethin', darlin'."

"Anything," she whispered.

I slid off the bed and reached under the mattress. "I will love you forever, Savanna Mitchell. When I said our vows, I meant every single word." I grabbed her hands and held them. "I just think that after all we've been through, maybe it would be nice to do something for us."

"You mean, besides the trip?"

"Savanna Mitchell, will you do me the honor of marryin' me again?" Her mouth dropped when I slid the anniversary band onto her ring finger.

She wrapped her arms around me. "I might have to think about it," she teased.

"Don't think too long. The family will be here next weekend to watch us do it."

She looked down at the ring again and smiled. "I guess I can go through with it again. I mean, you're pretty much the best man to ever exist on the planet."

"I'll take that as a yes, then."

"Hell, yes!"

"Noah and the girls are going to give you away."

She looked surprised. "You've already told them?"

"Well, I didn't think you'd say no." She cuddled up next to me and stared at her new ring. "Just so you know ahead of time, Miranda and Amy are already fightin' over how you should wear your hair. You'd think this was our first rodeo."

"You know how they are."

"Speaking of women, I have enlisted our girls to do the decorating this time. They did such a fantastic job with Joe and Barbie's wedding, that I just know they will make ours perfect. Well, with paper flowers and glitter, of course."

"Oh boy, that sounds scary." She giggled.

"It's going to be. Have you even tried to clean up glitter? The shit sticks to everything." I was thinking about banning it from our house.

She laughed at me again. "I appreciate how hard you worked to keep up with everything while I was sick. I mean, it must have been hard doing things you never had to do before."

"I never realized how hard you worked, until I had to do it all myself. Being a mother is a full time job. It never ends either. When I get home, my job is done, but your job is like being on call twenty four seven. You're my idol, because there is no way I could do it every day. You're an amazin' woman."

Savanna smiled as she ran her hands down my chest. She continued until she had my length in her grasp. "How about we stop all this talking and you show me just how amazing you think I am?"

I rolled on top of her. "My pleasure."

Epilogue

"I can't believe it still fits."

Miranda stood back and admired me in my original wedding dress. "It's perfect."

"Should I wear the cowboy boots, too?"

She nodded. "Of course. Did the girls like their sundresses? Ty's mom worked all week on them."

"Yeah, they love them. She got the sizes perfect." I couldn't believe she'd made them for me.

"It's time for your hair and makeup." Amy came walking in carrying a tool box of products. Miranda smiled and they dug in. They'd already decided that I was wearing my hair down. Miranda was doing my makeup, while Amy did my hair.

In the next room, I could hear the girls getting dressed. My mom was in charge of getting them pretty. They wanted to surprise me, even though I'd already seen their dresses.

I had to admit that this time around, all of this seemed so much fun. Everyone was relaxed and I couldn't wait to party with the family.

When it was time to walk down the aisle, my girls came running out.

Christian and Addy held hands as they walked right to their daddy. He was standing with his arms down at his sides, but as they approached, he held their hands.

Noah came walking around the barn. He was wearing jeans, a clean white shirt and a pair of boots. He smiled when he saw me all dressed up. "You look real pretty, Mom."

"You don't look bad yourself."

I put my arm in his and we walked down the small aisle. Since it was just our close family, Ty wasted no time being his normal self. I got halfway down the aisle and he started whistling. "Nice ass!"

The barn filled with laughter. "Shut up, party crasher!" I stuck my tongue out at him and noticed the girls were doing it too.

Colt was all smiles when we reached him. It felt so perfect to be standing up there with our three children.

Since we were already legally married, John had agreed to play the minister. He stood in front of us and let Colt take the lead.

He turned around and faced our family. "I'm goin' to try to make this short." He faced me again and took both of my hands in his. "The past eleven or so years have been the best years of my life. Lovin' you is the easiest thing I've ever had to do. Every single mornin', when I get up to start my day, I look over at you sleepin' and thank God for givin' you to me." He paused for a minute. "Several months ago, we had a big scare. Nobody ever wants to hear that they might lose the person they love. Life is precious, but I couldn't see myself gettin' by without you by my side. Savanna, you are the glue that holds our family together. I just want you to know that no matter how old we get, no matter what we have to go through, no matter how hard we have to fight, I'm going to stand by you for the rest of my life. I love you, darlin'. I always have and I always will."

"You broke the guy code to have her!" Ty joked. We heard him groan and turned to see Miranda's elbow in his side. He hunched over in his seat.

Colt laughed and looked back at me. "You were worth the fight," he whispered.

It made me blush. "You're the best I've ever had," I whispered back.

"We ain't here to watch you two tell secrets!" Conner added.

I took Colt's hands again and looked up at him. "It's hard for me to put into words just how much you mean to me. It was easier when we were first married to just say what was on my mind. After all we've been through, it's hard to find the words that can even compare to the way I've grown to love you even more. You say you watch me when I sleep. Well, when you're not next to me at night, I can't sleep. Sometimes hearing you snore comforts me. I feel like I need you to breathe. It's as if my whole reason for existing solely depends on your love for me. I never could have gotten through the last few months without you. You weren't just my caretaker. You were everything to me and the kids. There's something that I want to tell you." I turned to face our family. "I need to tell you all something, that I've never told anyone. It's kind of embarrassing, but I think if you hear it, you'll get a kick out of me telling you."

Colt had no clue what I was going to say. I took a couple deep breaths and looked up at him. "When I was around twelve years old, I wasn't exactly the prettiest of the girls. My hair was cut short. I had braces and everyone said I was built like a boy. Ty was the only guy that was nice to me, so I found myself hanging out with him all of the time. It just so happened that during that summer, his older cousin came to stay. Even at twelve, I knew beauty when I saw it. He was the most attractive human being that I'd ever laid eyes on. I swooned over him, along with all the other girls. The problem was that he made fun of me and so did the other girls. They said someone like him would never look at me. They said I'd never even get a boyfriend. I went home that night and cried my eyes out. I told myself that one day I'd be beautiful and someone like that gorgeous teenage boy would love me. I pretended he was my pillow and I made out with him every night." I started laughing. "Ty solved the boyfriend problem but, I think he only asked me because he felt sorry for me."

"Not true!" He added.

"Anyway, I never thought, in a million years that the same handsome boy would be the man that I fell madly in love with. I just wanted you to know that I pretended you were my pillow, even before I dated your cousin, even before you knew I was really a girl."

Colt and everyone else started to laugh. He leaned in and kissed me.

"Oh and just so you know, you kiss way better than my pillow."

"I'm goin' to throw up in my boot!" Conner announced. "Kiss her and lets get to drinkin'!"

"Fine!" Colt leaned down and planted a beautifully long kiss on me. We could hear the kids laughing at us.

Our vows weren't traditional. I don't even think we said our 'I do's'. All that mattered was that we shared our love with our family.

As the night progressed, Colt pulled me to the side. "So, let me get this straight. Technically, I was your first kiss?"

"If you count frenching with a pillow." I laughed.

Ty cut in, "Can you both stop discrediting me. I'm the whole reason you're even together. I think I should at least be able to see the new boobs in person, for my part in all of this."

Colt put his hand on Ty's shoulder. "I've already thanked you. I've even apologized to you. Now, as far as you seein' her new set goes, I think I'm going to keep them all for myself."

"It was worth a try." He walked away and smacked Miranda right on the ass. She screamed and turned around to give him a dirty look. Instead, he grabbed her and pulled her into his arms. She wrapped her arms around his neck and they started talking and smiling, like they were in their own little world.

Colt shook his head. "Sometimes, I still can't believe he was your first."

"He wasn't a good boyfriend, but he was my best friend. Does it really bother you, after all these years?" It was weird Colt was bringing it up.

"As long as I'm your last, none of that matters."

"You're my everything. How's that?"

"That'll do." Colt spun me around and planted another kiss on me. "I can't wait to take that dress off of you again."

"I can't wait either."

Christian walked over and pulled on my dress. Colt picked her up, even though she was getting way too big for that. "Mommy, when I get bigger, I want to get married here and wear a pretty dress , just like you."

I thought about the dream I'd had and couldn't help but

smile. Maybe God had given me just a peek at what I had to look forward to. It gave me hope that I'd be able to live a long, happy life, with the man and family that I adored so much.

End of Book 7

Look for Heather's story...Coming Soon!

If you enjoyed this book, please share a comment or review.

Let me know what you think of this book by contacting me at the follow:

http://www.jenniferfoor.com

http://twitter.com/jennyfoor

http://www.facebook.com/#!/JenniferFoorAuthor

http://www.jennyfoor.wordpress.com

Jennifer Foor lives on the Eastern Shore of Maryland with her husband and two children. She enjoys shooting pool, camping and catching up on cliché movies that were made in the eighties.

Printed in Great Britain
by Amazon.co.uk, Ltd.,
Marston Gate.